ICON

ICON

SERENA DA VINCI

CONTENTS

Icon

ICON BY SERENA DA VINCI

Disclaimer

This is a complete work of fiction. Any similarities to any people or places, whether fictitious or not, are all fictitious. The cities are fictitious representations of such, and any resemblance is unintentional and coincidental.

Trigger Warning

Closed practices, offensive iconography, violence, sexual assault, ritualistic sacrifices, sexism, racism.

I dedicate this work to my three muses. You hung on when I didn't want to continue. Thank you.

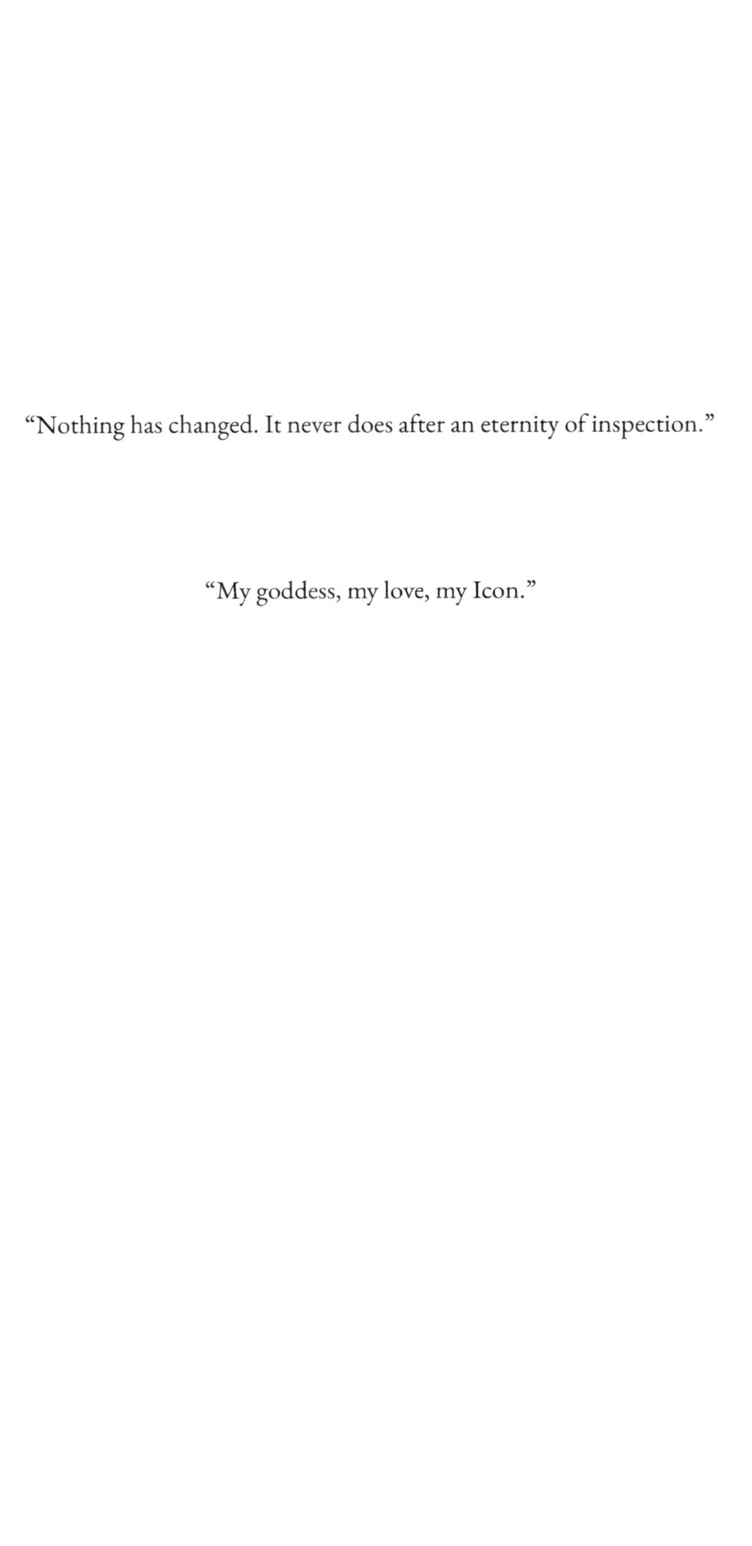

"Nothing has changed. It never does after an eternity of inspection."

"My goddess, my love, my Icon."

I stared out of the window of Creamy's Pies and Cakes Shop onto Gunter Avenue. Dusk was quickly approaching, and the weather had yet to improve. It was not exactly raining in Guntersville, Alabama, the small town that I have called home my entire life, but it was cold and wet.

Instead of raining, it was misting, even though that was not probably the proper term for it meteorologically. Misting was, though, the best way to describe the weather on the October evening the day before Homecoming. The Guntersville Wildcats would be playing their homecoming game tomorrow night, and the parade was held the night before the game. The high school kids had been working hard on their floats, and it seemed a shame that the weather was so bad.

"I hope it doesn't ruin the floats," I said to Larry Johns, the guy who owned and managed Creamy's, which was the last old-fashioned ice cream parlor in Guntersville.

Unlike other restaurants with ice cream parlors, which had burgers and fries, Creamy's served pies, cakes, and ice cream exclusively. Larry was a greaser, so he loved having a retro shop like Creamy's. Creamy's was across the street from where the last ice cream parlor had once been and a few doors down from the last place that rock legend Ricky Nelson had ever played. Many claimed that his ghost haunted that building.

Supposedly, when Guntersville City redid the sidewalks in front of that building, the commotion caused Ricky's ghost to roam from building to building on Gunter Avenue. Larry claimed to see him near the back door occasionally, but I never saw him.

Larry said, "Yeah, it does seem to suck. Why are they having it at night anyway? I thought they used to do this the day of Homecoming. What happened?"

"I don't know. I think it's weird that it's not during the day. How can people see the floats and the different girls chosen to represent school clubs?" I asked.

"Well, maybe we're too old to know anymore," laughed Larry in response.

"Speak for yourself," I said. "I'm still in my twenties."

"You're old enough to be a lawyer, aren't ya?" Larry retorted.

"I might be old enough, but no one ever believes it or takes me seriously," I answered. "Besides, it's not like it pays the bills. I'm working here and might have to take on a third job to pay my school loans."

"Don't whine, Alva Loomis. I'm more understanding than others. No one wants a lawyer around to work since they think you'll sue them at any moment, or you're undercover or something. And I'm willing to work around your court schedule."

"I know you are, Larry Johns, and that's why I love ya!"

I gave him a big hug, which was purely platonic for both of us. Larry had been married with kids for ten years. Although I was single, I had a few guys that I kept contact with on a regular basis. I was a serial dater, with no recent relationship lasting longer than two months at a time.

I did not have a fear of commitment, but I was a decisive person and knew when a guy was a waste of time. I believed in dating as many guys as I could in hopes that I would figure out what type I wanted. Some things that I could not tolerate as a teenager had become essential as an adult, so I knew that experience made me wiser. It was not like I slept with them anyway, which was another reason that most guys would not stick around for more than a few dates. I had discretion in that department, which was another reason that I was currently single.

I was not a saint, but I was not the opposite of that either. When I was eighteen, I had been in a hurry to marry my high school sweetheart, but my father had told me that he would not pay for me to go to college if I married. My mother died when I was six, so I did not have anyone to intervene for me. My older brother, Craig, could have helped me, but he was not interested in my love life.

We decided to wait, and after I graduated from college, Billy Flowers, my fiancé, refused to set a date. I knew then that he was not serious about me. He never bought me a real ring. I always wore his class ring to symbolize our engagement. He had a job and his own house, which I stayed at sometimes on weekends. He had room for me in his life, but never in his heart.

After I dumped Billy, I went to law school on a whim from a suppressed childhood dream. I passed the bar exam and began a private practice. I do not much have money, so I rent an office for a few hundred dollars a month in a nearby building. It is a one-room office, and the bathroom is down the hall and shared with the other offices. With my electricity bills and minimal phone and net service, I almost break even every month with my slowly growing clientele and court-appointed work.

For my personal bills, such as rent for my apartment and student loans, I work at Creamy's. However, life is getting more expensive, and I am looking to take a third job. I talked to my cousin, who works at home doing telemarketing. That might be an option, but I will have to make sure they are not doing anything illegal or unethical before I take the job. A call to the ethics hotline should help me cover my butt.

It was a slow day at Creamy's, but we had to prepare for the rush after the parade. The parade would run straight through downtown past our shop and all the way down until the main street intersected with the next highway. Gunter Avenue was also a state highway, but no one referred to it as that until they were out of the downtown area.

After the parade was over, people would come inside and get a snack instead of joining the traffic jam that was behind the parade. Some had made reservations to celebrate Homecoming tonight, while others were coming in tomorrow night before and after the game.

Creamy's was rare to downtown Guntersville because it stayed open late—until midnight on weekends, and until ten every other night of the week. It paid off because we were always busy, but I had to share my hours with four other people. That was another reason that I had to find a third job. Larry was awesome to work around my schedule, but he also used that as a reason to keep others around because of its unpredictability. So, I had to share my hours because of my uncertain schedule.

"Let's get the reserved signs on the tables in the back so that walk-ins will have to stick up front," said Larry.

"Okay, but I doubt they'll want to sit in the back anyway. They probably want to see the parade without getting wet."

"They can't see anything from here in the dark. Let's just set it up to be careful."

We began setting up the reserved signs on all the tables in the back room. Larry did not want to close the room off entirely because he said it was bad luck. He also thought that if he closed the door, the ghost would show up, but he never would admit that to me.

"Do you want the two side rooms to be left alone?" I asked.

"I think we only have enough reservations to fill the back room. If they get weird about being in the back, we'll just move them up front or in the side rooms."

"Reservation for Smith—table for twenty at eight, and another reservation for five at eight in the name of Potts," Emily hollered from the front.

Emily Reed was the youngest waitress at Creamy's. She was only nineteen and still friendly with most of the high school kids, which explained why she was taking reservations from her cell phone instead of the shop phone.

"Emily, how many kids are going to walk in, you think?" asked Larry.

"It should be fifty more, but you know, I am trying to get them to text or call me to let me know. It's too wet to have them standing outside, and I hate to turn any of them away."

"Keep up the good work," he said as we continued to set up for the rush.

My own phone rang from inside my front pocket. I picked it up to see it was my brother, Craig, who was a research assistant to a retired history professor named Dr. Johann Sockeye. Johann was working on writing the history of Alabama as commissioned for the next series of textbooks adopted by the state for public schools.

Although Craig was officially a research assistant, he was paid a little extra to be a personal assistant for Johann, as he did everything for his boss. According to Craig, Johann was too busy having deep thoughts to be bothered with cleaning his house or cooking his food. Craig did everything for Johann, which meant I rarely saw him. In fact, if Johann did not live nearby, I would never see Craig at all. Craig's voice sounded as calm as normal.

"I have the night off, and I want to bring my date to Creamy's at nine. Save me a seat since I know it's Homecoming this week. When's the parade?"

"Any minute," I answered flatly.

"Sis, you're so dramatic. I doubt it's that busy." Craig giggled.

"It's not yet, but it will be."

"Do you have court tomorrow morning?"

I knew where this was going, but I answered anyway, "No." As I predicted, he answered.

"Well, then you'll live."

"Tell that to my bank account. I don't know why I'm wasting time talking to you. I need to go."

"Okay, bye, sis," he answered and the phone went dead.

The parade buzzed by slowly, and when it was over, the rush began as we predicted. There were so many kids from the band that they nearly filled the entire back room since their parents joined them for banana splits. The band director had paid for each kid to get a banana split as a treat for doing such a good job in the parade. The dance line and flag team were there as well.

The cheerleaders and football team were supposed to be coming on Friday after school. That would take up the entire back room. Larry was always cutting deals to get big groups to come into Creamy's for celebrations. He had a special price for birthday parties, which were difficult to book considering there was no savory food to serve. However, every weekend, we had a birthday party or two, which kept us busy.

Of course, we were very busy tonight because of the parade. I managed to save Craig a two-seater in one of the side rooms for his date. Larry did not mind, which made it easier on my guilt when people had to wait for a place to sit because we ran out of room. No other reservations were held for that late, but I was eager to see Craig and his date Sandy.

This girl was new to me but not Craig, as he had been dating her for some time. I never got to meet her until tonight. I knew that my hair was frizzy from the humidity in the air and my makeup was sweating off my face and absorbing into my pores. I had hoped to see Sandy another night and under different circumstances, but tonight was the night to meet Craig's new girlfriend.

Exactly at nine, Craig walked into Creamy's with a short girl with black hair halfway down her back. She had thin lips, but her smile concealed it. Craig was smiling at her as much as she was smiling at him. They looked so happy. Craig was taller than me, he was six foot three, but he looked silly standing next to Sandy, who was shorter than me. I guess she was around five foot tall, almost six inches shorter than me.

Craig had curly, blonde hair and a golden tan, year-round. I was neither pale nor tan. My hair was long, straight, and brown. My eyes were the same color brown as my hair. Craig's eyes were also the same color brown. Otherwise, we did not look related.

Both Craig and I had long waists. This meant for Craig, he looked shorter than he was unless he stood next to someone. For me, this meant that although I was very pretty, I could never be a model. Along with my shorter stature, my short legs were not ideal for standard clothes. I always had to buy pants in the petite section. As for my short legs, I made up for it with a beautiful face, which I kept covered in glamorous makeup, and my curves, which were standard for girls from the South.

For the record, though, my dark brown eyes are my best feature. My long eyelashes frame them along with my application of makeup that would make the silver screen starlets proud. I look high class because I know how to wear my makeup and not let my makeup wear me. Otherwise, I would just look silly or cheap, which I do not.

My lips are not as full as I wish, but I have made peace with that a long time ago. I make up for it with careful application of lip-gloss in shiny tones. My smaller lips are just pouty, which is fine since men have complimented me over the years on them. Of course, their review could have been biased for obvious reasons. I am quite the good kisser. Whatever the reason, at least my lips are not as thin as Sandy's.

Sandy was freckle faced with pale skin and blue eyes. She was cute but not beautiful. Craig always went for the same type of girl. Craig was in the same way cute but not handsome. He was a good match for Sandy if one plays the game of matching couples on their level of attractiveness.

"Alva, this is my girlfriend, Sandy Beam. Sandy, this is my sister, Alva. Where do we sit?" asked Craig.

After we said hello to one another, I showed them to their table and took their food order.

When I brought them two vanilla milkshakes, Craig spoke to me.

"So, you feel better?"

"Yeah," I answered. Things were slowing down, so I did feel better.

"When's the last time you talked to our father?"

I bit my lip as I thought, "A few months."

"Well, you should reach out more because he's always asking about you."

"Maybe you should quit telling him how I'm doing since he doesn't think he has to call me and ask me personally."

"Alva, you don't call him either."

"I call him sometimes, but he never calls me. I can't think of the last time that he called me."

I glanced at Sandy, who was getting uncomfortable at our slightly heated exchange.

"We shouldn't do this here and now. I'll call him next time. He can call me this time."

"Okay, I'll tell him." Craig shrugged with his answer.

"Don't do that. Just leave it alone, Craig. I love Father, but we're not close. He's in another state now, and we talk more now than we did when he lived down by the lake. I really don't want to do this now."

"I'm sorry. I came here for a reason besides letting you meet Sandy. Father called and said that Uncle Leon finally found someone who is interested in buying Aunt Dawn's place. I think we should go up there tomorrow and look at it one last time just in case it sells soon. When was the last time you were up there?" asked Craig.

"It's been almost a year because I was afraid that Leon would get me for trespassing if I went up there."

"I understand your concern, but Leon said it was okay for us to go up there because the real estate agent will be up there tomorrow showing the house. I suppose he wants us to be supervised, but at least we can go inside the house instead of staring at it from the road. Do you have any time off tomorrow?"

"Yes, I don't have to be at work until four. I can meet you there around lunch."

I looked at Sandy and asked, "Will you be there?"

"No, I have to work until five," she answered.

"Well, it's a date then. I will see you there at noon. Don't be late!" said Craig.

"Okay," I answered as I went back to work.

I wanted to speak to Craig some more, but I was very busy despite the slowdown. By the time I made it back to speak to Craig and Sandy, they were gathering their things to leave. Craig handed me the ticket and his money, which included a generous tip. Craig made much more money at his one job than I did at my two jobs combined. He hugged me as we said our goodbyes.

I handed the money to Larry after they left. Larry gave me the change for my tip, and I continued to work. Cleaning up would keep us there until eleven if we hurried. Luckily, we were able to make it out in time for me to get home well before midnight.

I walked home, which Larry hated because I was female and alone. Sometimes he would walk me to my taxpayer apartment, which was across the street from the Courthouse. My whole life revolved around Gunter Avenue, it seemed, which was fine with me. I had grown up in the country, and I preferred to live in town.

When I was six, my mother killed herself, which was hidden from me until I was almost ten years old. Father had acted like Mother died from a mysterious illness, and he immediately sent us to live with my Aunt Dawn while he mourned.

It had happened a week before school let out for the summer, but I never returned to school until the next year. We spent that whole summer at Dawn's house. We reluctantly returned home to stay with my father, but Dawn kept us every day after school and on weekends. We spent every holiday and summer there as well. Father did not seem to mind. He kept to himself and never remarried.

Dawn was my father's sister, and they had another brother named Leon. Dawn left everything to Leon when she died as a spinster in her sixties. The death was very difficult for Craig and me. I was glad that it happened after I graduated from law school, although I had to leave my bar preparation course to attend the funeral.

That was a few years ago, and I would visit the house as often as I could. I never went inside. I only parked on the road in front of the house and stared at it. I cried when I did this, but this was my way of mourning her loss. She filled the void left by my mother, whom I barely remembered.

I feared Leon would be angry with me if he caught me because he was a suspicious man. I was surprised he got the house instead of my father. I knew that neither Craig nor I would have a chance at getting it, but Leon was such an awkward choice. Leon waited a while, but he eventually put the house on the market.

None of us had enough money to buy it, even my father, although I doubt, he wanted it. I prayed that I would get enough out of debt to offer to buy it, but once it formally went on the market, I knew I had run out of time. Now there was a serious buyer interested. It was as good as gone.

My new home was less than five minutes away from Creamy's. This mist had let up enough to allow me to walk leisurely down the sidewalk. I had a small jacket on that kept me warm and dry enough. I could smell ice cream on my clothes, which made me a little nauseated.

I had been hungry earlier, but I had lost my appetite by now. I wanted to get home and take a hot shower before crawling into bed. I hoped that my dreams would not be horrible nightmares about visiting Dawn's abandoned house. I dreamed of Dawn's house at least once a week since she died.

Tears welled in my eyes as I opened the door and climbed the stairs to my apartment. After I was inside my little home, I stripped down and jumped into the shower. I finished the cry that I had started after I got out of the shower and under the covers of my bed.

It seemed that I cried too many times in bed, but that was where I did my reflective thinking for the day. This cry was a deep one, coming from my gut, as I wailed from within my abdomen.

I wanted to call Craig, but I was not very close to my brother. He was almost as distant to me as my father because he was very similar to our father. Craig was stoic and private like him. When my father left to live in another state, Craig had moved with him to go to college there.

He had only recently returned to Guntersville a year ago to work for Johann. He had secured the position before he returned to Guntersville, and it was the reason he returned.

My cry began to settle down as my tensions unraveled. Hard work had gotten the best of me and my body betrayed me as I did the thing that I hated the most—I fell asleep.

I knew I was dreaming, which I always could discern. I was not at Dawn's house, but instead, I was on a train. A beautiful man was sitting beside me. I recognized him in my dream, but my conscious mind had no idea who this handsome stranger was. His dress was old fashioned, and I felt like we were on one of the first trains ever made for passengers. He got up and walked into another compartment. He said he wanted to get some tea. I stayed there and stared at a couple with a baby, who sat across from me.

Something felt wrong, and I heard a horrible crunching noise. I could see the train was crushing and twisting when I looked out the window. I pushed the couple into a corridor, and then everything went black.

I woke up suddenly from the dream. It was a fictional dream, but the emotions felt so real to me. I wondered what kind of metaphor this was for my current situation. I was too scared to go back to sleep, even though that was not a nightmare in the scary sense. It was just an odd dream, but at least it was not set in Dawn's house. It was twenty minutes past four in the morning.

I stayed awake until seven trying to figure out the metaphor for that dream. In the end, I decided the train represented what I associated as my childhood home—Dawn's home. The good-looking man was my future that had left me while I clung to the past. The couple with the baby was the past me—parents and all—that I longed to save on some subconscious level. The rest of the dream seemed obvious. Though insightful, I hated dreaming.

I got up at eleven and got ready for my meeting with Craig. I went ahead and put on my Creamy's uniform, which looked like something a Greaser chick would proudly wear. We had the same uniform in seven different colors. Each day was something with black, and todays was pink and black. Tomorrow would be red and black.

Larry knew how to beat a theme into the ground, but at least the outfits were cute and comfortable to work in every day. I could wash them myself, which was a big plus since dry cleaning was something I had to do for my suits that I wore to court. Dry cleaning bills added up, and money was not a luxury that I had now.

I finished my outfit with matching pink earrings, lipstick, and fast drying nail polish. I love to color coordinate, so I decided to grab a pink headband to make the pink theme complete. Pink was a good color for my hair and complexion, so I wanted to milk it for all it was worth.

I never knew who might come into Creamy's, and I wanted to look cute enough if some guy showed up all alone, which rarely happened. I could hope, however, and I even began to think about the beautiful man from my dream. If only he was real, I could imagine going on a date with him.

My phone rang in my pocket as I was locking the front door to my apartment. It was my brother, and he sounded impatient.

"Hey, where are you? It's five after."

I had been so busy getting dolled up that I had took too long getting ready and was late.

"I'm on my way. I'm on the causeway." That was a lie, as I was five minutes from the causeway, but he did not need to know that.

"Are you really there, or are you still at home?" Craig knew my scam because I always lied about how far I was since I was always late.

"Yes, I'm passing the chicken plant, so, I got to go before I lose my signal."

"Fine, bye."

I ended my call and jumped in my Jeep. I was ten minutes away from Aunt Dawn's house, so I had to hurry and make time in the spots where the cops never had a place to hide out and give speeding tickets. Almost the whole drive to Dawn's was void of cops, so I made it there in seven minutes instead of ten. Craig was probably angry when I got there, but I could not tell either way. He was calm faced as usual. He leaned against his pickup truck.

"Hey, I thought you were at the chicken plant almost ten minutes ago. That was quite a drive since you took so long." Craig's tone was calm.

"I'm sorry, Craig, I got behind a big truck. It's only a two-lane road, after all," I huffed as the humidity took my breath away.

It was much warmer than it had been the day before, and I was over-dressed with my hooded sweatshirt over my uniform. I removed it and slung it into the passenger seat of my Jeep. Craig ignored my dramatics and spoke to me as if I was a child.

"Alva, please don't act all weird. I got you here early so that we could walk around the outside before the real estate agent got here. I know you're emotional about this, but don't put them off the house or anything embarrassing like that. It's obviously not meant to be that anyone in our family will ever own this place again. We must move forward in life, not backward. The real estate agent will be here in a little over twenty minutes, so we must hurry and walk around the property before they get here. We don't want them telling Leon that we were acting suspicious, even though he thinks we're already suspicious for wanting to see the house in the first place."

"I got it, Craig, but what is your point with all the scolding?"

"Just act calm, and we'll get through this together. The guy who is going to look at this place is a developer from Birmingham, so please do not get upset if he says something about bulldozing this house down."

A dagger pierced my heart with that statement. I choked back tears as I walked the cleared-off portion of Dawn's property with my brother. We did not have much time to see it before we returned to our vehicles. The humidity had me sweating profusely, and Craig told me to use my handkerchief to dry myself off before the real estate agent got there.

According to him, my sweat told on us—how long we had been there and that we had been snooping around the property. I was mad and embarrassed by his continual scolding, but I complied. I wanted to fix my face anyway since I had not even got to work yet and already was melting in the October heat.

Although it was Fall, Fall in Alabama meant heat waves up to the eighties on some days—like today. The humidity was always there but was a little worse from the precipitation that had been going on all week. It was a good day for Homecoming, however, but a bad day to be me.

A few minutes later, a black SUV full of people pulled up to Dawn's house. I could see the magnetic sign on the door that said the vehicle belonged to a real estate agent. I sighed and waited for the destruction of my childhood. The SUV stopped behind our parked vehicles and the engine turned off as silently as the engine of the new vehicle had run.

The four doors opened at the same time, and a middle-aged man and woman got out of the back, while a man with almost the same face as the middle-aged man got out of the passenger side of the front seat. He looked about my age.

I felt a tinge of guilt, as I was relieved that I had fixed my face and combed my hair a few minutes ago. I noticed he was not wearing a wedding ring. There was another pang of guilt in my mind, but I ignored it.

The real estate agent was a strange looking man who was also about my age. He, however, wore a wedding ring. He also wore a gray suit with a red bowtie. He had a pointy chin, short brown hair, and round glasses. All in all, he was quite nerdy. I did not trust him mostly because of his bowtie.

However, I was prone to hating the man who was facilitating this whole situation because of my near predatory need to keep this house from selling. I knew that this nerd was not going to be defeated.

I knew he would sell the house. I could feel it. The anger kept my tears from coming to the surface, and I faked a smile and extended my hand to the man, who introduced himself as real estate agent Gene Shelton.

After my brother introduced himself, Gene said that we were meeting the Rowling Family: the father Joe, the mother Madge, and the son Hank. Hank was extremely good looking. When he smiled, his whole face smiled. He had sky blue eyes and brown hair that was straight but combed back to conceal how long it was.

He looked extremely preppy, which usually was not my type, but I could make an exception for someone as good looking as Hank Rowling. Hank made eye contact with me immediately, but my brother intervened by putting me in a bad mood. He spoke directly to Joe.

"Mr. Rowling, I understand that you're interested in developing these forty acres into a subdivision. We used to live here with my aunt, so I hope you don't mind us looking along with you for one last time."

I looked at Craig with fire in my eyes. He ignored me and continued to speak.

"My sister here is an attorney, and I am a research assistant. We can't afford this place, so please don't feel threatened by our presence. If we were going to put a bid on the place, we would have already done it. We just want to see the inside of the house for the first time in many years."

Hank's good looks no longer had any power over me. He did not exist to me anymore. I saw him as the enemy, even though he had said early on that he was just visiting the area with his parents, and he would not be involved with the subdivision.

"Let's begin the tour," Gene said as he unlocked the front door.

We followed him as he pointed out the various features of the house, as if Mr. Rowling intended on staying there with Madge. However, Mr. Rowling insisted on seeing the home as if he was not planning on plowing the house down to make room for fancier accommodations.

I thought I heard him mumble something to Gene about keeping the house for headquarters while the subdivision was built. I also heard him tell Madge that he could save this house for the last thing to remove before he replaced it with a new house. He made various despairing remarks about how country and old fashioned this house was.

"I think it has character myself," Hank said to his father, but I could tell he was saying that to me as a courtesy.

I had enough. Hank's attempt to compliment my humble upbringings felt like a derogatory remark. I fell behind the group intentionally to have one moment alone in Dawn's house.

I was in the kitchen, which was the room we used the most. We stayed in there to do our homework. We stayed in there and talked while Dawn cooked. We sat around the table and listened to family stories about our ancestors while we enjoyed the food Dawn prepared for us.

The table was still there along with the chairs. I sat down and stared at the windowsill behind the sink. The liquid soap that Dawn used to wash her dishes was still there. I almost burst into tears when I saw that tiny, sun-bleached bottle. However, I composed myself just long enough to hear Gene say from the hallway leading to the back of the house.

"And everything that is in the house stays, so you can just do what you like with it. The family already removed anything of value, so you'll probably be better off donating the lot to charity or chucking it in the dumpster."

Gene chuckled and I imagined his Adam's apple bobbing up and down and the bowtie bobbing with it. My blood began to boil. I stood up and walked out of the house. I could not take any more of this. I attempted to slam the door on my way out, but the effect was lost on the spring that allowed the screen door to shut in its own pace.

I leaned against my Jeep, as I was unable to leave because I was blocked in by the SUV. It was too hot to sit inside of the Jeep, and I was too broke to waste gas money and turn on the car for the air conditioning. I pondered on the different ways of handling the situation but came up with nothing but more frustration.

I knew that it was only a matter of time before someone came looking for me, which could only be Craig, as the rest were strangers. Oddly enough, however, the person who came looking for me was Gene. He was alone, which was surprising as well. He leaned on the Jeep with me, which was silly considering how dusty my Jeep was and how nice his suit was.

"You, okay?" he asked.

"Yes, I'm fine," I answered, which was a lie, but I was not going to let the enemy have the pleasure of my pain.

"I understand this is rough on you, but I am under the impression that Mr. Rowling is going to chuck everything in the house. I bet I can get him to allow you and your brother to go through and get whatever you want. He might appreciate the free help in cleaning out the place" he smiled as he spoke to me. I did not smile back.

"Listen, I am not in the mood for you and your fancy clients to come in here and act like you're doing me charity by allowing the poor rednecks to go through the junk. I know how much this house was listed for, and no one from Marshall County would ever be stupid enough to pay that amount."

"This place does come with forty acres of land. This is prime development real estate."

"Only a dummy from Birmingham would think that it is a great deal to pay so much for a nearly condemned house with a bunch of land that is mostly ditches. The other land around here that is not even built on is for sale, so why wouldn't he grab that up if he were so smart? It's a lot cheaper too. That shows me two things—you're a crook and he's a fool."

Craig cleared his throat from the front porch and interrupted my speech. Behind the screen door was the face of Mr. Joe Rowling. He looked furious. Craig was probably uncomfortable, but his face did now show it. Neither did Gene, as he was as calm and smiley as usual. He adjusted his bowtie and spoke above my head to Mr. Rowling.

"Well, let's tour the premises to see how lovely this farmland is."

"There's no need. I have seen enough. We can leave now," said Mr. Rowling

The tone in Mr. Rowling's voice stopped Gene Loveless' sales pitch dead in its tracks. He reacted to the authority of his client, who seemed to never hear no for an answer. With great politeness, Gene bid us farewell as he loaded the Rowling family back in his SUV. Hank looked at me with a grin that told me he was pleased with my speech. He was the only one that was legitimately happy. The rest were either uncomfortable or furious.

After the SUV left, Craig looked at me and spoke.

"Well, it was not as bad as I thought, but I doubt you did any good. Mr. Rowling was sold on the place. Gene told me he was going to tell you that Mr. Rowling was willing to let us go through the place, and I saw how that went. Oh well, whatever, Alva. See you later."

With that, Craig loaded up in his truck and I in my Jeep. We left at the same time. Gene Shelton had hastily locked the place before he left, and Craig had made sure all the lights were off except the front porch light. The road back to my apartment seemed longer than it had been when I traveled to Dawn's house.

I had two hours before I had to leave for work. It was nice enough of a day for me to walk to work, so I parked my Jeep and went inside my apartment to freshen up before I had to leave. I did not know what I should do in that time, but I was tired.

I sat up in my den in a chair that had an ottoman for me to prop my legs up. I grabbed a book that I had checked out from the library and began to read. This was the wrong thing to do, as I began to nod off almost immediately. My right foot fell asleep, so I moved to the ottoman after I jiggled it back to life.

My eyes were so heavy, so I closed them as I rested the book on the table beside me. I began to drift off and took a little catnap before work. I had another dream, but this time I was not in a train. I was in a boarding house. I sat in a bathtub. I had a male servant attending me.

I was wearing some type of flimsy dress that hid my nudity from my servant. I was in lavish surroundings, and I knew that I was in a school boarding house. My sense of entitlement was natural to me in this dream, although it was something the real me was not accustomed to feeling.

I yelled at the servant to bring me a bottle of oil that he promptly brought and poured into the bath water. He complied, but he did clumsily. I reached to slap him, but he grabbed my hand and kissed it instead. I pulled him, and he fell into the tub with me. We both laughed and kissed. I placed both of my hands on his face. When I touched his cheeks, his face changed from an anonymous Romani faced boy to the face of the man from the last dream. His familiarity made my passion surge, and I kissed him again.

The phone rang, and it woke me with a jerk. I did not have the time to finish the exciting dream, and I was also cheated the time to reminisce on its promise. I groggily cleared my throat before I answered it.

"Hello?" I asked.

"Hey girl!" screamed my cousin and best friend, Kim. "Were you sleeping? You sound just awful."

"Yes, I was, and you interrupted the greatest dream," I answered.

"Well, I'm sorry about that, but I can make it up to you. What are you doing tomorrow night? You got to work?" Kim asked.

"Actually, I work only through lunch. I'll be getting off at one," I replied.

"Well, good to hear 'because I want you to go out with a group of us to Birmingham. We're going to go to that big mall and maybe see a movie and get something to eat. Do you want to come?" she asked as if it was a rhetorical question.

"I don't think so, Kim. I really had a bad day and don't feel like doing anything other than sleeping this weekend. Sunday is my day off, and I want to get a head start on sleeping Saturday afternoon."

"Oh, you can't be so lazy. All you ever do is sleep late! Why don't you do this for me because I promised you'd come?" Kim whined into my ear.

I wondered what she meant and whom she had promised, but I did owe Kim so much. She was always there for me when I needed her, and she went out with me whenever I wanted and wherever I wanted. I agreed, and she squealed in response. I hung up the phone and saw it was time for work. I freshened my eyeliner and lipstick after I brushed my hair. I was at work exactly at four.

CHAPTER 2

Work went quickly that night because we were so busy. Many kids poured in and some of the girls wore the giant corsages that were customary for Homecoming. I was there cleaning until one, which was difficult because I had to be back at ten the next morning. After I got off on Saturday, I would have to hurry up and get ready for an evening in Birmingham, which was almost two hours away from Guntersville.

The next day, things went as I thought they would on Saturday—very slow. I was so tired, but the adrenaline of work had gotten me to wake up for a while. As I began to think that the day would never end, it was the end of my shift, and I went home.

I left with a shuffle instead of a bounce, but I knew that Kim would cheer me up and make me feel better. We had been best friends for so long, and yet we managed to keep our good relationship intact. She was a single girl like me, and she currently had no one special in her life.

That was why I was so surprised to see that I had been roped into a triple date, which for me was a blind date, even though it felt like a sabotage date. I knew something was up when she came to my apartment to get me and began a speech.

When Kim broke the news to me, her eyes got wide as she spoke.

"Don't get mad, but I have been talking to this guy from work. He is so cute, but he's a triplet. He wouldn't go out with me unless I could get his brothers a date, and my sister Betty agreed to go with one. I knew you wouldn't mind going with the other, but you were in such a weird mood yesterday. I was afraid you'd say no, and I had kind of already told them you would do it. So please don't screw this up because I think he's the one!"

I rolled my eyes and spoke.

"Fine, I'll do it."

She took me out to the minivan she borrowed from her parents. It was the only vehicle to which she had access that was big enough. The guys looked the same, except mine had a large birthmark on his face that looked like a giant, brown mole. He wore glasses. The other two did not. He had curly hair that he did not do anything with except allow it to frizz out, unlike his brothers, who wore gel in their hair. He was the dork brother. He was my date. He smelled like flannel and thrift store musk.

My date's name was Ted. His brothers were Tad and Tom. Tom was Kim's dream man. Tad was Betty's blind date. Everyone was having a good time, except Ted and me. Ted remained silent, and so did I, as neither of us had anything to say. I was too tired to be friendly. I kept nodding off during the drive.

When we got to the mall, we walked around forever but bought nothing. Ted made smart remarks about commercialism, which irritated me. Although I was too broke to buy anything, I was not against shopping. I planned on shopping again when I was back on my financial feet. It was too much for me. Ted was too irritating. I had to get away from the group for a moment.

Before I could go, Kim grabbed my arm and asked me.

"Where are you going? We're just about to get something to eat. There are a few restaurants here in the mall on the first floor. What sounds good to you?"

Ted interrupted our conversation.

"I think that seafood restaurant is great. Let's eat there."

Everyone else agreed. I did not even have a voice in the matter. Kim knew that I hated seafood. She pretended not to remember.

"It's settled then. Let's go there," she said.

The thought of a nasty fish dinner grossed me out. I followed them to the restaurant door and told them to get a table while I went to the restroom. When they were out of sight, I simply left the restaurant.

I walked over to the restaurant across from the seafood restaurant and decided to use the restroom there. It gave me a good excuse to wander. I began to stare at the menu posted on the wall of the entrance and was tempted to get something to eat there instead.

I heard Ted's voice coming from somewhere behind me announcing.

"I'll go see where she is."

I panicked and sprang for the nearest exit, which led outside to a plaza area. I realized that Kim might see me through the windows of the restaurant, so I started walking toward the garden area of the plaza. There was a catwalk that led to somewhere else out of view, so I took it. The place where it led looked like condos.

I saw a man walking in front of me. He was holding a six-pack of beer. One of the beers fell onto the ground but did not shatter. He did not seem to notice it, so I yelled out to him.

"You dropped your beer. That could be dangerous for kids around here."

He turned around and spoke.

"There's no kids here. The owner of this place doesn't allow them."

I recognized that face. It was Hank Rowling. He seemed a little drunk but sobered up when he recognized me.

"I know you. Alva Loomis, isn't it?"

"Yes, hello, Mr. Rowling."

"That's my father. Call me Hank."

"Okay, hello, Hank. How are you this evening?"

"I'm fine. Just having a good weekend that's about to get better once I relax with my six friends here."

"Right now, you only got five friends—at least until you pick up that one off the ground," I said.

Hank did not seem to notice my tone. He swooped down and effortlessly got the stray bottle.

"Why don't you join me?" he asked.

Before I could answer with the obvious no, my cell phone rang in my purse. It was Kim, and I knew she was mad. I reluctantly answered. Her voice screeched.

"Where are you, and what is the deal?"

"Sorry, I had to go outside for a minute to get some fresh air. I'll be right back in a second, Kim."

"Don't bother, Alva. We're driving down the interstate now. Ted had an allergic reaction to some shrimp in the appetizer, and we're following him in the ambulance to the hospital right now. You're going to have to call a cab to get a ride to the hospital. I'll call you and tell you which one."

"I'm so sorry about that, Kim. But you know I can't go to hospitals since Dawn's death."

Kim knew I had a phobia of hospitals. She sighed and spoke.

"Well, call Cousin Jimmy in Fultondale to see if he can let you stay at his house for the night. The ambulance driver said that we'd be there probably all night. I'll pick you up tomorrow on the way home."

"Okay, then. I will talk to you later," I said.

Kim hung up without another word. I knew she was mad at me, but she would get over it. She always did. The blood kept us together in ways that normal friendship would have not allowed.

Hank had been watching me talk on the phone to Kim with a pleasant smile on his face. He seemed to enjoy me getting riled up, which was somewhat intriguing and somewhat annoying. His cute face helped make it lean more in the positive way than anything else.

"Everything all right?" he asked.

"Well, I suppose," I answered. I did not want to go into it because Hank was a stranger.

I dialed Jimmy's number, but he did not answer. I called all the numbers I had for him, but no answer. He did not respond to my text messages. I was stranded and feared that I would have to go to the hospital after all. I called Jimmy's sister Peg, and she informed me that Jimmy was at Gulf Shores for some festival. Peg lived in Georgia, so I was stuck.

"I'm kind of stranded," I said to myself out loud.

Hank thought I was talking to him, so he responded.

"I guess you can hang with me for a while."

I hesitated, and Hank spoke.

"I promise I won't bite. We can just sit out on the patio of my condo and drink beers. I'm about to make dinner on the grill. Care to join me for some food?"

My stomach growled and I remembered how hungry I was. I decided it was just as blind as the date I was on before, so I agreed. Hank led me to his place, which was very nice from the outside. He handed me a beer, and I opened it and sat on a lounge chair on his patio.

Hank brought raw meat out on a platter and began to cook it in front of me. He handed me an unopened bag of chips and dip, which I opened and began to eat.

Dinner was nice, and after I had two more beers, I felt relaxed enough to open for conversation with Hank. Hank began with a surprise statement.

"My dad's not going to buy the place. You put him off it. He was insulted and all. It was so great." Hank chuckled.

"I'm glad."

"I knew you'd be, Alva Loomis, attorney at law."

"What is it that you do, Hank?"

"I'm a freelance journalist. I'm really a trust fund baby, but journalism is my career—officially," Hank replied in a matter-of-fact manner. I liked his style.

My phone buzzed again, it was Kim.

"Ted is doing okay, but we are staying the night. Did you talk to Jimmy?"

"No, he's in Gulf Shores," I answered.

"Oh, man, Alva, that sucks. I guess you're going to have to get a hotel room. Do you have the money?"

"No, I don't," I said with panic in my voice. I could not handle a hospital. Kim knew this well, but she was about as broke as I was.

I felt bad because I ruined the evening enough with my selfishness. I spoke.

"I'll charge it on my credit card." That was a lie, but she did not need to know. I had maxed out my credit cards, but I would deal with it later. She needed to focus on her almost boyfriend, who was probably distraught over his brother's brush with death.

I hung up the phone and answered Hank's inquisitive look.

"My cousin is at the hospital with a friend, and I'm stranded. I can't go to the hospital, so I need to get to a hotel. I think there's one in the mall, so I better get going."

"Do you have the money for a room?"

"I have a card," I responded.

"I can let you stay in an empty condo here if you like. They're all furnished. I have one you can sleep in for free."

So, he was the landlord. Landlords had keys to all the units, which was almost the same as sharing a room with him. I raised my eyebrow.

"You're the landlord."

"No, my father is, but I show the empty ones for him."

"Well, no offense, but I don't know you and you will have keys to the doors, so..."

"No, it's not like that. There's a dead bolt on the doors that can be locked from inside but can't be unlocked with a key at all. As long as you're in there, you're safe."

I shrugged. I was desperate, so I agreed. Hank took me to the condo, which was across from his. True to his word, the doors all had bolts on them that did not have a keyhole. I felt safe, and he left me alone. The place was completely stocked, including water and snacks that was from an unsuccessful open house last week. I found the master bedroom and went to sleep.

My phone rang the next morning. It was Betty.

"Where are you?" Betty asked.

"I'm at the mall pretty much," I answered.

"Well, can I come there and take a nap?" she asked.

I told her where I was, and within the hour, she was there. It was still quite early; in fact, it was barely daylight. She had a taxi drop her off because Kim was stuck at the side of her new man. According to Betty, the tragedy had brought them quite close. Kim was so glad that she was no longer mad at me.

Betty took a nap and then a shower. Hank had given me some toiletries along with a hot breakfast for us both. When Betty was dressed again, she came out of the bathroom holding her phone.

"Kim just called and said that she won't be home until late tonight. I must work early tomorrow, so I need to find us a way home. Got any ideas, Alva?"

Hank, who had just dropped in to deliver us some lunch, answered her.

"I can drive you two home. It's no problem." He smiled from ear to ear. He was so good looking.

"I don't know, Hank," I said.
"Thanks. Hank, is it? We'll take you up on that offer. When can you take us?" Betty asked.

"Right now, after you girls eat your lunch," Hank said.

I was too tired to argue and knew that we had safety in numbers. We rode home with Hank after we had finished our lunch. He dropped us both off at Betty's house. She drove me home, and I crashed into bed. My day off was totally ruined, but I could get some of the rest I had promised myself.

That night, my dreams were all over the place. I do not remember any of them in completeness, except one. *I dreamed that I was some girl in pioneer times. I had agreed to ride on a wagon with a guy a few years younger than me. I felt that he was too young to bother me, but he placed his hand in my blouse and attacked me.*

The rest of the dream was a blur, but before I woke up, I heard an internal voice say, "They blamed you and put you to death for fornication, even though he raped you. That's why you became a lawyer. The injustice still haunts you."

The next morning, I was in a bad mood from my dream. I knew it was something symbolic of my situation, but I hated to think about it. I caught myself assuming it was me processing the odd blind date that I had, but when I realized I was analyzing my dream, I stopped thinking about it.

Monday was always a slow day until after school. However, Larry started a preschool special that included one of his employees reading a story for story hour at Creamy's. Ice cream cones were only a dollar if the kid attended the story hour.

Today was my day to read the story, and I tried to be cheerful for the children. They always wanted to speak during the story, and I ignored them when they started talking. Some of the children that had been to a structured preschool would raise their hands, but I ignored them also.

When story time was over, Larry handed out the cones at the counter. I enjoyed being around children. In fact, they cheered me up. I smiled as I cleaned up the story time area. Larry would have a puppet show next week, but this week was story time only. As I put the books away, I saw someone standing in my peripheral vision. I turned around to see Hank Rowling standing beside me with a huge grin on his face.

"Hey, Alva. I see that I missed all the fun already. Care to recap the gist of it?" Hank asked playfully.

"You have the money, Hank. Go and buy the book," I replied in an equally playful tone.

"Why, Alva Loomis, are you flirting with me?" Hank asked.

I turned red but found boldness and answered.

"Yes, you're cute enough."

Hank liked my answer and did not turn red at all. He obviously was here to see me, so I felt that the direct approach would be fun for a change. Since his father was not going to buy Aunt Dawn's house, I felt he was no longer the enemy.

I walked back to the front and Hank followed me. I turned to him and asked.

"Would you like to buy something?"

"I will take a strawberry shake," he said and handed me a five-dollar bill.

I took the money and gave it to Larry after I made the shake. The change was my tip. After I handed Hank his shake, he asked me for a date. I agreed, and he said that he would meet me at Creamy's at six, which was two hours after I got off work. I had enough time to walk over to my house and get ready and walk back to meet him. He was still a stranger, so I felt leery of letting him in my apartment. Especially after the strange dream I had last night.

At six on the dot, Hank picked me up for our date. He was dressed in clothes that were about the same as he wore earlier in the day. I had changed into a nice dress with a sweater. Hank's face lit up when he saw me.

"You look beautiful, Alva," Hank said.

"Thanks, Hank, you look nice as always," I answered with a coy smile.

Hank took us to eat at a restaurant by the lake. It was nice to sit out on the patio since it was a mild day. The lake gave us a breeze that kept the heat from making us sweat.

We spent the entire evening speaking about Guntersville. Hank had been researching it, and he seemed to know a little more about the historical Guntersville than I did. I was more informative on the current Guntersville. The balance made an interesting conversation.

After supper, Hank asked me if I wanted to see something beautiful. We were already at the foot of the mountain, so after I agreed to his surprise, Hank drove up the mountain to show me a bluff view of Guntersville. It felt like Inspiration Point, but it was a spot in the middle of a neighborhood, so we could not linger too long.

"Isn't this lovely?" Hank asked in total awe of the blinking lights of the small town. The lake was as well, and the lights reflected on the calm waters.

"Yes, it is, Hank," I answered. I had seen this view before, but never in the dark. It gave me an idea.

"Have you seen this in the daylight?" I asked.

"Not yet," Hank replied.

"Well, we should do this tomorrow if you'll still be in town. What do you say? Lunch will be my treat," I said.

"Okay, but I'll pay for lunch if you choose the restaurant," Hank answered.

I agreed.

"I will see you at ten thirty at Creamy's."

"Do you not want me to see where you live?" Hank asked.

"Sorry, no, I just am used to being there all the time. I live across the street from it, diagonally that is," I replied.

"Well, let me take you home tonight, and I will pick you up there tomorrow. Is that okay with you?" Hank asked.

I agreed and gave Hank directions to my apartment. He felt my reservations about trusting him, so he let me out of the car without walking me to my door. He told me that I should come down and meet him the next morning at his car. I told him goodnight and went up to my apartment. I called Kim to check on Ted.

"He's doing fine. He never wants to see you again. He said that you were too materialistic for him. He seems to think that his allergic reaction was karma for agreeing to date a woman who loves shopping," Kim informed me.

"Well, that is fine. He was a little odd, even for me," I replied. My ego hurt, but I would live.

"On a happy note, I am really getting serious with Tom. We decided to go steady." Kim squealed as she spoke. We were too old to use those terms, but I knew what she meant.

"Well, that's great Kim. I hope you two do well. You home yet?"

"Yes, I just got home two hours ago. Thanks for taking Betty home. She tells me that you met a guy of your own named Hank. Do tell!" Kim purred.

"He's just a guy that I met last weekend. His father almost bought Dawn's place, but he didn't. He's a preppy guy journalist type, but I like him," I responded.

"When are you going to see him again?" Kim asked.

"Tomorrow," I said sheepishly.

"Well, good luck, girl! I'll talk to you later, as Tom is getting out of the shower," Kim said in a whispery tone.

Kim and Tom were getting more serious. I hung up the phone and went to bed. The last few days had been tiring, so my sleep came quickly. That night, I did not have a dream at all.

The next day, I met Hank at his car in front of my apartment. I decided we should eat at the sandwich place just a few feet away, so Hank got out of his car, and we walked to lunch.

Hank enjoyed the place, and after we ate, we went to his car to drive back to see Guntersville in daylight from the bluff. The view was prettier to me in the daytime, and Hank appreciated it very much. We spent ten minutes there before we felt a neighborhood resident might get alarmed and call the police.

As we pulled away from the bluff, Hank said, "There's a historical place on the road that cuts to the other side of the bluff. When my parents were looking for property in Guntersville, the owner of a house in the neighborhood said it was visited by historical tours sometimes. Do you know what I'm talking about?"

"I have no idea. What is it called?" I asked.

"I don't remember, but it's some kind of rock or something. I haven't been there for a few months since my parents have been scouting Guntersville for almost a year now," Hank said.

A cold chill went down my spine as I realized that Aunt Dawn's place was closer to being sold than I had realized. It was the final decision time that day when I had met Joe Rowling. That was all over now, so I felt game for a history lesson of Guntersville.

"Take me there," I said.

When we got up to the house, Hank commented that it must have sold since the sign was now missing and a car was in the drive. A new name was on the mailbox that said, "Cooper." The name sounded familiar. There was a family that owned a funeral home with that name outside of Guntersville, in a community called Claysville.

There was another familiar thing at the house. It was the truck that belonged to Cliff Marcel, who was a simple man that owned a gardening business. The truck was parked in front of a shed that was almost thirty feet from the house. The doors were open, which meant that he was somewhere inside the shed.

The shed was closer to where we were going than the house where someone named Cooper lived. The little road narrowed more considerably near the property line. It was the size of a driveway by the time we got to the rock. Hank turned off the car. We got out to see the historical rock of Guntersville.

Hank made it their first and stopped dead in his tracks. He spoke in a forced calm tone.

"Alva, don't come up here. Someone is up here. I think she's hurt."

He walked closer to the rock, which was at the edge of the bluff. One false move, and he would tumble down the side of the mountain, though the slope was not dramatic enough to hurt him too much. I could not see what he saw on top of the rock from where I stood. The rock was positioned with such a tilt that only the topside was visible to me.

"She's not hurt, Alva. I think she's dead. I'd ask you to identify her, but I don't want you to see this. I think she killed herself. Her wrists are slit. I don't see a note anywhere, but it could've blown down to the lake by now," Hank said. He had removed a hanky from his pocket and covered his mouth to keep from vomiting.

I called the cops from my phone. It was in my pocket. Hanks was in the console of his car. He was frozen, unable to move. I think he feared she might be alive. He stared at her with the intent of seeing the tiniest move.

Before the police made it up there, a scream came from behind us. It was Cliff.

"I heard you say that you were calling the police because someone is dead. It's not Miss Morgan, is it?" Cliff asked with fear in his voice.

"I don't know, Cliff," I said with caution.

Cliff did what I did not want him to do. He ran to the rock and looked at the woman. He screamed her name. It was Morgan Cooper, co-owner of the Cooper Funeral Home in Claysville.

Hank tried to stop him, but Cliff grabbed Morgan and held her tightly. Cliff was mentally disabled enough to be noticeable, but not enough to be nonfunctional. His gardening service was quite popular.

Morgan Cooper hired him a month ago. That was what I heard later from Cliff as he told the police. Cliff had totally messed up the forensics on the scene, as he grabbed her and held her with tears in his eyes until the police pried him off her. Hank had to explain that Cliff was nowhere near the rock when we got there. That pacified the police enough to not arrest Cliff on the spot, but he was asked to stay there for questioning after they finished with us.

Morgan had slit her wrists and laid on the rock to die. The police asked us if we saw anything that would indicate foul play. Morgan had donned a creepy, skintight black dress that looked like she bought it early for Halloween. The police split us up to make sure our stories corroborated. After twenty minutes of questions, they let us go. When we left, Cliff was taking his turn answering questions.

Hank took me home. I called in sick to work. Larry understood and agreed with my reasoning. He gave me the rest of the week off as well. I drank half a bottle of brandy to put myself to sleep.

The rest of the week, I took a shot a day until the bottle was empty. I did not call anyone at all. No one noticed. Larry was running the shop. Craig was working for Johann and dating Sandy. Kim was into her new man. Hank disappeared back to Birmingham. Father was ignoring me like usual. I was alone. I was relieved.

The entire week, my dreams left me alone as well. The alcohol seemed to block my ability to dream. When the next Monday came, I was as rested as I could be. I went back to work at Creamy's.

Three weeks had passed since we found Morgan's body, and I almost felt normal again. The only dreams I had lately been of me answering endless questions to the cops about what we saw on that day. Otherwise, my nights were empty. I would close my eyes and then open them to the sound of my alarm beeping.

It was a Friday at Creamy's, which was also Halloween. We had to prepare for handing out candy and coupons for ice cream to all the trick-or-treat kids, which would happen at the shop. The shop also was holding a Halloween party for kids that went from dark until eight.

After eight, the party would be themed for adults, with a costume contest with higher stakes than the one for the children. The child who won in various age groups would get a free party at Creamy's for up to twenty kids and ten adults. The adult that won would win a two-hundred-dollar cash prize. To cover the costs, there would be a cover charge for the adult party, which went on until midnight.

We were required to dress up in costume, which was fun to me because I loved Halloween. I had originally thought of being a vampire, but the thought of a slinky, black dress made me think of Morgan Cooper. That was a name that I would never forget.

My choice of costume was a scarecrow. I borrowed some overalls from a patron of Creamy's. He also brought me a flannel shirt with red and black checks to wear underneath it. I went to the thrift store and found an old straw hat the day before Halloween. I also found some dried out corn there, and instead of using it for a decoration for my apartment, I stuck it in the front pocket of the overalls.

I used some lipstick to paint a red triangle on my nose to complete the effect. I wore regular makeup otherwise. My hair was hidden under my hat. I wore sneakers, as I did not own any shoes that looked scarecrow friendly. It was the best I could do under the circumstances and on my budget. Larry seemed pleased as I came to work that morning.

"You look great, Alva," Larry cheered, "I'm glad you put in the effort."

"Thanks, Larry, but where is your costume?" Larry was wearing his hair like he always did, but he was wearing a suit instead of his usual greaser gear.

"I'm the ghost of Ricky Nelson."

"Larry, Ricky Nelson did not look anything like that before he died!"

"This is the way he looked when I saw him last near the fire escape in the back. I'm the ghost of him, not the actual him before he passed," Larry said as he shrugged.

It was time to get busy for Halloween, and we did. All four of the employees were here today. One would go with Larry to the booth, while the rest of us would stay here and handle the Halloween crowd and pass out candy and coupons. Emily went with Larry, and I stayed at Creamy's with the others. I was in charge, which was a surprise.

Halloween passed quickly, as I had a wonderful time with all the kids and the adults who showed up for the parties. I was a little disappointed to not see Hank, but I supposed that he would come around again, if ever, once he got over the weirdness of our last date.

I did see my brother Craig, who showed up after everything was over when I was about to walk back to my apartment. Craig was not dressed up at all, and he looked as he always did—serene. However, though he had a calm tone, his words made me quite upset.

"Alva, you should not go walking around on Halloween night alone. There's a lot of creeps out there," Craig said to me on the sidewalk in front of Creamy's.

"Craig, get real. It's not like I got blonde hair and blue eyes," I jested.

"I'm serious, Alva, you should be careful not to end up like Morgan," Craig replied.

"Morgan killed herself, Craig," I snorted in an attempt not to burst out in tears.

"No, she didn't. The police came and questioned me today at Johann's place. It turns out that she was murdered," Craig said.

I was shocked.

"How do they know that?" I asked.

"Because she was drugged before her wrists were slit," Craig said.

"They told you that?" I asked in the shocked tone that matched my feelings.

"Yes, well, no. They came by and asked me questions about the last time I saw her, and after they left, I called a friend that worked with Morgan. He told me that the autopsy revealed that she had been drugged before her wrists were slit, and she was probably unconscious through the whole time she bled to death."

"Why were they asking you, Craig? I didn't know you even knew her personally," I asked.

"I didn't really, but I was friends with a guy who worked as an undertaker. He went to high school with me, Leroy Osmond, and I met Morgan through him. She was friendly and wanted to hook up with me. She tried to get Leroy to set it up, but I wasn't interested. It was never more than that," Craig answered.

Craig walked me to my apartment, and he left. I was surprised that he made a trip just to tell me about Morgan, but he might have been on his way home or on his way to see Sandy. Craig never told me anymore than what I asked or what he thought was essential information.

I suppose since I found her body, Craig felt that I would want to know. However, I wish he had not told me, as it made me have nightmares about finding her repeatedly until the alarm woke me up for another day of work at Creamy's.

The following Monday came abruptly. I lost the weekend, and it was now time for another workweek. I did not have to be at Creamy's until three, as I had to go to trial for one of my criminal cases that I had gotten from the court-appointed list. While I was at court, I saw a smiling face of a friendly attorney who had always helped me out when I had a question on procedure.

He was over seventy years old, but he was still the best criminal attorney in Northern Alabama. He specialized in capital murder cases, and he had yet to lose a client by death penalty.

His name was Ernest Beason, and he waved at me to come and join him while we waited in line for our turn to go up to see the judge.

"What you got here today?" Ernest asked.

"I got a public intoxication case. Pretty simple case, but the prosecution is cracking down on these lately. I'm going to try this one," I answered.

"Yes, I know how that is. I have a standard DUI case, but the guy didn't blow, so I think we can get a not guilty on this one for sure. Well, after I appeal it to Circuit Court," Ernest said from behind his file.

"I'm surprised you're here, actually, I never see you in city court," I commented.

"Well, I took this one as a favor to my great-nephew. It's really a charity case, as the guy is supposed to make payments, but you know what they say about criminal work? If the client doesn't pay you by trial, you'll never get paid. If you get them off, they will disappear after they promise to pay. If they get thrown in jail, they'll blame you and never pay you. They'll even threaten to turn you in for malpractice." Ernest waved to another attorney that stepped in line behind us.

"Well, I never get paid ever anyway," I said with a forced smile on my face. "If it wasn't for court-appointed work, I'd have no income. Paying clients don't come to me."

"Well, maybe things will change. It took me nearly ten years to get above breaking even. I had older attorneys to help me out when I needed them. That's what I try to do for you when I can," Ernest said.

"Thanks for that," I said.

Ernest adjusted the files in his hand and said, "I'm glad you are here, though. I just got hired to be Cliff Marcel's attorney for the Cooper murder. They're charging him with capital murder. I will need someone that I can trust to work on this with me, and if you do well, I will hire you as an associate attorney."

I was shocked. I realized that Ernest was saying that I would be working for free on this, but this was what I had wanted forever to happen. It was my door into a firm, and that would allow me the ability to quit my job at Creamy's and be a serious attorney. I immediately agreed.

It turned out that although Cliff was simple, his family was loaded. They lived in New Jersey and paid for his quaint lifestyle in Alabama. Cliff took a job to keep busy. I always wondered how he could afford the nice gardening equipment for his business. To me, Cliff simply had a learning disability, but to others, he had become a killer.

"We may have to seek the insanity defense if it gets hairy," Ernest said to me in a hushed voice.

"I am surprised that he would go for that. Doesn't he just have a little bit of a learning disability? He's never been declared incompetent, let alone insane, has he?" I asked.

"No, but the insanity defense comes from a place of the lawyer knowing better for the client who has lost capacity. If it is a matter of life and death for Cliff, I will have to raise that defense," Ernest said blankly.

The line moved, and Ernest went before the judge to try his case. He stipulated to the facts and announced for appeal, and before I could try my case, my client begged me to make a deal. We struck a deal with the prosecution, the judge approved, and I went home to change for work at Creamy's. I agreed to be at Ernest's office at eight in the morning.

That night, I dreamed of the mysterious stranger once more. It was the first time I had dreamed of him in almost a month. This time, he was a soldier in the Civil War; at least he was dressed like a Confederate soldier. He had been at war for so long that he did not make it back in time to watch me die. I had a fever that killed me. He clung to my lifeless body, and he screamed and cried that he had only missed me by minutes. He held a bottle in his hand that looked like medicine.

My alarm buzzed at seven in the morning. I got up and got ready to work with Ernest. I would have to be at Creamy's at four, so I would work with Ernest until half past three. That would give me enough time to change my clothes and eat some lunch before going to Creamy's.

Ernest's office was on the side street parallel to the Courthouse. He walked to court whenever he needed to do so. He claimed that walking to court made him as healthy as he was. When I got to his office, he immediately saw me in his personal office. He lit a cigar and began to tell me where the case stood.

"Well, Cliff didn't do it. He had witnesses that saw him at Marge Neely's house less than twenty minutes before you two stumbled upon the body. He had been there since half past six that morning," Ernest said as he puffed.

I realized that maybe my expertise was not all that Ernest wanted to tap into for his case. I was a potential witness. My blood ran a little cold at the ethical implications for this.

"Can I ethically be working on this since I may be a witness?" I asked.

"Of course, you are not at all a part of this. If they put your name on the witness list, I'll remove you from the case," Ernest answered.

I trusted my older colleague, but I had reservations about the legality of his claim. If I were exposed as a tainted witness, would Ernest use me to call a mistrial? And if I were never called to be a witness, would Ernest be using me to get an inside track to the possible prosecution's case, as I had been the one to discover her?

Hank had really found her, but I was there. I felt uneasy and resolved to call the ethics hotline later. Ernest did not seem as sweet and fatherly as he had been a few minutes ago.

I resolved to begin my work for the day. Ernest had me looking up case law on insanity defenses in Alabama. He also had me looking up other aspects of affirmative defenses for capital murder cases. He wanted me to make sure that nothing had changed since his last capital murder client.

So far, he did not have me compromise my ethical duties. I could look up this law regardless of whether I was involved. I was an attorney. I needed to look up the law. It was my job to know it.

Ernest took me out to lunch at a nice sit-down place on top of the mountain. He paid, and when we went back to work, he met with several clients while I did research in his firm's law library. There were three other attorneys that worked for Ernest's law firm, all as associates.

Supposedly, it was a rite of passage to work for Ernest. He never allowed a partner, it seemed, though he promised it in the past. The attorneys grew tired of not making partner and would eventually leave.

Ernest handled all kinds of law, but he hired attorneys to specialize in certain areas. He had a good real estate attorney that was female. She handled all matters concerning land and focused on probate and estates. There was a bankruptcy lawyer that was male and stayed in federal court almost every day. The other attorney was male, and he was a tax attorney.

The female attorney came into the law library and asked me if I had seen Ernest. Her name was Callie Altman, and she was about fifteen years older than me. I told her that I had not seen him since lunch, and she disappeared.

After about an hour, I heard a familiar voice in the hallway saying, "Thanks, so much." It was my Uncle Leon. I pretended to go to the restroom to investigate.

Leon, for once, had a smile on his face. He quickly recognized me and held the smile on his face because he did not want Callie to think less of him.

"Hello, there, Alva. I see you're working here now. I had no idea," Leon said.

Callie quickly answered for me, "She's interning here with Ernest. Today is her first day."

Leon nodded.

"Well, Alva, I guess since you're here, I can save a call to your father. I sold Dawn's place, and we closed on it today." Leon did not wait for a response but instead bid farewell to Callie and me. He walked abruptly out of the office and onto the street.

My mouth was open in shock. I looked at Callie and inquired.

"Who bought it?"

"I did," boomed another familiar voice. It was Hank Rowling. He had appeared from the conference room with a stack of papers in his hand, along with keys on a familiar key ring that Dawn used for years.

I wanted to punch Hank in the face, and he knew it. He wanted to talk to me and possibly save me the embarrassment of losing face in front of a colleague like Callie, so he asked me to speak with him in private in the conference room. Callie shook his hand once more before we retreated. Callie went to meet with a client waiting in her office.

After Hank shut the door, he interrupted me before I could begin.

"Before you say a word, let me just tell you why I'm doing this. My father was reconsidering buying it after he cooled his heels. I knew he'd bulldoze it down, so I bought it myself. I needed a place in Guntersville because I wanted to see you more often, and I have been assigned to work on the Cooper murder case by a major newspaper in New York. I don't plan on doing anything to the place but restore it. I wanted to keep something important to you alive, and who knows; maybe you could help?"

I wanted to cry and scream at the same time. I wanted to claw at Hank's beautiful face and kiss it at the same time. I was in shock. I tried to process the information. Hank bought Dawn's house to restore it. It would exist still, and he would allow me to visit it. If I played my cards right, I could marry him and own it one day.

My mind was racing too far ahead in this story. I calmed down.

"Okay, Hank. This is strange, but I guess I can trust you with the house better than anyone else. Are you really going to restore it?"

"Completely," Hank said, "and with your help to make sure it's accurate." He grabbed me and kissed me. I did not fight but reciprocated. He whispered.

"I missed you so much, but I wanted to see you in person instead of calling you. It seemed so impersonal after what we went through together. I bought the house on a romantic impulse the day after we saw that dead woman. The sale just closed today."

Hank kissed me again. I kissed him back, harder this time, and it took his breath away. He spoke raggedly.

"I was going to come to Creamy's today and surprise you. I would have never guessed you would be here, but this is a law firm. I thought you worked alone."

"I do, but I'm moonlighting here to get my foot in the door for an associate position," I said in response to his implied question.

"That's great," Hank said.

A tap on the door let me know that someone wanted inside. It was Ernest, who had already met Hank before, as he addressed him by name. Hank excused himself after telling me that he would see me tonight at Creamy's. I told him that I would be there at four. I found it hard to catch my breath, but I managed.

Ernest and I went over the relevant case law for the remainder of my workday. When it was time to go, I found my heart fluttering in anticipation as I made my way from the law firm to my apartment, and finally to Creamy's.

When I arrived, Hank was not there, but I knew he would come nearer to the close of business. I floated through my shift in anticipation of seeing him again. Every time I thought about our two kisses, my heart skipped a beat. I had to stop thinking about him because Larry kept asking me what was wrong.

What was wrong with me was Hank, who came walking through the door at nine. He had changed from a business suit to a light sweater and slacks. He smiled brightly as he saw me in my yellow and black uniform.

"You look like a cute little bee," Hank chimed.

When Larry was not looking, he grabbed my hand and kissed it quickly. Hank then ordered vanilla ice cream and apple pie with a slice of cheese on it. He drank black coffee with his dessert. When he was finished, he asked me when we could see one another again for a date.

I wanted to see him tonight, but I had to write a memo on capital murder for Ernest. I was supposed to give it to him first thing at eight in the morning.

Hank would be a distraction if he came to my apartment, and if I went out, I would never get anything done. I had to turn him down until tomorrow night, which was my night off from Creamy's. I would work at Ernest's office until five and go home.

I saw a light flash in Hank's eyes. He spoke.

"Would you like to come over and see Dawn's place? It is livable, believe it or not, and we could hang out there. I already have the phone and cable turned on there. I have a crew coming tomorrow to put furniture in the rooms void of it. I am bringing new mattresses and sheets to go on the bed frames that were left there. The couches were not there, but I have some true to period pieces coming at noon. It will all be ready by the time you get off work. How about it?"

I agreed because I wanted to see Dawn's house more than I wanted to see Hank. Well, maybe it was half and half, but I was not sure. I told him that I would see him at six.

Hank did not leave Creamy's until we closed at ten, and he did that reluctantly. He could not kiss me goodnight like we both wanted because Larry was around. I knew we would catch up tomorrow night at Dawn's place. It would not be the first time I had a make-out session in Dawn's living room.

I went home around eleven and worked on my memo. I fell asleep around two, which was hard to do after being wound up by research. However, I fell asleep just long enough to not dream that night.

CHAPTER 4

The next morning, I was excited enough about seeing Hank that I did not feel as tired as I should after minimal sleep. I had toiled on the memo so intensely the night before, but when I gave it to Ernest, he tossed it on his desk and said he would read it later. He had court at nine, so he left almost immediately.

I was alone all day with my thoughts on the case. Ernest had entrusted me with the case file, which contained the report on Morgan's autopsy. It even had pictures, which I ignored while I read the written report.

The report had a lot of medical language in it that I did not understand. However, Ernest had written notes beside it that explained what it meant in common terms.

According to the autopsy report, what gave away the fact that Morgan had not killed herself was the angle at which the supposed self-inflicted cuts had been made. It was an angle that came from a left-handed person from the other side. Whoever had done this had not thought of trying to make it seem like she did it by standing behind her to make the cuts.

There was some kind of drug in her system that had been metabolized to the point of her having taken it at least two hours before her death. She had eaten a lunch of chicken salad sandwiches and a leafy salad about the same time as the drugs. The bread came out with some of the drug infused in the undigested parts, so it made Ernest think, according to his notes, that the bread had been laced with the drug.

The drug would have made Morgan sleep through the whole thing. She would not have felt the two cuts on her wrists, or the two other small cuts that were unnoticeable to the untrained eye.

There was a small cut behind her right knee that was the size of a paper cut and a smaller cut behind her left ear that was the size of a pinprick. The medical examiner noted them in the report. Ernest's only note was the word "ritual" with a question mark behind it, which gave me the fear that if anyone else noticed that Cliff may be labeled a serial killer.

That afternoon, Ernest came into the office after a long day in court. He was visibly exhausted, but he tried to hide it. Ernest looked at me and spoke.

"Did you get lunch, Alva?"

"Yes, I brought my own, thanks."

"Well, good, I had to eat lunch with a bunch of stuffy attorneys. It was miserable and boring!" Ernest chuckled as he spoke.

"How was court, Ernest?"

"It was the same old story. We went through tons of stuff just to have the DA move to dismiss because he had no case. My client insisted we have the full trial, so I put on the defense and we won. There was not probable cause for the warrant, so we couldn't let them dismiss it just to re-file another day. That's the way to keep them from refilling the charges after they perfect the warrant." Ernest cleared his throat and said, "Well, now you and I are going to see Cliff."

We left his office to go see Cliff, who was still behind bars because the judge did not want to let him out on bail. The heinousness of this crime was cause enough to keep him, according to the judge. However, that was unconstitutional, according to Ernest, and he was going to get the judge to set a bond amount, no matter how ridiculously high.

After we arrived to see Cliff, it was a while before he came out. The guards seemed unafraid of him, but they forced us into a visitation room with glass and phones. My job was to sit and take notes, and offer the occasional question if Ernest missed something. Otherwise, Ernest would do all the talking.

Cliff seemed to be all tears when he saw Ernest. Ernest told him to calm down so that we could get something done, which somewhat pacified Cliff. The only thing Cliff said was that he did not do it because he could never harm anything, let alone a beautiful woman like Miss Morgan.

Cliff called her Miss Morgan instead of Miss Cooper. He had a difficult time saying her last name without stuttering. I had noticed that the day we had found her body, and the police questioned Cliff.

Cliff answered all of Ernest's questions, but I could tell that Ernest was not getting the answers that he wanted. Ernest finally gave up on getting the magical answer that would aid his defense of Cliff. In the end, Ernest told Cliff that he would get the judge to set a bond amount for Cliff. Cliff only nodded in response.

When we left, Ernest and I got into his vehicle and made it back to his office. On the drive there, Ernest spoke to me about the case.

"There's a great danger of this being called a ritualistic murder. If that happens, then they'll start searching for any other unsolved murders that fit the pattern from here to New Jersey. Cliff has lived lots of places over the years, so they might search the whole country. Anything that even looks similar, they will try to pin on him. It becomes a witch-hunt after that. We must stop it before it starts. Alva, I want you to investigate ritualistic murders and serial killers and write me a memo on it so I can have something to fire at them if they start that talk."

By the time we got back to the office, it was time for me to go home. Ernest told me to get the memo done in a week. That gave me enough time to do some research. I decided that I would go to the local university library to search it out, as I wanted to keep this as anonymous as possible. Ernest wanted a memo on information, and not the law, so I did not have to go to a law library, which was a relief.

I went home and got ready for my date with Hank. I had a few minutes to kill, so I decided to call Craig to ask him if I needed to get a special library card since I graduated nearly five years ago. My student library card had been my student ID, so that was no longer valid.

When I called Craig, he seemed busy, but he talked to me anyway. He was in the middle of the library himself. He whispered as he talked to me.

"What's up, Alva?"

"Sorry to call you in the library. Can you talk?"

"Sure, I got a minute. No one is up here in the archives anyway."

"I wanted to know if I could get a card to use the library as a former student. Do I have to do anything special to get it or will they deny me since I graduated?"

"No, they will give you a card. You're still in the system, even after you graduate. You just get a different kind of card. It's a real card instead of your ID. Why do you ask? You got some research to do?"

"Yes, I wanted to do some research for my personal knowledge." I remembered that Ernest did not want this to get out, and if Craig let it slip, I could be in trouble. I kept the secret from Craig, and he did not press me for more information. I suppose he figured that it was recreational since it was not in a law library.

"Well, when you come up here, let's have lunch," Craig responded.

"Okay," I answered.

"What are you up to tonight? I am free and wanted to have dinner with you," Craig so quiet that I could barely hear him. Someone must have come in the archives floor.

"I am going to spend time with Hank," I replied.

"Hank? The guy that you almost blasted to death because his father wanted Dawn's place, or is this some other Hank?" Craig inquired.

I forgot to tell Craig about Dawn's place selling. I would never call my father, but Craig would for me. I sighed and spoke.

"Craig, I forgot to tell you that Hank bought Dawn's place instead of his father."

Silence from Craig's side of the line, but I continued.

"He bought it because he wanted to keep it from being destroyed by his father. Joe was going to bulldoze it probably for sure, but Hank is going to restore it."

"Why would he care, Alva?" Craig asked. His skepticism was valid. I would wonder the same thing from his shoes.

"We're kind of dating or something."

"Is it dating or something—which is it?"

"Dating, I guess."

"Well, it must be serious if you inspired him to buy a house and restore it."

"I suppose, Craig."

"Well, good luck, sis."

Craig was about to end the conversation, but I wanted to make amends somehow.

"Craig, would you like to join us tonight? Hank has had Dawn's place cleaned up and filled with furniture so that it looks pretty good already."

"I don't know, Alva, that seems weird."

"Please, Craig, come with me. I want you to see it too, and I want you to meet Hank properly. He's nice."

"I heard that he was with you when you found Morgan's body. You two probably have a trauma bond, but you're an adult."

Craig was not saying what he wanted to say. He was not saying that at least Hank did not kill Morgan since he was with me when they found her. He was not saying that I should have told him that I found her instead of him hearing it through the gossip of Guntersville.

Craig never answered my question. I pressed.

"Please, Craig, come over with us!"

Craig agreed to come without Sandy, who was out of town. I hung up the phone with Craig to call Hank and tell him about the change in plans. Craig would not eat with us, but he would come over to Dawn's house around nine thirty to visit. Hank decided to take us out instead of cooking at Dawn's house because he did not have enough supplies there for that quite yet.

Hank picked me up at seven, and we had dinner at a great Chinese buffet. We opened our fortunes at the end of dinner to see what was in store for our futures.

"Though the door may close, the lock will never rust." Hank's fortune was odd. He laughed at it and threw it in the middle of his empty plate.

"Remember who you are." Mine was more poetic and generic, in my opinion. That could refer to a million things.

When the waitress returned to offer us a to-go cup for our sweet teas, Hank asked her, "Are all these fortunes always so hokey?"

The waitress grabbed Hank's fortune and read it. She said, "Yeah, they're always silly, but we always get the same ones here. There's about ten of them that circulate in each box. Her face looked puzzled as she reread Hank's fortune. She said, "That's strange. I've never seen this one. I've read all of them in this week's box."

The waitress asked me to see mine and she read mine. She was flabbergasted, according to her, because both of our fortunes were anomalies from the standard batch. She said before she went back to work, "I thought I've seen them all in my two years here, but I never saw those."

We shrugged it off as we paid for our food and left. We made a quick stop by the market to grab some of my favorite snacks and drinks in case I was to get the munchies later. This gave us about an hour to cuddle and kiss before Craig arrived. However, he was early and waiting for us when we got to the house.

"Sorry that I'm early, but I thought it would take me longer to get here through all the road work they're doing between here and the university, so I left earlier than I should," Craig said.

"Craig, you should've called us. We could have had supper together," I said.

"It's okay." Craig answered, "I already ate with Johann before I left. We were both in Huntsville today, so we met up and ate there. We always try to have some time each month to do a status of his project, which we went ahead and got over with for this month."

"How's that going?" I asked.

"Well, it's fine. We have a presentation tomorrow at the university for the committee approving the book's progress. We seem to be on target," Craig answered.

With that, we went inside of Dawn's place. The clouds were growing thick and dark, and the moon was no longer visible, though it was full. It seemed the clouds were so full of rain that they were only a few feet above the trees. It was going to storm hard when it finally broke. I thought I saw the occasional flash of lightening in the corner of my eyes, but I never could be sure.

We all toured the house to see the instant improvements that Hank had made. It looked nice and almost like home. Hank assured me that he would try to make it even better, but I was not certain I wanted a replica of Dawn's place. I liked the idea of Hank making it into his own. I would talk to him about it later once I had a chance to absorb the changes and reflect on my true feelings.

After our tour, Hank poured wine for us. After my first glass, the rain began to tap lightly on the tin roof. After my second glass, the rain began to knock, and by my third, the rain was pounding away. Hank looked unconcerned because he was probably used to tornado activity in Birmingham. It seemed like it hailed there almost every thunderstorm. When it started to hail, Hank seemed less nervous than I was—probably because he was used to severe storms and hail during thunderstorms.

I peeked out the window with hesitation because of my fear of being near a window when the lightening was outside. By this time, the lightening was flashing away, and the thunder shook the house while the hail rattled it.

I saw that the entire yard was covered in so much hail that it looked like snow. The flashing of the lightening provided me with the illumination to see the yard. I was glad that Hank and Craig parked in the carport, as it kept their cars from being dented and damaged.

The lightening flashed violently and crashed into a tree at the end of the carport. The tree split in two, which was quite a feat for such a large oak tree. Half went over to the edge of the yard. The other half fell right in front of the carport.

Hank was behind me and saw the whole thing.

"I guess we're trapped here until morning. I'll call someone first thing to get them to remove that dead tree," he said.

"I'll just get someone to pick us up and take us home," Craig said. Hank insisted.

"In this weather? I just heard on television that it's too dangerous to travel until the tornado warning is over, which won't be for another four hours. If the trees are down here, then it is probably the same for the rest of the roads leading up to this place. We're so isolated that I doubt if anyone knows yet that the roads are impassable."

"That's only if they are, Hank," Craig said.

"Oh, come on, Craig," I said. "Let's just stay the night. You can have your old room."

"What about you? Where you going to sleep?" Craig asked sarcastically.

"In my old room as well, of course, dear brother. Hank has taken the master as his own, and our two old rooms are guest bedrooms. He's got them all done up, as you saw, so let's just get some sleep." My head was spinning from the wine, and I was ready to sleep it off.

We all agreed to stay the night in Dawn's house. The storm was bad for a little while longer, but after a while, I woke up to find it was only raining steadily enough to soothe me back to sleep. Hank had found one of the old nightlights that Dawn always kept in my room and put it back in there. Its presence made me think of Dawn, and I realized that I might be falling for Hank Rowling.

I woke up the next morning to find that the electricity was off in the house. I crawled out of bed and saw that the streetlights were also out as well. It was still dark, although it was almost time for the sun to come up for the day. All the clouds had cleared away, but there was still a steady breeze that whipped the trees and bushes around in a frantic manner.

I was still very tired, but I decided to get up and use the bathroom before trying to go back to sleep. After I finished, I noticed light flickering down the hall leading to the kitchen. I followed it to find that both Hank and Craig were sitting at the kitchen table with a single candle illuminating the room. The candle was in the middle of the table.

Hank looked at me and apologized.

"Sorry, this is the only candle I have in the house. I need to add that to my list, along with flashlights and batteries. I did manage to find this tiny radio in the cupboard. The batteries are old, but they still work."

The radio was a tiny one that I bought when I was a teenager. I was shocked that Dawn still had it. I was even more shocked that the batteries, which were at least ten years old, were still working.

The radio crackled as Craig turned up the volume. Since I was no longer sleeping, there was no longer a need to be quiet. The radio announcer began to describe a tornado that had ripped through Albertville the night before while I slept.

"The damage is considerable. Police are imposing a curfew of eight, so please no one leave your houses until daylight. If you need help, there are rescue agencies that are set up to help you. If you are not in need, please stay in your house. It is too dangerous to drive through the damaged areas of downtown Albertville and the highways that run through those areas."

The male announcer continued to describe specific incidents of damage. Albertville was the city directly next to Guntersville. Dawn's house was near the city line between the two cities. We barely missed the tornado, it seemed.

In about an hour, we had electricity again. Craig and Hank made some breakfast while I called around to see if anyone could remove the tree from Hank's yard. Most of them were busy, but I finally found one who was willing to do it at the escalated price that Hank promised to pay.

Within the hour, the tree was moved enough for Hank to deal with it later. That was as much as he could get out of the man whom he had paid to move it out of our way. It turned out that the city had cleared the road leading up to Hank's house to work on the power lines.

Craig offered to drive me home, which he did quickly. Craig seemed anxious because he had his presentation today with Johann, who lived in Albertville. My heart sank. Johann lived in the area that had been hit the hardest by the tornado. Craig must have thought the same thing, as he was driving like a madman to get me to my apartment.

"Is Johann okay?" I asked Craig when he dropped me off.

"I have been unable to get him to answer his phone. I will go up to his house and give him a ride to the presentation, as we had originally planned."

"Craig, what about the police restricting access to that place? Will you be able to get in there?" I asked.

"I'll find a way," Craig answered before I shut the car door. He drove away in a hurry.

It did not take me long to find out what happened to Craig that day. My phone buzzed with a text message from Craig about ten minutes later.

"Cops won't let me in, but I'm going to find another way around to get in." About twenty minutes after that, I got another message from Craig that read, "I am about to be arrested. Please call Johann, as he is not at his house. His car is not here either."

I called Johann a few times but never could get in touch with him. His cell phone went straight to voicemail. I fidgeted until the phone rang from an unfamiliar Albertville number.

"This is Alva Loomis," I said when I answered the phone.

It was Craig. He had been arrested. However, he did not call me to bail him out. He asked me a strange favor.

"Alva, can you please go with Johann and assist him in his presentation today at the university. I found him. He decided to stay in Huntsville last night when he heard that over one hundred tornadoes were set to strike the South this week. His friend has a storm shelter, so he stayed with her. I know you want to bail me out, but I will deal with that this afternoon. I will get a bondsman to come here, but he can't be here until six because of the weather damage. So, please go with Johann today. I have the number of where he's staying. His cell phone is dead."

Craig gave me the number and told me that Johann was expecting my call and my help. I was in shock because Craig did not even tell me why he was arrested. I assumed it was because he tried to go against the cops' roadblock. However, I did not know for certain. For now, I would help Craig out because this was important to him and meant his job. If Johann lost his funding, he would no longer need Craig. So, I called Johann to see what he wanted me to do.

Johann was very nice, as usual, and I met him at the student union center for the presentation. Johann was confined to a wheelchair, so he wanted me to pass out the handouts and turn down the lights for the power point slide show he was going to show. I would just be there to make things go quickly and to fetch anything unexpected that was needed, such as extra copies or water.

The presentation went smoothly, and Johann was very courteous to me. After everyone left, Johann began to speak to me about Craig.

"I feel horrible about what happened to Craig. He was arrested because of me, you know."

"What happened?"

"Well, Craig snuck around the barricades to get to my house. He told the cops that I was disabled and may be seriously injured or near death without my medical equipment, which is powered by electricity. However, the cops told him that they did not care what he was there for because only medical and city personnel could pass through the barricade."

"Believe it or not, though, that is not why he was arrested. He was arrested because he caught people rummaging through my damaged house. It was not destroyed, but a tree went through it. That pushed some of my things out, and Craig tried to scare them away, but one man beat him up. When the cops saw that it was Craig, they recognized him as violating the barricade and arrested him. The guy who did it played innocent and his girlfriend who was waiting in the getaway car lied and said Craig attacked that man."

I was in shock. I knew that if Craig said he did not do it, he did not do it. Johann agreed with that but did not offer any help. Of course, I was a lawyer, and Craig would never let on to Johann that I was anything but successful. He probably refused to let Johann post bail for him. Of course, it was technically unprofessional to ask that of his employer. Johann never brought it up, so Craig must have told him that he had it taken care of, which he technically did.

My mind began to race about going to Albertville to see about getting Craig out of jail. I did not have any money to pay a cash bond, if that was what was required. I did not have any real property to put up for the bond. Craig was correct in calling a bondsman. I would go to the jail and wait for him to get out around six. It was currently only one in the afternoon. Since I was still in Huntsville at the university, I would have to kill time somehow to keep my mind from going crazy with worry.

I walked over to the cafeteria for some light lunch. I was too nervous to eat very much, but maybe doing something regular like eating would help me feel better. It had been a while since I went to college here, and the cafeteria was completely different than it had been the last time I was there.

I walked past the different hot meal stations and went to the cold sandwich case. I picked up a chicken salad sandwich plate. I remembered Morgan's last meal and cringed. I chose a fruit salad instead.

After I paid for my food, I found a seat off in a corner. I went to the unoccupied side of the cafeteria seating because I wanted to disappear from everyone's attention.

My plan worked because I was able to sit in the solitude of my thoughts, which surprisingly were focused on Cliff Marcel. I knew that Craig's issue would take care of itself. Maybe I was a little bit in denial of what happened today. No matter the reason, I was glad to not be upset for my brother. I would be upset later, when I needed to be.

For now, I needed to worry about Cliff, whose life may be forfeit if someone decides he is a serial killer. He is not a killer. I just knew it.

When I finished my lunch, which I mostly picked at, I left the cafeteria and went to the library. I decided to go ahead and get my library card today. I could do some research later.

After I got my library card, I looked at my watch and saw that it was only two. I still had more hours to kill before I could go to Craig. I went ahead and asked directions to the proper section of the library to begin my research on ritual and serial killers.

I was too embarrassed to ask about the crime section, so I asked about rituals instead. The person sent me to the mythology section, which surprised me. It was in the basement of the library, and the criminal section was on the top floor. Since I was already there, I decided to browse around.

I knew that this was the wrong section of the library for me. I did not need to know about religious rituals or cultural rituals. I needed to investigate ritualistic killing in respect to serial killers. However, I was already down there, so I checked around just to make sure there was absolutely nothing for my research. It is easier to eliminate things in research than it is to search out infinite possibilities.

After I had my fill of mythology, I left the basement and rode the elevator to the top floor. I began my research on serial killers. After about an hour of that, I knew that Cliff was not one. I took notes for my memo to Ernest, who was probably on the case as I was doing this.

Luckily for me, I was able to get him to let me off work today. Larry understood as well. I would go back to both jobs tomorrow.

I wanted to check the time on my phone. However, my phone was missing. I searched around the top floor of the library, and when I could not find it, I returned to the basement to look for it.

As I rode the elevator down to the basement, I remembered putting the phone on a shelf of books while I had tried to stack and balance a couple of large books in my arms. Once on the floor, I rushed to the spot where I had left the phone, but it was not there. I knew that was when and where I lost my phone.

After I checked the entire floor, I went looking for someone who worked in the library to see if they had found my phone. Of course, no one was to be found. I began rummaging through all the offices and workrooms to see if there was a person inside that could help me.

So far, I was the only person on the floor. Most of the offices were locked and all the workrooms were dark and vacant. Finally, however, I found a room that had the word "refreshment" on the door. I turned the knob, and it opened. The light was on, and there was a man inside drinking coffee at a small table positioned in the middle of the room. In his hand was my phone.

When he saw me looking at the phone, he spoke to me.

"Yours, I presume?"

"Yes, thank you so much for finding it. I can't live without my phone." I answered breathlessly. I tried to regulate my breathing before I took the phone from his hand. He patiently sat the phone on the table beside his coffee cup.

The man did not seem to notice my huffing. Instead, he smiled and spoke.

"Glad that I could help you sustain life. I personally do not get cell phones. I think they're an invasion of privacy. I do not like the idea of someone being able to find me at any time, any place."

He rummaged through the pockets of his jeans and pulled out a phone that made mine look quite inexpensive and archaic. He sighed as he spoke.

"Yet it is required to live and survive in this day."

As if the spell seemed to lift, he was snapped out of his philosophical distraction and smiled brightly. He shoved the phone back in his pocket and spoke.

"I am so sorry. Where are my manners? My name is Aren Willows."

Aren dug out a card from his messenger bag and handed it to me. Even his business cards were nicer than mine. Aren explained.

"I am the Department Chair of Mythological and Religious Studies." The card said the same, along with the strange spelling of his name, which I would have guessed was "Aaron" instead of the way it was spelled.

Aren left out his title in his introduction, which made him officially Dr. Aren Willows. Aren appeared too young to have made it through that much schooling. He had wavy, black hair, with only the slightest silver strands mixed amongst the curls. He was taller than me, and I would guess he was a few inches over six feet tall. He had dark eyes that must have been hazel, for one moment they appeared to be brown but the next they appeared to be green. He had a nice tan, and the few creases in his face and the slight crook of his slender nose only made him more attractive.

Even though Aren had a sophisticated look about him, he had also the look of a man who knew of hard labor. He wore the nicest clothes. He had on jeans and a button-down shirt that would fit in at a rock concert. His shoes were made of beautiful leather that probably cost more than one month rent for my apartment. His watch was of a brand that I never imagined I would see a person wearing without it being a knock-off.

Through all the nice clothes, somehow, Aren did seem tough. He looked like a Greek soldier, but he was not. He was here, smelling of cologne and lotion. He was not holding a sword. He was holding a cell phone—my cell phone. I had forgotten to take it from the table. He smiled at me patiently as I finally reached out and took the phone.

As I took the phone from Aren, his fingers brushed mine. I felt electricity in that moment. I always thought that was a figure of speech, yet I felt it. It did not hurt like it did when I got a shock from wearing socks on carpet. Instead, it vibrated and tickled right under the threshold of pain.

It startled me, and I almost dropped my phone. Aren must have noticed it as well, but instead of surprise, he looked relieved. I must be imagining this. He probably only noticed my reaction. His relief must only be from me not dropping the phone onto the tiled floor. I must look like a crazy woman to him.

I was crazy. I had not even said my name. I cleared my throat and spoke.

"I am Alva Loomis." I blushed as I rummaged through my purse to pull out my small business card case that looked like it should hold cigarettes instead of cards.

Aren took my card and read it silently. He said, "Attorney at law." He smiled and said, "You seem like a lawyer to me."

"Really? I never get that. Most people never take me serious as an attorney. They think I am too soft spoken and always too young." I blushed again.

"I would have guessed attorney right away. You seem like the kind of woman who wants to fight against injustice. Don't be meek. You are very intelligent."

"How do you know?" I asked in a defensive tone.

Aren's face became serious for a moment, but he quickly smiled again and answered.

"Because you got through law school, Alva. That is not easy. And you passed the bar exam. Most people can get into law school, but they fail out and never graduate. Others make it but fail the bar exam. You must be smart to go so far."

Aren slipped my card into his wallet.

"I will call you if I ever need legal advice."

"And I will call you if I ever need mythological advice." I paused and said, "Wait, do you know about rituals as well?"

"Of course, that is my area of expertise. What's your question?"

"Well, I know you know about cultural rituals and religious rituals, but do you know anything of rituals that serial killers perform in their crimes?"

"I am trained at noticing patterns. If there is a pattern, I will notice it. I am not a psychologist or a criminal expert of any kind, however. If you have a scenario, I may be able to see if there was a religious or mythological message in the ritual."

I bit my lip and thought a few seconds. I could not just tell Aren about the case without Ernest's approval. Ernest would probably assume that it would be over the top to consult an expert in mythology for a criminal case. Ernest would never agree to pay Aren either. Aren interrupted my thoughts.

"I won't charge you for this, and I am willing to sign a confidentiality agreement."

I blinked as he said, "I have worked with attorneys in the past."

CHAPTER 5

I decided that I would think about Aren's offer as we said our good-byes. I really thought that Aren was intriguing, and an excuse to work with him closely would be welcome to me. However, how could I convince Ernest that this was required for the case?

My answer came quite unexpectedly as I was exiting the basement. I had been so preoccupied with my thoughts that I did not notice that someone had made a pile of books on the floor at the end of the book-shelf. This pile was slightly in the walkway created between the main two sections of bookshelves that divided the floor in half.

I tripped over the books and stubbed my big toe through my shoe. I was grumbling as I leaned over to pick the books up and place them in a book cart that was only a few inches away from the lazy reader's dis-carded pile.

As I put the last book in the cart, I noticed the cover art. It was of a crow, but it was done in an artistic way that made the silhouette seem more human than bird.

As a chill went through me, I realized that silhouette looked familiar. I remembered Morgan's lifeless body in a black, slinky dress that was so tight it clung to her like a second skin.

The sleeves, collar, and hemline all had been cut to look shredded, so I thought. But as I looked at this bird, I saw that the tightness and the jagged hemlines were meant to mimic something else—feathers.

Someone wanted Morgan to look like a crow. The report indicated that the dress was brand new, with hardly any physical evidence from Morgan's house on it. It was so close to Halloween that it was the kind of dress that could be at any of the hundreds of Halloween shops in the area.

Ernest had checked on that dress, and it had been sold in thousands of Halloween shops for the first time this year. It was also available online as well. It was almost impossible to trace the dress, but there was no evidence that Cliff ever bought such a dress.

I looked at the book to see if it would help me in my studies. However, the cover art was just that, and there was nothing in the book that would point me in the right direction.

I needed to consult Ernest and see if I can ask Aren for help. I could probably find it on my own, but it would be better for Cliff if we went for the expert in the field if someone was using mythology as a type of ritual in how he displayed the victims.

A cold chill ran through me as I realized that this was in fact a serial killer. Morgan may have been the first victim, but he was performing rituals. I needed to stop him, and I needed to clear Cliff's name.

When I went to see ernest, I was relieved that Ernest was there after five. Everyone else had gone home, but he remained. He looked relaxed for the most part, but his eyes looked troubled.

"Alva, how are you?"

"I'm okay." I decided not to speak of Craig now. I wanted to know where he stood before I began to air my dirty laundry around town, especially among my colleagues.

"What are you doing here this late?"

"I saw that your car was here, so I tried the door, and it was open. I wanted to talk to you about the Marcel case." Ernest nodded, and I continued.

"I think there may in fact be some kind of ritual here. I think the person who did this is trying to make a religious statement."

Ernest dropped his head and rubbed the sides of his temples. My news had upset him. He removed his reading glasses but never looked up.

"What kind of religion? Christian?" he asked.

"No, I think it's older than that. I think it's like what we'd now call mythology," I answered. Before Ernest could argue or question me further, I explained.

"I think that Morgan was put in a costume to represent a crow. There's some kind of cultural reference to that. I know that we don't really have a stigma about black birds like they used to, so I assume it is something older. So, I think we should look to mythology to see if there are any other patterns that we can use to figure out who this person is and disprove that Cliff did it. And I met the Department Chair of Mythology at the university, and he has worked with lawyers on other cases. He's willing to be a consultant. He'll sign anything we need, and he'll do it for free."

Ernest perked up and spoke.

"That's great thinking, Alva. Good eye for detail and great initiative to make that contact. I'll get the form for the expert witness to sign."

I was surprised that Ernest did not at all get upset or dismiss my ideas. I gave him Aren's card, which he photocopied and returned to me. He used it to insert Aren's name into the form that was standard for all consultants and experts. He printed it out and gave a copy to me for Aren to sign.

"Make sure to keep up with your time from this. Have Dr. Willows sign this before you do anything with him."

Before I left, Ernest inadvertently answered my question about why he was eager to sign Aren up for his services.

"Cliff's family's pockets are deep. The more billable hours, the better."

After I got to my car, I looked at the clock. It was a quarter past five, which gave me enough time to make it to see Craig when he got out of jail at six. It usually only took a few minutes to get there from here, but since the storm damage, I needed the extra time to navigate through the maze of debris and closed roads.

I hoped that the roads leading to the police station were not closed. I doubted it since the police station was essential to keep order in a town.

However, if it came down to it, I would use my lawyer status to get access to jail. They could not deny a prisoner constitutional rights.

The main highway was closed except for one lane each way, which made it very difficult to move efficiently. People were making it worse by slowing down at especially damaged areas to gawk. I detoured onto the old highway that is the Mainstreet that ran through downtown Albertville.

Many side streets were closed in Albertville, but I was able to get to the police station. It was a few minutes after six when I finally arrived, but Craig was not outside waiting for me. I decided to go inside and see if he was waiting in the lobby.

There was no sign of Craig in the lobby. However, there was a bondsman that I recognized from court.

"Are you here for Craig?" asked the bondsman.

"Yes, I'm his sister Alva Loomis."

"I recognize you from court. You're an attorney, right?"

"Yes, I am. Where is Craig?" I asked impatiently.

The man held a clipboard in his hand. He said, "I am waiting for them to let me back there. It might be a while. It could be almost an hour. They're slow as it is, but the storm made it much worse."

The man's cell phone rang, and he excused himself outside to answer it. I took a seat in the lobby and stared at the floor. It was cement and shiny. The little gravel particles that were sealed in gave the floor its own pattern. That was the extent of the decorating, I suppose.

As my stress increased, the little pebbles seemed to move. I closed my eyes, but the dizziness got worse. I tried to regulate my breathing. It finally hit me. Craig was arrested. He did not do it, but no one believed him. There was a false witness.

I did not know how Craig would beat this. To beat the appearance of impropriety, the prosecutor would make an example of him because of me. It was all politics in a small town like this amongst the lawyers and city government. There could be not even the slightest indication of favoritism to the relative of an attorney.

An hour and forty minutes later, Craig emerged. I somehow managed to make it without passing out. The bondsman was called back there for about thirty minutes before Craig came out with him. Craig went into the small courtroom adjacent to the lobby. It was empty, but an officer had him sign multiple forms before he could go. The bondsman had already left since his part was finished.

I did not say a word to Craig. The officer explained to Craig that he would get his day in court before he was considered guilty. Craig smiled a crooked smile at her, and we left after he finished signing everything that she put in front of him. He took his copies and folded them as we exited the building.

Craig's car was impounded when he was arrested. The cops refused to release it to him that day, and they used an excuse about the tornado to justify it. They told him to pick it up tomorrow between the hours of eight and noon. Craig did not argue with them as they said this on our way out.

I drove Craig to his home. He never said a word to me. I wanted to ask him so many things, but I could not bring myself to break the silence between us. I knew that what he was charged with was not the worst thing in the world, but that did not mean it should be taken lightly. All these thoughts went through my mind as we remained in silence.

As Craig exited my vehicle, he finally spoke.

"Thanks for letting me just not say anything. You really understand me, Alva."

He closed the door. I remained silent even though I was raging on the inside. Craig had been charged with something he did not do. I was a lawyer, yet I could not prevent injustice from happening to one of my own.

My silence continued as I drove myself home. Craig was wrong. I did not understand him at all. I just could not bear to open my mouth to argue.

By the time I got home, I was crying hard. It was like a dam broke inside of my head. I just had held it in so long that it finally exploded. I was glad that it was too dark to see me inside of my car. My make-up was everywhere. I had black mascara stains on my shirt. My eyes stung with salty tears and eyeliner.

I could barely see to get myself out of the car and into my apartment. When I finally got inside my home, I scrubbed my face and changed into my pajamas. I could not afford fancy matching pajama sets that boutiques sold. Instead, I wore old t-shirts and gym shorts to bed. Most of it was what I had worn to gym class in high school, so it was too small to be of any use in public. The shorts were very short, and the shirt had become a tank top with my belly showing.

I pulled my hair back from my face before I had washed it clean. I rinsed out the sink and began to soak my mascara-stained shirt in cold water. It was possible that I could save this shirt. I did not have many nice work shirts, and this was one of them. I had wanted to look nice for Johann's presentation.

As I soaked my shirt, I heard my phone ring. It was not very late in the evening, but I was unable to deal with anyone right now. I ignored it. However, whoever was calling was persistent. As soon as the phone would stop ringing, it would resume ringing seconds later.

After four times of this, I went to shut my phone off. However, the screen told me it was Hank. I was frozen with terror because I did not want him to know that I was avoiding him. It was nothing personal. I did not want to talk to anyone right now.

However, Hank's next strategy was texting, which he began. He sent me three texts in a row. I opened them.

"Alva, please answer your phone."

"I need to talk to you."

"Don't avoid me. I can see you walking around your apartment."

Hank was outside. I composed myself and answered when the phone rang. "Hello?" I tried to sound surprised, but it was not working.

"Alva, please let me in. I've been out here for almost an hour. You won't answer your phone or your door. I'm worried about you."

Hank must have found out about Craig somehow. Or maybe he was worried about me due to the tornado. There was also a killer on the loose. There were reasons to worry.

As I reached for the door, I thought of how Hank was still relatively a stranger to me. I did not know him at all. He could have been a killer for all that I knew. Maybe he did not hurt Morgan, even though he did know where she lived. He had been with me for a few hours, but it was possible that he was able to drug Morgan, cut her and be there just in time for the chicken salad surprise.

I made a note to myself to speak to the owner of the place we ate that day to see if Hank had ever been there. Hank had acted like he never had been there before, but the waitress seemed too friendly with him. She may have been flirting, or maybe he had been there before but pretended otherwise.

The person who brought Morgan the sandwiches had gotten them there. Most people did not know that, but the ingredient list tipped me off. There had been sugared pecans in her stomach. The Cream Puff Restaurant put those nuts in the chicken salad mix.

I snapped out of detective mode and back into reality when I heard Hank pounding on the door at the bottom of the stairwell. I left my apartment and ran down the stairs to let him inside. He had a dozen pink tulips in his hand. Where he got those at this time of year was a mystery to me. However, I was so happy. Those were my favorite flowers, though I preferred red, pink was just lovely.

Hank followed me to my apartment, and once the door was closed, took me in his arms and kissed me. I was completely oblivious to the fact that my face was swollen from crying. Only when he pulled away did I feel the pain. Hank noticed me squirm and inspected my swollen cheeks.

"Are you okay? I knew something was wrong. Did someone hurt you?"

Hank's eyes seemed to boil momentarily at the thought of anyone doing me harm. That made me realize that he would not hurt me. He was protective over me. That was a good thing.

Hank leaned in for another kiss, but this time, it was on the forehead and very gentle. My forehead was the only place that was not red or swollen. It did not help that I had enthusiastically scrubbed my face. I had irritated the skin more than it already was from my crying session. However, cold cream would solve my problem. I would wait until Hank left for me to put it on.

Now, it did not seem that Hank would go anywhere. He plopped down on the couch and spoke.

"Tell me what's going on." His words were confrontational, but his tone was tender. I sat beside him and began to tell him about Craig.

By the time I got through my story, Hank was leaning forward, with his hands on his face and his elbows propped on his knees.

"This is what I hate about small towns. They are so corrupt," said Hank.

"No, it's not like that. Besides, big towns are just better at hiding it, that's all," I said.

I was a small-town girl. I would not have some big city preppy boy telling me about where I lived.

Hank noticed my irritation and apologized.

"I just assumed you wanted to hear something like that. Sorry, this place is lovely, or else I would not have bought a house here."

I smiled.

"Oh, I thought you bought that house because of me."

Hank pulled me close and whispered in my ear.

"Well, you were the deal breaker."

We kissed again. This time it barely hurt my face. Most of the irritation had gone as my cheeks had cooled down. However, Hank was making them warm up again. With every kiss, I blushed a little more.

It was getting close to nine, so Hank offered to take me out before the restaurants started closing. I turned him down, and we agreed to talk tomorrow and see about getting something to eat when I felt better. Hank was very respectful, as he did not press me to stay any longer.

After Hank left, I sat down on the couch and tried to relax. Although I was no longer upset about Craig, Hank had gotten me wound up in a completely different way. It was nice, but I wanted my heart rate to slow to its normal speed for more than five minutes at least once today.

That was not going to happen, it seemed, because my phone rang again. I laughed at myself because it had made me jump. Hank must have forgotten something. I flipped my phone open without even looking at the screen.

"Hello," I said in an exaggerated friendly tone.

"Hello. Is this Alva Loomis, attorney at law?" a man spoke on the line. This was not Hank.

It was too late for a client to call me, so I was irritated because I felt it inappropriate for a client to call me at almost nine on a weeknight. However, I kept my cool when I spoke.

"Yes, it is. How may I help you?"

"This is Aren Willows. I hate to bother you, but I assumed that you would not go to bed before nine. I am more of a night person myself, so to me, this is early. I did not wake you, did I?"

"Oh, no, of course not. I was going to call you tomorrow. I talked to my boss, and he said we could use your services as an expert. He really appreciates your public service since that's what you're doing by throwing us a freebie. I may be able to get some money to reimburse your expenses, if push comes to shove, Mr. Willows."

"Please call me Aren. I can just write off my expenses on my taxes. I would love to help. I find the legal industry enthralling," Aren said.

I tried not to laugh at Aren's comment. He was being gracious. It was possible that someone from the outside thought legal work was exciting. There were enough television shows about it. I snapped out of my amusement and spoke.

"When can we meet for you to sign the confidentiality agreement and get a look at the case?"

"Well, I am available tomorrow night. Night is the best time for me. I am indisposed during the day," Aren answered.

"Oh, yes, you have classes during the day," I commented.

"No, my classes are all at night. Everything I do is pretty much at night," Aren chuckled. "Like I said, I am a night person. However, I can meet you at five, which is right after sundown, tomorrow. I don't have classes this week because of Fall Break."

"Where would you like to meet?" I asked as I grabbed my notebook and wrote down the time.

"I can come to the law office. Is it in Guntersville?" Aren asked.

"Yes, well the office address on my card is my personal office. I am working with a firm in Guntersville for this case. However, I won't make you drive all the way here since you're working for free. I will meet you at the university. We can meet at your office." I dug in my bag for his card. His office information was on there.

"Sure, I can meet you there. I have an office in the building next to the library."

"That's convenient," I responded.

"Yes, it is. We can walk over there if we need to look up anything that I don't know or have in my office," Aren said.

"Okay, Aren," I said. "Meet you at five in your office. Thanks for calling and take care."

Aren hesitated for a moment, as if he wanted to say something else, but must have decided against it since all he said was, "See you tomorrow then."

It was only after I hung up the phone that I realized that Aren was probably calling me for a date. I had cut him off. If it were a legal reason, he would have brought it up after we spoke of meeting for business reasons. His hesitation must mean he was calling me socially and not professionally.

I giggled because I was flattered. Aren was good looking and sophisticated, but he had to be at least ten years older than me. He did not look that old, but his level of education and career stature told me that he was at least in his late thirties.

I did note when I met Aren that he was not wearing a wedding ring. It is a single girl's natural reaction in the company of men to look at the ring finger. However, I was focused on Hank now, so I was relieved that I had cut Aren off. It was not professional to get involved with someone you worked with; since Aren and I would be working together closely for at least a little while, I knew I had dodged a bullet.

I put those thoughts away from my mind as I began an outline for the memo on ritualistic killing for Ernest. In no time, I would have my memo completed. After I worked a while, I stopped for the evening and climbed into bed. I had to be at the law firm at eight, but I had to split my day at Creamy's. I had a four-hour shift from noon until four. That would give me enough time to dash to the university and meet Aren at five. I knew Ernest would be okay with my half day because I would resume law work from five until at least ten, with or without Aren at my side.

As I drifted to sleep, I made a to-do list in my head for the next day. I already had it written out in my planner, but it helped me to shut my brain down by running through lists. It was my version of counting sheep. It worked because I slept soundly.

CHAPTER 6

My eyes popped open the next morning exactly one minute before my alarm was supposed to ring. That put me in a bad mood right away. I knew it was going to be a rough day.

I begrudgingly slid out of bed to begin my day. I was a little bitter about losing a minute of sleep that was due to me. I fussed about it internally while I took my shower and finally stopped after I had my morning bowl of oatmeal.

I left the apartment and walked to the law firm. It was a nice day for walking. There was a little breeze that was just cool enough to make me feel invigorated. The wind snapped around me until all the grouchiness blew away from me in the morning breeze.

I arrived at the law firm exactly on time. Ernest was already there in an early meeting with a client. Ernest kept his loyal clientele by working around their schedules. He often had early and late appointments and even would meet on weekends to accommodate work schedules.

I was about thirty minutes into my workday when Craig called me. He sounded groggy, which was a change from his usual neutral tone.

"Alva, can you take me to get my car?"

"I'm at work right now, and I will be working all day until late tonight. Sorry, I can't help you," I answered.

"I need to get my car today, and you are the only one who can take me. Please. I'm desperate, Alva."

"What about Sandy?"

"She's still out of town. Please, I am calling you as a last resort," Craig pleaded.

"I was supposed to work here until eleven thirty. I guess I can ask to leave early," I said.

"Thank you so much," Craig sighed.

"I'll call you back and let you know when. It will probably be sometime around eleven, at the latest. I must be at Creamy's at noon for the lunch rush," I responded.

We said our goodbyes, and I went to talk to Ernest. He just finished with his early morning client, and I caught him before he left for court. Ernest agreed to let me leave at ten thirty if I would pick up the lunch for the firm at the Cream Puff, which was only a minute or two walking distance from the office.

I called Craig to tell him that I would be there at eleven sharp. He responded with gratitude, but he also made a snide remark about working for free should mean setting my own schedule.

Before Ernest's secretary called in the order to the Cream Puff, she checked with me to see if I wanted anything. I turned her down, and when it was time to pick up the order, I scooted out of there as quickly as I could.

When I got to the Cream Puff, I saw Jolene, the waitress that had served me the day that Hank and I went. That was also the day that we found Morgan's body. Jolene had been the waitress that had seemed way too friendly with Hank. That reminded me to ask her about the sandwich that someone had brought Morgan that fateful day.

Hank had acted like he had never been to the Cream Puff before, but he never said it one way or another. His unfamiliarity was implied. He acted too eager to be there, as if it was a new experience for him. He had many questions about the menu, which made it seem like it was his first visit to the Cream Puff.

Hank had been in Guntersville many times, and it is possible that he ate there. I never thought to ask him. Now that it was important to know for legal reasons, I decided to ask Jolene instead of Hank.

Jolene was gathering the multiple bags of the law firm's lunch order when she saw me. She smiled big enough to show me every one of her teeth.

"Hey, we're almost done here. Let me check the ticket to make sure that we have the right number of plates in here."

After she counted and said it was ready to go, I handed her the money. While she gave me change, I made what I hoped appeared to be casual conversation with her.

"So, Jolene, how's business been?"

"Great, honey. How about ya'll?"

"Things are good. Just recovering from the tornado damage. It really slowed down the legal work for us attorneys. I live in Guntersville, so I didn't get any damage. How about you; do you live in Albertville?"

"Oh, no. I live right off the highway here in town, but one girl that works tables here had to quit because her house was destroyed. The insurance company is going to write her a check, and she's moving to Michigan to be with her family." Jolene stuffed napkins in the bags before she pushed them forward for me to take them.

I looked up and asked, "You still dating Roy?" Roy was Jolene's boyfriend of nearly four years. She kept waiting for a ring, but he was still in school.

Jolene's face lit up and said, "Yes, he's about to graduate in the spring. Then we'll probably get engaged after he gets his first big job. How about you? Are you dating that good looking Hank Rowling?"

She took the bait. I answered.

"Yes, we are dating. We just started, so nothing serious yet." I paused to pretend I was thinking and asked, "How did you know his name? Have you met him before?"

Jolene smoothed her hair and said, "Oh, yes. He first came in with his family months ago. He comes here quite often. I thought he would've brought you here for his weekly visits, which have really been almost everyday lately. He just loves our chicken salad sandwiches. He can't believe how awesome it tastes with our candied pecans. He wanted to know what brand of sweet pecans we use, but I had to tell him we make them candied ourselves."

Jolene continued, "Of course, we're not allowed to give out any recipes, so he was so disappointed. He wanted to make it himself when he was bouncing in between here and Birmingham. He said he was thoroughly addicted. In fact, he came in twice the day before you brought him. He got lunch and then came back later to get a to-go order."

"Oh, really? That chicken salad must be quite popular."

"Well, yes, it is. We usually run out by the end of the day. Whatever we don't sell is bought up in bulk at the end of business from one loyal customer or another. Everyone loves it. Your boss Ernest comes in for it all the time. So does your brother. He comes in with his boss, Johann."

I had gotten what I wanted, but I wanted the conversation to wind down naturally. I asked, "Does he now?"

"Yes, they come in for their little work sessions a couple of times a month. They rent out the back room and spread out their work and eat a platter of chicken salad with crackers. Your brother does not really like the sandwich bread we have here. Johann loves the croissant we serve it on, but he's always watching his bread intake, so he usually gets it with wholegrain crackers instead."

"Well, it's just so good," I said as natural as possible.

"Oh, I didn't know you liked it. You've never ordered it."

"Oh, it's nice. I just always crave soup when I come here," I replied.

Jolene leaned in and whispered.

"Well, maybe it's too popular, if you know what I mean." When I did not respond she continued, "Cliff Marcel ate here every day before he got arrested. I hope no one realizes that because it could hurt our business."

I did not know what to say. I just placed my hand over my lips to imply that her secret was safe with me. Jolene nodded and spoke.

"Well, you're his lawyers and all. Tell him if he likes, I can ship him some to the jail. He was always so nice. He was a good tipper, and he would mow my lawn for free since he was my neighbor."

I knew I had found a goldmine in Jolene. I would let Ernest know that she may be able to help us as a character witness. However, Jolene did not help me with my need to find out who served Morgan that drugged sandwich, as it seemed all of Guntersville ate the famous chicken salad. I took the bags and left after giving Jolene a large tip.

After I dropped off the lunch, I realized that I had spent way too much time talking to Jolene at the Cream Puff. I went as quickly as I legally could in my Jeep to Craig's house.

When I got there, Craig was waiting for me outside. It was only a few minutes past eleven, so I was still good on time. Craig jumped in the Jeep, and we drove to the police station to get his car out of impound.

Traffic was surprisingly light, and I could navigate the back roads efficiently enough to save us time. Many streets were still closed, but I was able to avoid them with ease. I wanted to drop Craig off and go, but before we parked at the police station, he asked me to go inside with him. He wanted an attorney and a witness in case they tried to arrest him again for another bogus charge, such as disorderly conduct. His paranoia was somewhat justified, so I parked and escorted him inside the police station.

The cop that helped us recognized me from court, and that seemed to make things go smoothly. The cop was always nice to me, and he never gave me problems. I wish he had been there the day the Craig was arrested, but he was somewhere else that day. He was probably guarding the stores damaged by the tornado to keep looting from happening.

The cop's last name was Turnip, which always made me laugh and remember him easily. He left us for about five minutes and returned with a small bag full of stuff. The bag was bright orange and had a skull on it.

"I hope you don't mind, but we did not have any bags left, so we put all your stuff in this Halloween store bag that we found in your car. It's not like anything in here was contraband, so we just itemized it here," said Turnip.

Turnip produced a list of contents and handed it to Craig. Turnip ordered.

"Please read this and initial on the bottom in the box that says it's all here and you take possession."

Craig briefly read through the list and signed off on it. He had already signed multiple forms and paid his impound fee. Turnip handed him the keys and told us to meet him outside in the impound lot.

As we left the building, I questioned Craig.

"I didn't know you dressed up for Halloween this year. What were you?"

"It wasn't my bag. It was Sandy's. She likes to role play, so she stocks up once a year at costume stores."

Craig said this highly personal statement in the same casual tone that most would use to describe the weather. I blushed slightly because it was more information than Craig had ever given me. He might have done so because he anticipated my follow-up question, which was now unnecessary. He knew like everyone else in town that Morgan had worn a Halloween costume as she laid dying on that rock.

Turnip allowed Craig to leave in his car without comment or incident. He waved at me as I walked back to my car and left. I had to get home to change clothes for work at Creamy's. I would barely make it, but I would be on time.

When I arrived at Creamy's for my shift, I found a box of roses with my name on it. My heart skipped a beat as I opened the card and saw it was signed by Hank. There was no message, other than the generic "Thinking of You" that was part of the printed design of the card.

I put the flowers under the counter. I called Hank when Larry was not looking. I got his voicemail, but I left him a message.

"Thanks for the flowers, Hank. I cannot see you tonight, but I will try to call you tomorrow. I must work late tonight. Talk to you later, bye."

About an hour later, I got a text from Hank.

"Got your message. Couldn't talk earlier because I'm working. Too busy with work myself to do anything tonight. So don't feel bad. I'm glad you like the flowers, but they pale and wither compared to you. Talk to you later, love."

My heart skipped another beat. Hank used the word "love." Did he mean to finish that statement, or was that a pet name? I assumed it was a pet name, but that was uncommon for around here. Of course, Hank was not from here.

The bliss of the moment carried me through the end of my shift. I left with the box under my arm as I walked triumphantly to my place to change clothes. I put the flowers in water. I did not have a vase that was big enough. I put them in a plastic pitcher, which made them more mine in some sense. I laughed while I got ready for my meeting with Aren. My minimal attraction to Aren had faded in Hank's light.

My buzz continued as I made my way to Huntsville. It was dark by the time I got there. I parked in the library parking lot and walked into the library to meet Aren. I forgot where in the library he had said to meet, so I went downstairs to the spot where we had met for the first time.

After I could not find him anywhere in the library, I went to the front desk on the main floor. There were two geeky looking students that were working at the information desk.

When they made eye contact with me, I spoke.

"Excuse me, do you two know Dr. Aren Willows?"

"Yes, I know him." The chubbier one answered.

He waited for another question, so I obliged.

"Have you seen him in here today?"

The two looked at each other and laughed as the thin one answered.

"It's a little early for Dr. Willows. He usually doesn't get here until well after dark."

The other butted in and spoke.

"Yeah, we are beginning to wonder if he's a vampire. He never comes out during the day. In fact, I don't know one person who has seen him in the daylight—at least not outside. He's kind of the school's urban legend."

The two began to laugh again, but when they saw some woman in a suit come their way, the chubby one continued.

"I'm just kidding. He's a great guy. He's so smart. He knows everything humanly possible about mythology and history."

The other one spoke under his breath.

"It's hard to forget what you've seen firsthand." The chubby one nudged his friend, who began to chuckle under his breath in the same manner he had spoken.

The woman must have been important because the two snapped out of their merriment as she joined them behind the counter. She was not facing me and was looking through a folder. The thin guy spoke in an official tone.

"If you are looking for Dr. Willows, ma'am, might I suggest you try his office in the building next door. I believe there is a listing of the offices with the room numbers on the first floor when you enter that building."

Then I remembered. I was supposed to meet Aren in his office instead of here. I thanked the two young men, who had begun to straighten up their work area. The only response I received was a nod from both before I turned around and left.

I was fifteen minutes late by the time I made it to Aren's office, but he did not seem to notice. He was at his computer typing away as he stared at notes that were scattered on his desk. There was no receptionist to greet me when I entered the suite that held five offices, all dark and closed apart from Aren's.

I knocked lightly on the open door. Aren stopped typing and looked up at me and spoke.

"It's so lovely to see you again, Ms. Loomis. Sorry, there was no one here to show you the way, but my receptionist, Jacobi, left at five."

"Oh, that's okay. I'm sorry that I'm late." After a moment, I added, "Please call me Alva."

I saw something flash in Aren's eyes. A light drew me in, but then I pulled back. It felt very hypnotic for a moment. I remembered the vampire comment and shuddered a little. I did not believe in the supernatural. However, something was a little off with Aren.

I stared at Aren for a moment. He did have some wrinkles, but they appeared to be artistically placed instead of worn into the skin. Otherwise, his skin was perfect. There were no visible scars or freckles. Hands that surely wrote many notes were without callus. There was not even a hangnail on his perfectly manicured hands. His hair was perfect, and the silver strands, though few and far between, looked more like highlights than a sign of age. In fact, they appeared more golden than silver in this light.

Aren stood up and smiled at me. He was so attractive, even more attractive than I had noticed before this moment. My heart did not race, but it felt like it was slowing down. He was calming me down. I felt such peace in his presence. I was being pulled in again. I had to shut it down before I was lost. I cleared my throat.

Aren turned around and grabbed a notepad and a pen.

"Let's sit here at my workstation and see what we've got." He walked over and shut the door to his office and said, "Discretion, of course."

We were now alone. I gulped.

My briefcase began to slide down my hip. This brought me back to the task at hand. I walked over to the desk and sat at one of the two chairs in the area that Aren called his workstation. I opened the briefcase and pulled out the agreement for Aren to sign that would seal his lips and keep all his work under the umbrella of work product and legally undiscoverable.

Aren spent a few moments reading the agreement. I told him that he could consult an attorney if he wished. He answered.

"I will call him right now. He's expecting my call."

Aren went over to the fax machine and sent the document through while he dialed the number of his attorney. He offered me coffee, which

I accepted gratefully. A few minutes later, the phone rang. I excused my-self to the restroom while he spoke to his attorney.

I did not need to use the restroom, so I just stared at myself in the mirror. I thought about Morgan Cooper. Then I thought about the two goofy library assistants that called Aren a vampire. I knew there was no such thing, but I knew that humans could be like vampires. I thought of Morgan once more. She had slit her wrists, but where was the blood? I never saw blood on the scene when I was there.

I reached into my briefcase, which I had to keep with me until Aren signed the confidentiality agreement. I pulled out the file on Morgan. I flipped through the file. There was no blood in the pictures. No blood anywhere. Someone had drained her, but where was the blood? No one had caught that, as it was not mentioned in any of the reports or state-ments.

Since I knew a vampire was an impossible scenario, it could mean only one thing: Morgan was moved. She had not died at her property. Someone could have caught it in containers, but what would they do with buckets of blood? I choked back nausea and fear as I considered the near impossible.

I shook my head and closed the file. There is no such thing as vam-pires. A person could pretend, however, to be a vampire. A person sick enough to dress her up like a vampire princess and put her on a ceremo-nial rock. I decided I would ask Aren about vampire mythology when we began, if we ever began.

I went back to the office and saw that the door was again open. Aren heard me coming and spoke.

"Come in, please. I have it all signed and ready to go. I made a copy. Here's the original. Shall we begin?"

I handed Aren the file, which he began to thumb through slowly. He pulled out pieces of paper that interested him, which included the pho-tos of Morgan's body and the autopsy report. He jotted down notes on a piece of paper he had labeled "Confidential."

After he seemed content with his initiation into the case file, he spoke.

"What are your thoughts on this?"

"Well, I think it's strange that she's dressed like a vampire queen with her blood drained. It is possible the person was really into vampires. What is the mythology on them?"

"I see where you would get that, but vampires would never do this kind of work. Slitting the wrists is not vampire style. There would be only two puncture wounds, from the teeth, of course. And if she were supposed to be the vampire, then she would not have been the one who was drained," said Aren.

I could not believe what I had just heard. I heard Aren speak of vampires as if they were real. I looked at him and asked, "Theoretically?"

"Theoretically of course."

Theoretically could have meant the existence of vampires, or it could have meant if that was the motivation of the killer. I was too embarrassed to clarify, as it was too absurd to do so. Of course, Aren would use such concrete terms because mythology was what he dealt with day-to-day. If he added "theoretically" or a disclaimer to everything he discussed concerning mythology, he would never get to the point. Vampires were just another mythology of which he had knowledge.

"If this was not a vampire pattern, what other pattern would you see?" asked Aren.

I tried to remember what I had thought before about this case. What had made me consult Aren in the first place? I remembered a book with a black bird on it. The bird almost looked like a woman in a black dress. That reminded me of Morgan.

"I thought she looked like a black bird in that dress. She was on top of a mountain, after all. So maybe someone thought she was a giant crow or something. They set her free when they placed her up there and sent her onto the next world."

"Well, the importance of black birds is a popular mythological and religious theme. The crow is in many stories of creation and destruction.

She gives life in some cultures, and she takes life in others. I am not certain that she is intended to be a bird, however. Were there any feathers found near her body or in her home?" asked Aren.

"None at all," I answered.

"Yes, that may or may not be significant. What else?" he asked.

"She had four cuts, so maybe that was important. Maybe four had something to do with a religious symbol." I paused and then blurted out, "Poor Morgan! To think that she ended up being buried in a service held by her own family's business. They owned a funeral home, after all."

Aren's eyebrows went up and he spoke.

"Her name was Morgan, *and* she ran a funeral home?"

"Yes, why?"

"Those were not four cuts, but three wounds. This is a bird mythology all right, but it is not a black bird in general. It is a crow. It is based off the mythology of Morgan Cooper's namesake—the Morrigan. That is the triple goddess that brings death. Morgan worked in a funeral home. She had three different wounds that, according to this report, were inflicted at different times over the course of three days. Whoever did this was someone who was familiar with Morgan enough to spend three days with her and no one knew the difference. Someone had seen her the day before at work, according to this one statement. She was not missing at all. So, whoever it was, did this when she was not looking, or made it seem like an accident. The first two cuts were small and could be laughed off, but the last would require her to be drugged, as it says."

"Are you saying the three cuts represent something?" I asked.

"Yes, and in the mythology, the goddess was wounded three times, but that was part of the mythology that symbolizes her triple nature. Of course, she was the goddess of warrior death. Had her funeral home recently buried a veteran?"

"They did all the time, but about a month before her death, they buried someone who died in the line of fire. I remember because the whole town shut down and attended a service to honor him," I said.

"That explains why whoever did this chose her. They chose her because she had done the work of the gods. This person dressed her up like this goddess and killed her, but why?"

"I don't know. I guess we need to keep looking for more patterns. What about the blood?" I asked.

"Well, it's not a vampire. I honestly do not know why the blood is not there. Maybe the person took it to drink or use in some other ritual. Let's go and see what other gods and goddesses drink blood. It may help us establish a pattern to find other victims, and if we're lucky, we can prevent another one."

Aren went to his bookshelf and pulled out a book. He flipped through it in silence while I shuffled through the case file. I kept hoping something would jump out at me and give me an obvious answer, but I did not have such luck.

After Aren studied a while, he had a conclusion. He spoke.

"The Morrigan was a shape shifter. She could appear as a woman, but she also shifted into animal forms, one of which being the crow. This report says that the rock overlooked the lake. That confirms to me that this person was using the Morrigan as inspiration because she was known as the washer of the ford, which is a body of water. She washed the blood of warriors off their armor in that ford." Aren continued.

"As for the missing blood, the Morrigan would take the blood of her foes and present it as a token to her other foes as a warning and a mockery. She would personally extract the blood from the corpses. There is no telling where Morgan Cooper's blood is now, but that is why the blood is gone. The killer was acting the Morrigan myth out on this poor female who just happened to be named Morgan. I suppose her providing a send-off to that warrior made someone think of her as the Morrigan."

"But why would they kill her?" I asked.

"I don't know, but it seems like that is the pattern. This is a ritualistic killer."

My heart dropped, as I knew it was what I had feared. There was a serial killer in Guntersville. At least the killer had passed through Guntersville. It was only a matter of time before someone else realized this and applied it to the suspect, which was currently Cliff Marcel.

Cliff was not the killer. I had to find out everything I could on this. The place to start was the Morrigan ritual. I asked Aren, "What else is there?"

"Let me compare the complete myth to the case, and I will get back with you. I can write a brief report on it if you wish. I can have it ready tomorrow by the time you get here. That is, of course, if we're meeting tomorrow. Are we?" asked Aren.

There was hope in Aren's voice. He did not try to hide it.

"Yes, of course. Same time or something earlier?" I asked.

"Definitely same time. I will see you tomorrow here in my office."

We said our goodbyes as it was well after ten in the evening. I went home and fell asleep missing Hank and avoiding thoughts of Aren.

CHAPTER 7

I just knew I was asleep. I could feel it. I was dreaming, yet I could not stop my mind from acting as if I was awake. *I stood in the front yard of my childhood home. It was the home that I had lived in before my mother had taken her own life.*

That home was no longer here in present day. My father moved us into a new home immediately. He sold it quickly and quietly. The new owner plowed the house down within a few months. Cows were there for years until a chain store bought the pasture for a new store. Now there was a supermarket there.

However, I was not in the supermarket, or the farmland version of the property. It was the way it was before my life was forever changed by my mother's death. I was standing on the front porch of the house that was once my only home.

The sun was brilliant in the sky. Its warming rays drew me from the safety of the cement and brick porch. It beckoned me. I walked through the green grass. The blades tickled my bare feet.

As I stood at the edge of the yard near the fence that bordered a pasture, I saw that the sun grew in the yellow sky. I felt it draw me into its light, and I was now being pulled toward it in the sky.

I stared at what looked like the sun, but it was not the sun. It was a ball of golden light that was just a little too large for me to wrap my arms around it. Yet I attempted to embrace it. I was not afraid. Though it glowed like the sun, my eyes could bear the light, and its touch did not burn me.

I said, "I am not afraid," and immediately, I was somewhere else. I was standing on land once again.

The beautiful orb of light was now a beautiful woman. She glowed with the same intensity. I released her from my embrace and looked at her.

I was not alone with this woman. Someone else was with us. It was another woman. However, she was not like this woman, but like me. I looked to my left and saw that this woman was my mother. She was as young as I remembered her before her death.

I turned my gaze away from my mother and to the mysterious woman. My attention on her was too intense for me to bother speaking to my mother. I would wait to see what this woman, this goddess, wanted of me.

However, the woman spoke not a word. She only stared at me with a sweet smile on her face. I smiled back at her. I began to inspect her beautiful, glowing garment. It seemed to be made of light.

I looked at her skin to see if she had light glowing from her pores. Then I noticed something. There were tiny smudges of soot all over her skin. Her garment was flawless, but her skin was dirty.

I pulled back. Something was not right. I felt fear and distrust. This woman was no goddess. She was a deception. I looked to my mother, but she remained entranced with the woman's illusory divinity.

My eyes snapped open. It was such a horrible dream. I did not like this dream. I missed the ones with the handsome stranger. However, I was now awake and needed to get ready for work.

I did not feel like getting out of bed, but more sleep might mean more dreams, so I suddenly felt motivated. I also had work to do. I had no choice but to get ready.

After I finished my morning routine, I was ready to leave. I dressed in my Creamy's uniform because I had to be there at ten. I would stop by Ernest's office and quickly tell him that I could not really work today. He should understand because I would work with Aren tonight. However, lawyers are sometimes unpredictable.

When I got to the law firm, I was relieved because it was still too early for anyone but Ernest to be there. I did not want anyone to see me in my bee gear, which were what today's colors for Creamy's were. Everyone in town knew I worked at Creamy's on the side, but it was still embarrassing for me when other lawyers saw me. Most of them never came in the shop. It would be awkward if they appeared.

I walked into Ernest's private office because the door was open. Ernest was alone with his cup of coffee. He held a newspaper in his hands. There was a half-eaten bagel in a wrapper near his computer. Ernest looked up and spoke.

"Hello, dear." It was good of him not to mention my server's gear.

"Ernest, I cannot work here because of Creamy's. I must be there by ten, and it seems a waste to only work here for two hours. So, if you do not mind, I will just leave. I must work with the consultant this afternoon, so I did not think it would be a problem."

Ernest took a sip from his coffee and answered.

"Well, I see it's only almost eight. Why don't we get a little out of you before ten?" Ernest was not letting me off the hook. It figured.

I looked down at my outfit and blushed. Ernest smiled and assured me.

"I know it's delicate, but we need you. I can hide you in the back suite, which has its own restroom and exit. You'll be completely invisible."

I knew I did not have a choice. I was only fortunate that Ernest understood and had some version of mercy on me. At least there was a secret pocket that he could tuck me into while I worked. I knew that no one ever went in the back part of the building where that suite was. I would be safe in there. I nodded and Ernest spoke.

"Well, then, that's settled. How is the progress? Do we have a serial killer on our hands?"

"Yes, I think so. I must do a little more research, but I can give you a status right now."

"Oh, don't worry about it. I figured it was something like that. I will just wait for the report you give me at the end of the week. I must be in court in an hour, so I don't want to start something I can't finish."

I began to leave at my unspoken cue, but Ernest interrupted me.

"So, how is that Hank fellow doing?"

Ernest wanted gossip instead of business. I answered.

"He's fine. Why do you ask?"

Ernest reached from under his desk and pulled out a small potted plant. It was a beautiful purple flower. I had no idea what kind of flower it was, but it reminded me of an orchid. Ernest answered.

"He left this for you about thirty minutes ago. Here's the card."

Ernest handed me the card and plant. He did not wait for me to open it. He spoke.

"He seems like a good young man. Maybe there's a future between you two. I have to say that I never would have imagined that the young man that bought Leon's place would have started dating Leon's niece. At least Hank tells me you two are dating now."

"Yes, we are."

"A man like that should not have to try so hard. Be careful."

I did not know if he was joking or warning me. I was confused.

"What do you mean?"

"Oh, I do many divorce cases. Most every lawyer I know is divorced many times over. I am on number four. Lawyers just make difficult spouses, that's all."

I left the office after Ernest's remark because he received a phone call. He waved me on as I motioned for the door. I would talk to him later. As I went to the office that Ernest had directed me to, I pondered on Ernest's loaded comment.

I knew Ernest had meant something else, but he was back-pedaling. Maybe he knew something about Hank that I did not. His firm did handle the closing. Something may have come out in those proceedings that made Ernest suspicious.

Of course, to an outsider, it was suspicious that Hank bought Dawn's place. I knew that he had done it as a grand romantic gesture, but it was a little odd, no matter how amorous. It seemed strange to Craig as well, although he did not press the point.

However, maybe Ernest meant something else entirely. He did say that someone like Hank should not have to try so much. Hank was good looking, charming, and rich. He did not have to work it like he was. But to say that was to say that I was not worthy of such effort. I knew that I was, so I put the thought out of my head.

I took the potted flower with me. It seemed that Hank had wanted to brighten up my office, as the card had indicated. I did not have an official office at Ernest's firm, so it was moot. However, it was the thought that counted, and that made me quite happy. I texted Hank, who said he was in the middle of work. He would get back with me later.

I then remembered that Hank had mentioned that he was assigned the Cooper murder case. He was a freelance journalist, who had negotiated with some New York newspaper to work on it. I was working for the attorney of the only suspect, so Hank was the adversary in that respect.

I did not want to tell Ernest because it might get me in trouble. I also did not want to risk Ernest trying to use me to sway Hank's story. It was unethical, and frankly, it was a risk. Journalists sometimes trick people into opening and then put a damaging spin on it.

Besides, Hank could write an innocent story that his editor could turn into something tabloid worthy. Journalism was all about sensationalism. Therefore, I would be careful around Hank. He did not know I was working on the case yet. At least I did not think I told him. Hopefully, I did not. I would keep it that way.

I sat in the office and went through the case file once again. Nothing new stood out to me. I went through my notes so far and began a rough draft on the memo on ritualistic murders. This work kept me occupied until it was time for me to sneak out of the backdoor. Ernest was already gone to court, so I locked it on my way out.

I walked down the back alley that led to Creamy's. It seemed eerily dark for that time of day. I remembered for the first time in a long time that I was a vulnerable young woman. Someone could hurt me at any moment. I could not fight anyone off because I did not have any training for that kind of stuff. I did not know how to use a gun or a knife. It was not like I owned either one. I suppose that if someone attacked me, I could count on adrenaline and instinct to help. However, I would rather not test the theory.

I did not remember this alley being so long. It seemed that Creamy's was on the other side of eternity. I crept through the alley, which was littered with empty crates and garbage dumpsters. I held my breath. I told myself it was to avoid the nasty smells coming from the dumpsters. However, I was really trying to hear everything possible, and breathing would be an extra noise that I could avoid making.

I heard a sound of something rattling through bottles and cans. It came from about three feet ahead of me. The source of the noise was invisible because it came from a doorway that was deep enough for me not to see the person or thing that made the noise. I heard a cough. It was a person. It was a male.

I exhaled momentarily and held my breath once more. I began to pick up the pace because the door was for a building that was currently vacant. No one should be there or had been in there for almost six months. Therefore, whoever was in that doorway was either rummaging through trash or they were messing with the door. Either way, they were up to no good, and I needed to get away from potential trouble.

By the time that I passed the doorway in question, my stride had almost become a jog. I kept my gaze forward, and the man in the doorway was a blur of white, brown, and black.

I had almost made it to the backdoor of Creamy's when I heard someone call after me. The raspy voice said, "Hey, Miss, wait up!"

I began to fully run when the voice called again, "I said wait up!" The voice was getting closer. I heard the footsteps slam into the asphalt behind me. Whoever was behind me was running after me.

I almost put my hand on the doorknob of the door to Creamy's when someone grabbed my free arm and pulled me back. I gasped in silence, which impressed me because I assumed that I would scream. I wanted to slam my eyes shut, but I faced my attacker and waited for the worst.

"Miss Alva, it's me, Cliff Marcel. What are you doing out here by yourself?" Cliff stood in front of me. He had a bag of recyclables in his hand. He was taking out the trash. But what was he doing free?

I gulped and tried to collect myself. I smiled a crooked smile and spoke.

"Cliff, you scared me."

Cliff put the bag down on the ground and spoke.

"I'm sorry, Miss Alva. I just did not think it's safe for you to be walking alone. You are a young lady, after all. I just wanted to walk you to work, but when you ran from me, I felt bad. I thought that you might be scared that I was some strange man instead of me. I wanted to let you know not to be afraid."

I had finally caught my breath as I answered.

"Oh, Cliff, thank you. I didn't realize it was you. But I could never be afraid of you."

Cliff looked more serious as he spoke.

"Well, you should be afraid to be alone. I won't hurt you but someone else might. There's a killer on the loose, you know."

"I know, Cliff. We'll find out who did it so you can go free."

"Hey, don't worry about that. You let Ernest and the cops do that. You just keep yourself safe for now. What would we do without you?"

I paused as I heard something deeper in Cliff's voice. Something that seemed a little too intelligent from what I expected from a simple soul. Cliff would miss me, but of whom else was he speaking when he said we? I wondered momentarily but then assumed he meant it as an expression and nothing more.

Apparently, Ernest had succeeded in getting a bond amount set for Cliff. His family's wealth would have been able to satisfy any amount, according to Ernest. Obviously, it was true.

"Cliff, when did you get out on bail?" I asked.

"The hearing was yesterday. Ernest said that you were working at Creamy's. I got out this morning, first thing."

I looked down at the bag of bottles and cans on the ground. I spoke.

"What are you doing in that empty office building?"

Cliff grinned and answered.

"Well, I can't really work right now. No one will let me work his yard because of the trial. I'm just cleaning up this old building that my parents own. It's really mine, but they have the deed on it. Since things are so hard for people, no one can afford to rent it. I need to keep busy, and I don't want it to get too dirty in there. So, I'm cleaning it up."

At that moment, the backdoor to Creamy's opened. Larry jumped a little at seeing someone there unexpectedly, but he hid it well. He played it off for surprise rather than fear.

Larry looked at me and then at Cliff. His expression went blank, and he spoke.

"Alva, you're almost late. Come on inside and get to work." Larry nodded at Cliff and said, "See you later, Cliff."

After we went inside and Larry shut the door and locked it, I spoke.

"Larry, you shouldn't shun him like that. He's innocent."

"He might be, but you don't need to be alone in the alley with him or any man. I would have acted the same no matter who it was."

"Larry, you have been alone in that alley with me. And what if it was Craig?"

"You're related to Craig, that's different. Besides, I'm your boss, and you can trust me in a dark alley."

"What about Hank?"

A voice came from behind us and inquired.

"Yeah, what about Hank?"

We both turned around and saw that it was Hank who had spoken. He was jesting, but he had startled both of us. Caught off guard, Larry answered.

"Hank is a great guy. That would be fine. Just stay away from Cliff, please."

Larry walked away in his usual tactic to end a conversation that he was uncomfortable with, which irritated me to no end. Hank remained and inquired.

"Cliff Marcel? As in the man that is accused of murdering Morgan Cooper?" He did not wait for an answer. He ordered, "You stay away from him, Alva. He's a murderer. Why that judge ever granted him bail, I will never know."

"He's not a killer. He's innocent," I snapped.

"I have so much evidence against him that I could stand in for the prosecution, and I'm just a reporter. It's a clear-cut case. He's done. I don't care what magic rabbits that sleazy Ernest Beasley has in his magic hat of deception. There is no jury in Alabama that would let that man walk," Hank said with a smirk.

My face tensed, which Hank must have noticed because he assured me.

"Alva, I know you're an attorney also, but you're not *that* kind of attorney. Ernest Beasley has been getting killers off the hook for almost forty years now."

To change the subject, Hank reached into his pocket.

"I'm so sorry that I upset you. I just wanted to come by and surprise you with something." He pulled a key out of his pocket. It was metal, but the metal was painted pink.

When I hesitated to take the key from his hand, Hank spoke.

"This is a key to Dawn's place. I want you to feel free to come there any time, whether I'm there or not." When I did not move or speak, he said, "I think of it as our place, though it's more yours than mine."

Something was between Hank's fingers of the hand that held the key. It was shiny and dangling. It was Dawn's old keychain. He saw my eyes light up, so he took my hand. He gently forced open my fingers and placed the key and keychain in my hand. A small tear made its way down my face. Hank wrapped his arms around me, and when I looked up into his eyes, he kissed me.

We were in the back of Creamy's, so no one saw us. The kiss was deep, and it would have lasted for hours if I could let it. We spent at least ten minutes kissing before I made it out to work. Hank came out and sat at a table. He spread out there and worked on his laptop until it was time for me to leave at four.

We had found a way to spend the day together, and it felt natural. It felt almost like home. I was sure it would take a little more time before it was completely organic. However, at this rate, that could be the next time I saw him.

It felt like I had known Hank my entire life. I wonder if that was what love felt like. Maybe I would know soon enough. Maybe deep passion was only for people in lust. Love must be more like comfort and structure. There was passion, but it was more about trust than fire.

Hank and I would have a late dinner tonight at his place. I told him that I would meet him there at eleven. He had the kitchen ready to go, so it was nice to see if he was as good a cook as he claimed. I had his grilled food before, but that was the minimal cooking skills of a bachelor. The breakfast he made me was cereal and cold milk. This was something to look forward to, and the thought made me smile.

Hank decided to stay at Creamy's after I left. He and Larry were becoming friends. Hank had not warmed up to Craig yet, but Craig was not the warm kind of person. It would take a little longer to get anywhere with Craig, but that would happen with time. I was content to make Hank a part of my life. I had patience and time to develop this into something permanent.

Before I left Creamy's, Hank handed Larry a bag and spoke.

"Here's the books I borrowed from you. I appreciate it."

The bag was bright orange and had a skull on it. It was the same type of bag that Craig had in his car. It was from a Halloween store. I did not want to say anything because Hank was a reporter who would follow through on the tip-off, be it accidental or not. The bag could have been Hank's or Larry's. I would never know.

After I left, I had just enough time to quickly change clothes and get my briefcase. I had a duplicate copy of the file that I always left at the office, which was something Ernest required. It also made it easier to not have to lug it around everywhere I went. If I had it with me earlier, Hank could have gone through it. That was why I kept everything in my personal copy of the file secure at home while I was at Creamy's. I would make copies of new notes and take them with me each morning to the office.

When I got to Aren's office, he was talking to his assistant, Jacobi in the reception area. Aren briefly introduced us before Jacobi left for the day. It was right at five, so it was time for Jacobi to leave.

Aren's usual cheery face looked concerned. As I followed him to his office, he did not make any friendly conversation. I was a little disturbed by his change in demeanor. It was pretty much dark outside, but Aren had his blinds closed in his office. It seemed much drearier than I remembered.

Aren acted tired, but he did not look it. In fact, he looked refreshed and a little younger than he had yesterday. The once silver strands that had seemly become golden were less noticeable. Where there had been a few here and there were now almost nonexistent. Minimal golden hairs remained, so he had not dyed his hair, which was now thicker and shinier.

If Aren was a vampire, he had fed recently. He looked rejuvenated. The strange way he was acting may have been the hunger for more. I was increasingly nervous as Aren closed the door behind us. We were now alone once more. I fought off the cold shiver that went through the pit of my stomach.

To act natural, I sat down in the same spot that I had yesterday. Aren sat down beside me. He handed me some papers.

"Here is my report. It details the connections to the Morrigan with the Morgan Cooper case."

I did not want to sit and read it in front of him. I placed the report in my briefcase.

"I'll look at it later. Let's get started."

Aren had a strange look on his face.

"Is that not okay?" I asked.

"No, that's fine," said Aren with a shrug.

"Well, what's wrong then?" I asked.

Aren sighed and said, "This," as he handed me another piece of paper. It was a story of an unsolved murder from New Jersey. He inquired.

"Didn't you say the main suspect is from New Jersey?"

I looked at the paper as I distractedly affirmed his question. The paper was a printout from a newspaper archive. It was a story written about six months ago. There was an unsolved murder case from a few years ago that the cops finally abandoned.

The victim was a woman around Morgan's age who had worked for a message delivery service. She had beautiful, long blonde hair that fell in waves to her waist. The picture was of her pre-murder appearance. However, there was a vivid description of how she was arranged at the crime scene.

She was adorned in a costume that had been bought at a local costume store, but there was no way to trace who bought it. She wore a white dress that came to her ankles. It was a Roman nobleman costume. Around her neck was a broad, gold fabric necklace that had come from a superhero costume. She was found lying on top of a white blanket with white feathers sewn onto it.

The way she was killed was quite different than Morgan. The killer strangled her with the fabric necklace. The necklace had a plastic stone glued to it, but it fell off in the struggle and was found at her feet. The killer displayed her body in an empty lot that was recently zoned to become a cemetery. Her name was Marla Oberg.

My mouth dropped open. If anyone found this out, Cliff would be finished. Even I began to have my doubts about his innocence. Cliff was from New Jersey, but I was not sure what part. This did not look good. I was speechless.

"Despite this, I still think your guy did not do it. I read through the profile of him that was in the file yesterday while we were working, and I don't think he can do this. However, according to this, Marla Oberg was found one hundred miles from where Cliff's parents reside," said Aren.

"What am I supposed to do with this?" I asked Aren.

"I don't know. I'm sorry to put this at your doorstep, but I was doing some searching on unsolved murders that involved women and feathers. This is what came up."

"I know this looks bad, but maybe it was just some girl in a costume who got strangled at a failed rape," I said.

"I thought of that, but the blanket was not a blanket, but a cloak of feathers. The necklace and the cloak tell me this person was modeling the victim after the goddess Freya."

Aren opened a book and showed me a drawing of Freya. She was dressed in a white, almost sheer dress and had golden hair that went past her knees. The necklace was there as well with amber stones set into the thick golden band. She wore a cloak of feathers.

Aren pointed at the cloak.

"This is made from the feathers of falcons. Falcons are the birds that were used as the first messenger service known to man." His finger went up as he pointed at the necklace, "And this necklace was what caused Freya much torment and trouble. It seems fitting to her tribute that the necklace would be what killed her."

Aren's comment seemed callus to me. However, he may be separated from it since there were no crime scene photos of Marla Oberg to bring it out of the abstract.

"Now what really brings this home for me is where they found her. The police found her in a vacant lot that was supposed to become part of a nearby cemetery."

I did not say anything, so Aren elaborated.

"Freya is the owner of the Field of People. That is where she receives half of the souls that were slain in battle."

I did not get it, so Aren continued.

"The Field of People that were slain is a modern equivalent to a cemetery. This lot would have doubled the size of the cemetery at that time, so it is half of the cemetery. She was the first one there. She was the one that was there to greet her half of the slain. Get it?"

"Oh, okay. That's deep."

"I know. Do you really think that Cliff is that intelligent to come up with such an elaborate metaphor?"

"No, I don't, but who?" I inquired.

"I don't know," Aren answered. "Whoever did this was very precise. They even ripped off the stone from her necklace and placed it at her feet. That is symbolic from a story of Freya. And her name is Marla Oberg. Marla is a derivative of Mary, and Mary was the replacement of Freya for the Scandinavians when the Catholic Church forced Christianization on them."

"Wow, that is too much planning for Cliff. However, he's the only person I know that has been in both places, so it can really hurt us if anyone finds this out," I said. "This just makes a weird day for me get much worse. Cliff scared me today by accident, and believe me, if I had known about this, I would have been more scared than I was."

Aren still looked worried.

"This is why you seem so upset? Because of this?" I asked.

"Yes, this really hurts the case. However, I know that he is innocent. I can just feel it."

"How do you know that these are not two unrelated murders? Is the goddess connection enough?" I asked.

"I looked at a lunar calendar, and both were committed on the full moon. That is a pattern. It's too difficult to search out murders that happen on every full moon because most reports do not catch that fact, and people traditionally do more crime on full moons."

So, there was nothing we could do. No one had noticed the goddess pattern, so it was just a murdered girl in a costume. The New Jersey article had said that cops thought the girl was attending a local medieval festival that was held a few days before she was found.

The murderer was clever to cover his tracks. Morgan's death was near Halloween, so it was an excuse to dress her up and kill her without the goddess pattern becoming evident. Marla Oberg's costume was rational because people dressed like her when they went to the festival that was held in the same city.

"It figures that you would drop this in my lap right now. I almost saw it coming. I had a weird dream about a woman dressed in white with golden hair. She didn't look like this, but it was somewhat similar."

Aren looked concerned then he asked me to explain the dream to him. When I did, the color drained from his face. I reached to touch his hand because he looked as if he was about to become sick. His hand was ice cold. That coupled with his pale face made me think of Aren as a vampire. I jerked my hand back. Aren did not seem to notice.

"Are you okay? I can get you something to drink from the vending machine downstairs if you like. Have you eaten today?" I asked.

"I am fine. I don't really need anything to eat," he answered.

Another chill ran through me, but this time it started at the base of my spine and went up to my neck. I placed my hand on my neck and rubbed it gingerly.

Aren's concern turned to me. He spoke.

"I know this dream seems to you like it was just your mind trying to reason and solve the case. You probably told yourself that you were working it out in your mind and predicted this next piece of information. However, dreams are not your subconscious working it out. They mean something."

"What do you mean?" I asked as another chill ran through me.

"Modern society analyzes everything, but the ancients knew what dreams were. Dreams were the message service of the gods. When a person could not commune directly with a god, they would receive a dream of instruction. Maybe it's not always so dramatic, but that's why people dream prophetic dreams. They're warnings of things to come, and not a reflection of what already happened."

I laughed.

"Aren, I didn't know you were such a mystic." When Aren did not smile, I fidgeted. I said, "Next thing you'll tell me is that vampires are real as well. Is that why you said it wasn't their style? Are you some kind of vampire?"

I chuckled my question, but Aren's face grew more severe as he spoke.

"No, I am not a vampire. There are no such things as vampires."

I was embarrassed that Aren did not realize I was joking. At least I wanted him to think I was joking.

"I'm just teasing, Aren. I am so sorry. I am not acting professional. I should not jest with you. I apologize deeply," I said.

Aren did not acknowledge my apology but instead spoke.

"These dreams are very serious. You should not ignore them."

He said dreams instead of dream. How did he know that I was having other strange dreams? He did not, so that was strange.

"Don't you mean dream?" I asked.

"That's what I said dream," he said.

I did not argue because it was too personal to explain my other strange dreams to him. I did not want him to call them prophetic. I shrugged it off to me mishearing him. I questioned him.

"What do you want me to do about this dream? If it is a warning, then what warning is it?"

"I am afraid that it means you could be next."

CHAPTER 8

I did not attempt to hide my shock. Aren was not only being irrational, but he was being a little dramatic. I knew that dreams could sometimes warn people of disasters. I mean, we have all heard the stories. However, there was no evidence that those things were not as mythological as Aren's body of knowledge.

I stared at Aren.

"Really? That is your response to me?"

"I know it's crazy, but I just don't want anything to happen to you. I think that the closer you get to the truth, the more likely that the killer will come after you to prevent being exposed. Even if you discount this dream, that is a rational possibility."

"I think that's a little premature. I have only attempted to discredit the case against Cliff. Who really did it is so beyond me at this point. I don't know where to even start to find that out. Right now, I just want to get Cliff off the chopping block."

"Alva, you must understand that the person may have planned it to look like Cliff did it. Maybe this person is related to him. That would explain why there were similar deaths in both locations."

"This is not very helpful, Aren. All you are doing right now is trying to freak me out, and that's not good. I don't need to jump at everything that bumps in the night, okay?"

"No, that's precisely what you do need to do. You need to suspect everything and everyone." Aren stared at me intently as he spoke.

"If I did that, that would mean that I would fear you as well. Is that what you want, Aren?"

"Yes, if that means you stay alive. I have nothing to hide from you. I am not the one who did this, so you can examine me under a microscope if it helps keep you focused. Focused people don't die as easily. At least not without a fight."

Aren's voice had such concern that it was touching. Human compassion seemed so rare that when you felt it, it was like a breeze of fresh air. I understood his point, but it still seemed a little bit overdramatic to me.

I was about to tell him that he could calm down when I looked down and saw the headline of the article. Underneath the title was the name of the author. It was none other than Hank Rowling.

I tried to hide my reaction of shock and fear, but Aren sensed something had startled me. He asked me what was wrong, but I just told him that I was thinking of the reality of what he had been saying. That seemed to placate him enough, as he did not persist in finding out why I had changed my mood all the sudden.

Hank had told me that he was a freelance journalist. I should not be shocked that he wrote this article. If he was hired to cover Cliff Marcel's trial, it was possible that was because of his past writing of this article had qualified him to win the job. It was just a coincidence. Hank probably specialized in murder cases.

I pushed my thoughts of it aside because there was no point of freaking out over this. I knew Hank was a great guy and not a murderer. Just because he covered both crimes after they occurred did not mean anything.

My mind shifted once more. If there was a connection between these two murders, it was only a matter of time before Hank realized it. That was if he had not already. That may be the reason he took the job in the first place because he realized something from his work on the last article. If he did connect these murders in the media, we would never recover. Also, the case would become federal. That would completely change the game. A knot formed in my stomach.

"Okay, what now then?" I asked Aren.

"We need to consult with someone who may be able to help us figure out what is going on here."

The look on Aren's face made me think that I was not going to like his solution.

"What kind of person?"

Aren paused as if he was thinking of a gentle way to answer me. He finally spoke.

"The person is like me. They know much about mythology and mysticism."

I leaned back in my chair.

"Aren, I don't think I can get Ernest to agree to this. And without his approval, we cannot tell anyone anything about the case."

"Don't worry. I won't have to tell him anything. I will just ask him about the mythologies that this person is focusing on and see if he sees a comparison between the two. I will lie and say I'm writing a paper on Freya and the Morrigan. He won't know the difference. I promise."

"Well, do I need to be there then?"

"I would like you there in case you have a question that I don't cover. I am pretty much going to get one shot with this expert. He's a little eccentric and sometimes reclusive. If you have any follow-up questions, it would be impossible to get him to agree to talk more than once with me about this. So, it would be better just to meet him with me. That way I won't have to relay the information back to you. He'd never let me record the interview," Aren said as he stared at the article about Marla Oberg. Aren saw my hesitation.

"Just come here tomorrow. I'll have him meet us here. Just keep all your case files tucked away until he leaves."

"What time tomorrow?"

"It will probably be later than usual. Let's say at seven instead. I'll call you if the time is earlier."

"Okay, that's fine." I would have to ask Ernest for an extension on my memo because it was due the day after tomorrow. He would probably agree.

There was a great amount of sadness in Aren's eyes. It could have been because I was leaving, but I doubted it. He did seem very worried about my safety. It was more than likely something personal that had nothing to do with me.

I met with Hank at his place for dinner as we had planned. It was going to be a late night, but it was okay because I had the day off from Creamy's and had requested a personal day from Ernest's law firm. I told him that I had a dentist appointment, but that was a fib because I had already cancelled it and never told him that I was once again available to work. However, since Ernest rode me today about working when I did not want to, I did not feel guilty.

Hank really was a good cook. He said he had spent a little while in culinary school, but I did not believe him. I thought it was one of those things that guys say to make you laugh, but it seemed he had meant it. Dinner was amazing.

After we ate, we stretched out and watched television. I rarely had time to do this on my own, so it was nice. However, when Hank began to give me a foot rub, I was too distracted to care about what was on the television.

Things went to their normal place, which for us was kissing and petting. I could tell that Hank wanted more like I did, but he never pressed me. However, tonight he seemed like he was ready. I pulled back because I was not sure I wanted it to get physical this early in the relationship.

Hank's big eyes stared at me.

"Would you like to stay with me tonight?"

I was not ready. I wish that I could abandon my internal code of behavior, but I could not. My mind went to the article that Hank had written.

"I cannot do that, Hank."

"How about you just sleep here. Nothing else must happen if we don't want." The intensity in Hank's eyes grew.

It was not about desire with me. It was about controlling what I wanted. Besides, I had heard this line before, and it never went well.

"No, Hank. I don't think that would be a good idea."

We kissed again. I felt a spark in my stomach, but then a knot replaced the spark. I remembered Marla Oberg. I pulled away and tried to change the subject.

"How long have you been writing?"

Hank kissed me again. When he came up for a breath, he whispered, "Later."

"Hank, let's just slow down and talk for a while, okay?"

Hank kissed me again and pretended that he had not heard me. He finally pulled away from my lips and began to kiss my neck. I groaned a little in frustration, but he thought it was a groan of desire. He moved to my ear and whispered.

"I have been writing for almost seven years. It's been my sideline throughout my various careers. Now I make it my main gig." He bit my earlobe gently.

"That's great. I would love to see your portfolio sometime," I huffed.

He purred in my ear, "Okay, baby," and gave me another nibble.

I pushed back and said, "How about now?"

Hank stopped dead and looked me in the eye. He said, "Seriously? Right now, and that's all you can think about?"

I sighed and he said, "Let's do that later. I don't know if it is here, and if it is, it's in a box somewhere."

I knew better. I knew that people kept that stuff in their computers and in hardcopy. However, it was possible that it was not directly saved on his current computer that was in his little office that was once the back den.

I could not press anymore without Hank becoming suspicious. I let it go, but I did not return to his lips. I sat a little distance from him on the couch and pretended to watch television once again. Hank did not seem to mind too much. He looked a little frustrated with me.

Hank stood up and said, "How about some dessert?" I followed him into the kitchen, where he pulled out a cake from the fridge. He said, "Rum cake—want some?"

I was not a fan of rum cake, but I wanted to lighten the mood, so I accepted a piece. It was better than any rum cake I had eaten before, but it was strong. I accepted a second piece because I was still trying to make him not mad at me.

That was a mistake because my head began to swim. This rum cake was strong, and it was more like a cake soaked in rum than it was baked into the cake. Was that how they made rum cake? I could not remember.

"What kind of rum is this?" I asked.

"The highest quality available in the area."

"You mean the strongest as well?" I asked.

"Well, I suppose, but I have a high tolerance. This is my mother's recipe, but I make it a little weaker than she does."

I felt strange as my head was spinning a little.

"I think this made me drunk."

"That's impossible, it's baked into it. The alcohol loses its potency when cooked," Hank argued.

"But did you also put a glaze on it or something? These tastes soaked in it."

"Well, yes, but that was ... wait I just blended it with simple syrup. I only cooked the syrup, not the rum for the glaze," Hank had an epiphany. He looked stricken as he said, "I'm so sorry. Let me take you home."

"No, wait. If you're not drunk physically, you may be legally drunk. Let's just wait a while," I said. Hank had eaten three pieces himself.

Hank scoffed, "Oh, please, I'm fine to drive."

I giggled and said, "That's what I always hear! I'm a lawyer who does DUI cases every week."

Hank persisted and said, "Come on, let me take you."

"No, way, mister. Not only would you get a DUI, but they would also throw a public intoxication on me the moment I stepped out of the car they were about to impound. It may not be the legal standard, but that's what they do all the time around here. Charge now and fight it later."

I hiccupped and Hank busted out laughing. The mood was lighter. My head began to swim once more and I felt weak. I asked Hank if I could lie down a while in my old room.

"Go and rest in my room because the guest bedroom sheets are at the cleaners."

Hank helped me to his room. I crawled into the bed fully dressed, minus shoes. I watched Hank leave the room in the direction of the kitchen. I closed my eyes and told myself that I would just rest them for a moment.

I opened my eyes but instead of the soft light from the light fixture overhead, I saw nothing. All the lights were out in the house, but I could hear the humming of the heat, so it was not a power outage.

I sat straight up in the bed. I looked at the clock on the side table. It was four in the morning. I was sweating, so I pulled the sheet off my body. I found that I was only wearing panties. I gasped and pulled the sheet over my exposed chest.

I felt something moving next to me, and I looked and saw that it was Hank. He was in bed with me. He was asleep. I lifted the sheet to look under to see his body. He was completely nude.

I was afraid that if I moved, he would wake up and see me. I reclined back down and waited for an idea of how to escape this situation. My head was still swimming, so driving was out of the question. It was too dark to see where my clothes were.

I tried to move my leg slightly to slide out of the bed undetected, but Hank began to stir. I would remain still and wait until he settled back down and into deep sleep once again. I closed my eyes to look asleep just in case he woke up and looked at me.

I opened my eyes again, but this time it was bright in the room. It was daylight, and Hank was still asleep beside me. I felt different and realized that I was now wearing the t-shirt that I had worn all evening. My shorts and bra were neatly folded on a chair nearby. The fold looked like the unique way that I always folded my clothes.

I rolled over and lifted the sheets to stare at Hank. He was dressed this time. He was wearing shorts and a t-shirt. I rolled back over and looked at the clock. It was seven in the morning. My head was a little achy, but otherwise, I was not hung over.

Hank woke and said, "Morning. Sorry that I did not wake you up, but you looked so peaceful. I just crawled in and joined you." He kissed me on the forehead and said, "I hope you're not too upset."

"It's fine," I said. I did a quick scan of my body status. It did not feel like I had been doing anything else other than sleeping. It was possible that we just slept together, and nothing more had happened.

However, I could swear that I woke up half naked, and was Hank not completely naked? I was not sure. It may have been a dream. It was quite dark last night when I was awake. That is, if I was truly awake and not dreaming the incident.

I am usually a light sleeper. I thought I would have noticed if someone had undressed me. It should have woken me up. Also, the clothes were folded in my unique style, so it must have been me doing it in my half-drunken stupor.

"Do you want some eggs and toast?" asked Hank.

"No, I need to get home. I have some errands to do around my place. It's my day off, so I really need to go ahead and go."

"Alright, will I see you later today?" he asked.

"No, sorry, I have to work this evening," I said.

"I thought you said it was your day off." he said.

I had slipped up.

"I don't have to work, but I have some research to do for a case I'm working on for Ernest."

"Oh, some real estate stuff?" Hank asked.

"No, but it is some legal stuff. Just your usual law update kind of things."

Hank's face grew serious.

"This has nothing to do with Cliff Marcel, right? You should be excluded since you were a witness."

Hank was connecting the dots, so I interrupted.

"No, just regular stuff."

I had lied to him, but it could not be helped. It was not as if he was telling all about his article on Cliff. We were somewhat even.

I got dressed and left with minimal follow-up questioning from Hank. He dropped the subject, but I feared that I had opened to some new trouble in both my professional and personal life.

I dared not tell him that I was supposed to be meeting with a couple of men tonight. He would probably be jealous. Hank seemed like the possessive type, but in a romantic way instead of a territorial psycho way. I was quite flattered by the attention that Hank gave me. I did not want it to stop.

When I got home, I got in the shower. When I had disrobed, I realized that my clothes and skin smelled just like Hank, even in places that he should not have touched. Maybe it was just his sheets that had gotten me to smell of his subtle cologne and skin.

I threw the clothes in the wash before I jumped in the shower. I would pretend that it was still because we slept together and not that we had been intimate. The act of actual sleeping was not that big of a deal. It did leave one vulnerable, but it was something that everyone did each day.

I had nearly forgotten about it by the time I was out of the shower and finishing up getting ready for my day. I did not have to be anywhere until seven, so I was going to sit around my apartment dolled up until it was time to go meet Aren.

However, things did not work out the way I had planned. My phone rang right around nine in the morning. It was Aren.

"Alva, we have a problem about my expert."

"What is it, Aren?"

"He's in Gadsden at a conference," Aren spoke impatiently.

"And?" I asked with equal impatience.

"He's only going to be there today. He's leaving tonight to go home," Aren answered.

"Well, that's no problem. We'll just meet with him tomorrow in Huntsville when he's finished with his conference." I was not getting the point of this conversation.

"He's going home to Gulf Shores tonight. He won't extend his stay for us. He said if we want to meet with him, we will have to come there."

"Is that supposed to be some kind of joke, Aren?" I was not in the mood for this.

"I will try to reason with him, okay? Let me call you back."

I agreed, and in about fifteen minutes, Aren called again. He said, "He's okay with it. He will be at my office at one. Can you come that early?"

"Sure, I'll see you then," I responded with little enthusiasm. This guy was already getting on my nerves, and I had yet to meet him. I asked, "What is his name anyway?"

Aren said, "His name is Paul Light."

We said our goodbyes. I hung up. I had to get my household chores done at a quicker pace. I also needed an extension on my memo for Ernest. I knew if I called, he would try to get me to come into work.

So, I decided to finish the rough draft of my memo and correct it for my unofficial copy. I struggled with whether to give it as is to Ernest. It had enough information, but I still did not know everything. In the end, I decided to go ahead and email it to him. This was the last thing I did before I left to meet Aren. The laundry and the dishes would have to wait until the weekend to get done.

I had eaten a hasty sandwich while I had toiled away at my memo, so I was not hungry. I made it to Aren's a few minutes late, but it did not matter because he was not there. Jacobi said that he had not been in all day. I waited for about thirty minutes, when Jacobi was finally able to reach him on his phone.

"Aren will call you on your phone. It's now time for my lunch break, so if you don't mind, I need to lock up the entire suite," Jacobi said.

"You mean that Aren is not coming?" I asked.

"Just talk to him. He'll explain everything."

Jacobi led me into the corridor, and I stomped all the way outside to my car. I was a little upset, but maybe Aren had a flat tire or something.

My phone rang. It was Aren. He sounded out of breath as he spoke.

"Alva, please forgive me, but there's been a big change in plans. I need you to come and meet me at my house."

I wanted to object, but I did not have the energy. Jacobi knew where I was, so he could tell the cops if I came up missing. The one time that Aren was supposed to meet me during the daylight was foiled. I sighed at the irony. I agreed to meet him and took directions.

Aren lived in a gated community, but he had called the guard to put me on some list. The guard let me in after I showed him my identification. All the houses were about the same size, but Aren's was by far the nicest.

I was not surprised when someone greeted me at the door besides Aren. The opportunity for the light to shine on his face when opening the door was lost. The person who seemed to be an assistant let me in and introduced himself as Aren's graduate assistant, Bob Porter.

Bob excused himself as he left. All the shades were drawn in the room where Aren was talking on the phone. I sat on a large leather couch and waited for him to finish.

He sounded angry at whomever he was speaking with, but he tried to hide it. When he was unable to do that effectively, he stepped out of the room. After a few minutes, he must have gone farther away, as I could no longer hear his voice.

Aren was using his cell phone. The landline began to ring. There was a large phone on his desk that looked like it belonged in an office instead of a home. The line flashed repeatedly, and I began to wonder where Aren was.

I stood up and looked out into the foyer where I had heard Aren go. He was not there. I could not hear him anywhere in the house. I walked around the foyer and listened at the different doors for Aren's voice. I could not hear anything, so I gave up and decided to use the restroom.

I tried a couple of doors until I found a hallway. This hallway was decorated with fancy oil paintings. Each one was in a gilded gold frame that was probably real gold. They were antique looking, that was for sure. Each one had a little light above it to showcase it. Otherwise, the hall was completely dark.

I could not find the light switch, so I used the lights above the paintings as my guide. There were a couple of doors at the end of the hallway, so I walked toward them.

I stared at each painting as I walked. The paintings were from different eras in history. Each painting had nothing in common with the other, except for two things. Each painting had people in it, and there was at least one man in each painting.

The man was not the same person, but each man had a similar look to him. I could not put my finger on it right away. It was not as if he was dressed the same, for each was of a different era. His face was not the same either. Wait. There was something similar. His eyes were the same. He had the same eyes each time in the different faces. Also, he stood in the exact same pose each time.

I reached out to touch the face of this strange man. Why did he seem familiar to me? No one else would see it, as it had to be a different man in each painting, right? I heard a voice snap.

"What are you doing in here? Please don't touch those. They're antiques." It was Aren. He looked mad.

"Who are these paintings of Aren?" I felt bold. Aren was hiding something.

"They're just random paintings that I have collected over the years. There is nothing special about them."

"Really, then who is this man?"

"How should I know?" Aren scoffed.

"Well, he's in every picture," I replied. "You should know something about the man you have twenty paintings of."

"What are you talking about? These paintings are of different people with some of them being hundreds of years apart. It is impossible that the same people are in those paintings."

"I didn't say people, I said person." Then I looked. There were people in the other paintings that had the same eyes as the others. I looked at Aren, and I saw the same eyes. I asked, "Aren, what are you?"

"I'm not a vampire. I know that's what you think. That's what everyone always thinks." He walked to the end of the hallway and opened the curtain. The sun shined on his face. He was unharmed. He said, "I told you there is no such thing as vampires."

"Then tell me what there are such things as?" I asked boldly.

"Immortals. I am one. The one we are supposed to meet is one as well."

"How many are there? Like you?"

"There are quite a few of us, but we are all different. I have already told you too much, so just trust me when I say that you are safe with me. You are safer with me than anyone else on earth. Now can we go? Paul won't meet us here. We must drive to Gadsden."

CHAPTER 9

I exclaimed, "What?" Aren did not speak. He just waited for me to deal with it. At least that appeared to be his strategy.

When Aren continued his silence, I spoke up.

"I think you owe me a little more of an explanation than that."

"What do you want to know?" asked Aren with patience.

Before I could ask, Aren followed up with a caveat.

"Of course, I'll answer your questions on the road—those that I can answer—that is."

I thought a minute, and a surge or peace went through me. I felt safe and calm. I decided to leave with Aren. It was irrational to go before I knew what it was that I was dealing with, but reason and logic seemed overrated.

We got in the car, which was Aren's car instead of mine. His car was like his house—elegant and expensive. The color was silver, but the inside was tan leather. It was quite comfortable. The seats were heated, which was nice on the mildly chilly November day.

After we got onto the interstate, the peace subsided ever so slightly, and I decided to speak again.

"So, you are immortal. What exactly does that mean?"

"It means exactly what the traditional dictionary would say of something that is immortal. I cannot die by force or nature."

"Is there any way you can die?"

"No, I cannot die at all."

"So, you will be here forever? Even after everything is gone on Earth?"

"I did not say that, but I will exist no matter what state Earth is in. That means even if it is destroyed or barren, I will still exist. That does not mean I will be here."

I heard a loophole, so I asked, "So where will you be?"

"That's a little too much information for you to know. If you are concerned for my mental health, the answer to your implied question is that I will never be alone."

"You'll be with the others like you—the immortals?"

"Among others," Aren answered in an ambiguous tone.

I could tell this was going nowhere, so I asked about Paul Light.

"Why is it that both you and Paul are mythology experts? Is it because immortals specialize in that?"

Aren almost laughed.

"No, we have just been alive for long enough to see every religion become mythology."

"And how long is that?" I wondered if they were like what people thought of vampires, who were once alive but slipped into immortality.

"I've been alive since the beginning."

"The beginning of what?"

"Earth. I saw the birth of humanity."

"Did you create us?" I asked sheepishly.

"No," Aren chuckled, so I did not say anything else for a while. After a long, awkward pause, he spoke up.

"I remember Earth as an infant. The whales were as big as mountains and dolphins were as large as whales. You should have seen the humans scatter if they were caught near the spot where the whale would surface once a day for air. They would scatter everywhere in fear that they would be taken under when the inevitable monster waves would wash on the shore to pull them under."

"If they were so large, how is it that the whales could surface that near to the shore? Wasn't it too shallow for them?"

"No, the first humans lived on quite a different landscape than the current ones enjoy. There was more water, less land. The land in some spots would be on the shoreline of water so deep that no one could reach the bottom. I mean, even now, in those places too deep for modern man to yet reach. There literally was a tiny shelf and then a huge drop-off in some places. That was always the best fishing lands, so the humans migrated there for the meat."

"The whales only came up for air once a day?"

"Yes, they were so large that their lungs had great capacity. They are different than the modern whale in many ways. One of those ways is that they stayed near the bottom of the deepest part of the ocean. It would take them all day to ascend and descend once again."

"Aren, that is so interesting." I smiled at Aren, who had become more at ease with me than he ever had been. He must feel a sense of relief that someone knew his secret. It must be a burden to hide amongst humans. I wondered if that was his true form, or if he really looked completely different than human form I saw. I had so many questions, but he did not like specific questions about his nature. He seemed to be more open to speak about history. I would be patient as he opened to me slowly.

We listened to the radio for a while. It was a welcome distraction. When we were about thirty minutes away from Gadsden, Aren spoke once more.

"I know you have many questions, but right now is not the time to get curious. I will answer what I can when I can. It's very important that you only ask me and not Paul or anyone else we might encounter in this journey for knowledge."

"Aren, why are we asking this Paul guy about it anyway? What do you think we can find out by consulting another person? It seems a waste of time and a bit of a tangent. We need to focus on the murder case and not mythology."

"I guess you're about to find out the truth anyway, so I might as well tell you why we're going to Paul. Paul is more than an expert in mythology and mysticism."

"I don't understand," I said.

"He's a soothsayer. Well, he has access to an oracle. I am worried that you may be next, so I want him to meet with you and see if that is in your future. Maybe if you personally know the killer, he may be able to see who it is."

"Paul's a psychic?" My mouth dropped open.

"Yes, well, he has access to one. So, he can let us meet her. They're in Gadsden for some kind of mystic conference. There's a collection of new age people in that area. This is how he makes a living. He travels to these conferences with his oracle, and he gets paid."

I leaned back in my seat and stretched.

"Well, it's not the weirdest thing I heard today. Let's go meet the psychic-handling immortal."

when we arrived in gadsden, Aren stopped to get gas. He called Paul while I went to use the restroom. By the time I was back in the car, Aren told me that we would have to meet Paul at a cabin he was provided as part of his stipend for the mystic conference he had participated in this week. He was leaving soon, so we had to hurry.

The cabin was very beautiful, and it was somewhere on the outskirts of Gadsden that was on the bluff of a mountain. All the windows were open, and every light was on inside and out of both floors of the cabin.

Paul was waiting for us and forced us to tour the entire cabin before he would get to business. Paul was tall and lanky, but he had broad shoulders that made him seem thicker than he was. He had dark hair and dark eyes like Aren, but they did not look related. His skin was not as dark as Aren's, but he was not pale. He had a healthy, golden tan.

Paul smiled non-stop, which made his full lips seem alluring. His face was perfect in appearance and proportions. He was quite the pretty boy, which was the opposite of Aren's rugged, manly appearance. Paul had a baby face, but in some ways, it looked quite seductive. The only bad thing about his body was his posture, as he did not stand up straight like Aren did. Despite being a few inches taller than Aren, he looked almost the same height.

From the first moment that Paul saw me, he acted like he knew me. I assumed it was the psychic part of him, but he seemed very conflicted over my presence. He was dismissive to Aren, but to me, he was attentive. It made me a little uncomfortable. After a little while, it began to bother Aren, who played it off as annoyance at Paul's stalling tactics.

Paul looked into my eyes as if he was searching for something. He waited and waited for me to recognize him. When I did not acknowledge him in the manner, he must have desired, he turned his attention to Aren, who was growing increasingly impatient with Paul.

Finally, Aren asked Paul to see the oracle. Paul asked Aren for money to pay for his services. Aren said that he did not find the dramatics funny, but Paul only laughed.

However, when I took Paul's hand in mine and asked him to please help us, he agreed. I thought I saw tears in his eyes for a moment, but he disappeared into another room too quickly for me to tell.

Paul returned in a few minutes and announced.

"She is ready. She's been outside hiking in the wilderness, but she's back now."

"You let one of your oracles walk around unattended?"

I did not follow what that meant, but Paul answered.

"Oh, I keep a little rope around her waist so that she doesn't get lost on her own. She is more functional than most of the others that I've had. She has her motor skills intact."

I began to get upset at the implications, when Paul turned to me and spoke.

"I do not take mentally impaired people. I take those declared brain dead. I get them before they pull the plug and rehabilitate them. Their family thinks they're dead, but the brain never dies. That is if you're willing to work with it."

I was a little upset and confused when a woman walked into the room. She looked clean and content. She sat in a chair and waited for Paul's instructions. However, Paul did not say one word. Instead, he took us out of the room and shut the door behind us.

Paul looked at me and inquired.

"Who shall go first?"

"I will go first," said Aren to which Paul motioned him to go. Aren went into the room. Paul closed the door once more. We were now alone. Paul offered me a seat on a couch. I took it, and he sat right next to me.

Paul had no issues with personal space since he invaded mine with great ease. He put his arm on the couch behind me. It felt like we were cuddling, and I had only been in his presence less than fifteen minutes. I thought I caught him smelling my hair, but when I looked him in the eye, he began to speak to me.

"What is your religion, dear?"

"I do not have a religion, Mr. Light."

"Oh, please call me Paul—unless you prefer to use my other name?"

"What other type of name do you have?"

"I have many names over the years, but currently, I have this name and a name that I use as a stage name."

I remembered how Aren had warned me to not ask Paul questions. I spoke.

"I think Paul is just fine for us."

Paul leaned in closer and spoke.

"Is it now? Do you think you'll change your mind soon?"

I had no idea what Paul meant, but Aren had said he was eccentric, so I just smiled at Paul and gave him a classic blank face. It was a face I had used many times to get myself out of trouble at home and in school.

Paul leaned back and smiled at me. He spoke.

"I only ask what your religion is because you seem quite calm for a Southern girl going to a cabin in the woods with two strange men to visit an oracle."

"Whatever do you mean, Paul?" I played dumb once more.

"I mean, Alva my sweet, that you are not acting like the Southern Baptist you ought to be, and I don't see a talisman around your neck.

So, why ever would a sweet thing like you be here with a bunch of devil worshipers like us?"

"You don't worship the devil, Paul."

"Do we not now? Then what crazy men are we to you?"

"Who said you were men?" Oh, no. I slipped up a little.

Paul tried to keep a straight face when he asked, "What are we then, my princess?"

"Immortals," I said as flatly as possible and without any emotion in my face.

Paul giggled as he exclaimed, "Is that what Aren told you we are?"

"So, you're not immortals?"

"Yes, we are immortal, but that's so vague. It's like marinara and Alfredo being listed only as sauce on the menu. They are completely different in taste, appearance, and texture. Although both are for pasta, you'd want to know more about it than the mere noun minus the adjective prior to ordering."

I wanted to ask more of Paul, but Aren interrupted. He may have heard us speaking because he looked upset at Paul. He still looked at me with calmness as he spoke to me.

"Go ahead, Alva. I will stay with Paul. We need to have a private word."

Before I could stand up and leave, Paul grabbed my hand to help me up from the couch. He said gently, "It helps if you let her touch you. She won't bite. A simple holding of hands like this will do." He leaned over to kiss my hand before he released it.

Aren looked annoyed at his theatrics but remained silent. I left to visit the oracle in a cabin overlooking Gadsden in the same manner as if I was going to pick up bread at the store. *How much knowing an immortal can change one's outlook on life*, I thought as I entered the room to visit Paul Light's oracle.

CHAPTER 10

I walked into the room where the oracle sat. She moved from a chair to a loveseat. There was enough room for me to sit beside her, so I did.

She had a blank stare on her face. I remembered what Paul had said, so I reached out and grabbed her hand. I held it gently and waited.

It was as if someone turned her switch to the "on" position. She broke her empty stare from the window to look me in the eyes.

"Thank you for seeking me. It means so much to me that you are here," she said.

"Thank you," I uttered.

"What is it that you wish to know?"

"I want to know who the killer is."

"There are many killers. I need a specific question."

"Who killed Morgan Cooper?"

"A man."

"What is his name?"

"He has many names. He has many faces. I cannot see clearly."

"What does that mean?"

"It means that I cannot see clearly."

I was becoming frustrated. I released her hand and asked another question.

"Did the same man that killed Morgan kill Marla Oberg?"

"Morgan who? There are many Morgans in the world."

I clenched my teeth and spoke with precision.

"Did the exact same man kill Morgan Cooper and Marla Oberg?"

"Yes."

Now we were getting somewhere.

"Who is this man?"

"He is a man."

"Why won't you tell me anything specific about him. All that I know is that he is not an immortal. He's a human like me and a man, but that's it."

"Yes, he is just like you."

"What do you mean? Is he a lawyer?"

"No, he is like you."

"A human?"

"Not exactly human, but something more."

"Not immortal?"

"No, not immortal but not human."

I was more confused than I had been before I arrived. I thanked her and stood up to leave. When I did this, my keys fell out of my purse. She caught them before they could hit the loveseat. Her fingers moved wildly all over the keys. She looked frantic.

"Can I have my keys back?" I asked.

She handed them to me but did not release them from her grip. She held onto the keychain that had once belonged to Aunt Dawn. She spoke.

"A group of three peas in a pod. Why won't you come back to me?"

She released the keychain into my hands and resumed her blank stare. Her switch was now in the "off" position.

Before I could leave the room, Paul and Aren rushed into it.

"Are you alright? Did she scare you?" Paul asked me.

"I'm fine. She just confused me, that's all."

Paul seemed to know more about what had happened than he was letting on to me. Aren seemed in on the knowledge as well. I was the only one in the dark. I looked at them.

"What is it that you're not telling me?" I asked.

"I need to check on her. I will be with you shortly," said Paul.

I thought this meant he would check on her alone. However, Aren remained with him while I waited in the other room. I was becoming more increasingly annoyed. What reason did I have to trust these two men who claimed to be immortals? I had no proof that such a thing existed. They could be yanking my chain.

I decided to eavesdrop on them. I cracked the door silently and listened in on their conversation. Aren spoke to Paul first.

"What did you mean when you said that?"

"I don't know. I was unable to get a solid read on it. I just saw that June was involved."

"You know that she hates it when you call her that. You better call her by the name she uses now."

"She's not here, so she doesn't know what I'm calling her."

"You know what this means? This means that we must go and see her. If her kid is doing this, then we need to find him and stop him," said Aren.

"What do you mean *we* have to go and see her? I'm not going!" said Paul.

"You must go with me. She won't see me and you know it," said Aren.

"I don't care what you do with your plaything, but I'm not participating," said Paul

"So, you'll let her go again? Tell me, Paul—where's your girl?" asked Aren with malice in his voice.

Aren and Paul had a silent face-off that meant nothing to me but scores to them. After a moment of silence Aren spoke.

"Did you think I didn't know? After all these years and you think you're so smooth."

"Fine, I will go, but I do this for love and not for hate, which is what I feel for you," said Paul.

I leaned closer, which was too close, because I pushed the door with my nose and it creaked. Paul and Aren stopped their conversation and looked straight at me. I was busted, but I did not care. It seemed like they did not care either, as they would not let on to me that it bothered them in the slightest. If they did that, it would indicate that their conversation was off-limits, which would show that they were guilty of something.

Aren's face went calm as he looked at me. He spoke.

"Come on in, Alva. Sorry that we are being so rude. We just needed to check on Missy here." He patted the now mute girl on the shoulder. She remained stoic as she was still in her "off" position. I walked into the room carefully and demanded.

"What is going on here?"

Aren and Paul looked at one another, and when Aren nodded, Paul spoke.

"Let me just make a phone call to change my plans. I will have my handler come and get Missy until we can conclude our business."

Paul left the room. He held Missy by the hand and led her out with him. Aren and I were now alone, and I wanted some answers.

"Aren, what is going on here?" I demanded.

Aren hesitated before he spoke with caution.

"It is now confirmed that you are in physical danger. The killer does know you. He's someone in your life. It may be someone you barely know exists, maybe you don't even know him, but he knows you. He's after you as well. That dream you had about the woman—the goddess—I think it means you're the next one chosen as the goddess in his ritual."

"That's crazy, Aren. My mother was there with me, and she has been dead for almost twenty years."

"She may be symbolic of a mother in the same way that the girl from New Jersey was the goddess that represented Mother Mary to the Catholics."

"I think that's a stretch, Aren."

"Well, think of it this way, Alva. If you're being symbolic, it can be a stretch to most people that the girl you chose is symbolic of a goddess, but if it means something to you, it fulfills your need to perform a ritual."

I sighed and sat down on the loveseat. Aren sat beside me. I could feel the warmth coming from his body. How could I have thought he was a cold, dead vampire? The heat was quite intoxicating. It aided in the permeating of his scent in the room. He smelled like soap, rain, and incense.

My head began to swim in it as Paul burst into the room and spoke.

"Okay, let's go to Nashville."

I gave Paul a blank stare and then gave one to Aren. Paul looked at me and asked Aren, "Did you not tell her?"

"I was about to, but you came in before I could get to that, Paul."

"Well, allow me to do the honor, Mr. Mysterious."

"I can handle it, Paul. Alva came here with me. She's, my responsibility."

"She may be your responsibility on the trip, but now that she's here in my house, she is my guest and my responsibility."

"This is not your house. It is just a cabin you were about to abandon to return to your domicile."

"Wherever I lie my head is my domicile and my domain. You should know that after so many years."

This was getting to aggravate. I interjected.

"Guys, please quit speaking in some weird immortal code. I am sure after eternity you two have beefs, but please chill for a bit. I am not going anywhere with anyone until I get some answers. I don't care who talks, but someone better talk before I call someone to come and pick me up and get me out of here."

Aren sighed and began to speak.

"Alva, I know we have assumed you to trust us so much, but we need a little more trust. I know you can feel it in your gut that everything we have said is true, don't you?"

I paused and reflected on my feelings. I did trust Aren and even weirdo Paul. I felt at home in both of their presences. It was so strange.

After I thought about it, I felt more at home with Aren than I ever did with Craig or even Aunt Dawn. I stared at Aren's necklace. It was a small, metal circle with intricate carvings that was on a chain of the same bronze-looking metal. The carvings began to move, as if it was not a circle but a wheel. There were many tiny wheels within the giant wheel. The other geometric objects began to dance, and I could see movement. I could see life. I could see eternity.

The room grew bright until all that remained was the tiny bronze circle. It churned and churned until I focused on the tiniest circle in the middle. Once I did that, I was gone.

I was no longer with Aren or Paul. I was no longer in Gadsden, Alabama. I was somewhere else completely. I was dressed in a long beige dress that went to my ankles. My skin was darker, but it was I inside of it. I could not see my own face, as there were no reflective surfaces near me.

I had something in my hand. It was metal and sharp. It was a dagger. I heard a voice urging me to hurry up before we got caught. The voice was male, and it said, "Hurry, girl, before the attendants come and kill us both." I looked down at the dagger in my hand before he urged, "Pry the cursed thing off already!"

The same symbol from Aren's necklace was on a clay pot. The emblem was the same size as the pendant on Aren's necklace. In fact, it looked just like it, except it was made of clay, though it was set inside and made from a different piece of clay, rather than a part of the larger pot.

I tried to pry it off, but it was no use. Although it was somehow attached, it seemed supernaturally so, as the clay was glued by some unknown force. I almost had it, it seemed, when I heard a yelp come from my companion, who had fled by the time I could see why he was scared.

I heard a voice boom.

"Do you dare disturb the temple of the Cursed One?"

It was the most beautiful man I ever laid eyes upon that spoke to me. He was perfect, and he was smiling at me. I answered boldly, "Yes."

"Do you not fear his curses upon you, girl?"

"No."

"Why not?"

"His curses are already upon me. He is the cause of my people's ruin."

"Do you really think that ruining an emblem on his drinking vessel will take his power away?"

"No."

"Then why do you do it?"

"I was the only one who would come here."

"And?"

"And my people have my lover. They won't release him unless I do this fool act."

"So, you acknowledge that a manmade symbol could never hold our power?"

"Yes."

"Then take it, my girl. Save your lover."

The symbol popped off in my hands. The man smiled at me for a moment, then he disappeared. I fled the temple.

"Alva, Alva?" a voice called. I walked down the corridor in Aren's home. The people in the paintings danced for me. One bowed as I passed. It was the same man from the temple. He stood next to the man I have been dreaming about for months now.

I tripped on the rug and landed on it. It was thick enough to make the wooden floor underneath not so hard. I swatted in the air to grab something to pull myself up again. I heard someone say, "Ouch!" Soft, warm flesh crashed into my hand.

Paul laughed and said, "She seems better already."

"Be quiet, Paul. She's about to open her eyes," said Aren.

I was back in the cabin in the woods of Gadsden. I was lying on the floor. Aren and Paul stared at me. There were two other people in the room: Missy and a man I did not know. He looked concerned for me, but Missy looked blank.

Paul saw me staring at the stranger and said, "Alva, this is my handler, Jake. He's here to take Missy back to my place until I can return."

"Hi, Jake," I said before the pain of landing on the floor awakened in my body. I followed my greeting with mumbles of pain. Aren rushed to help me up to the loveseat.

"Are you okay?" Aren asked.

"Yes, I think so. What happened?" I asked.

"Don't you know?" asked Aren.

"No," I said.

"You passed out and landed on the floor before we could catch you," said Aren.

Paul bit his lip and asked, "Do you remember anything at all?"

"No," I said. It seemed like I dreamed a night worth of dreams while I was gone, but I could not recall one image now. I stared at Aren's necklace for a moment and said, "That's pretty." Something was odd about it, but I did not know what. It was probably interesting because it was so old.

Paul brought me a drink of water. After I had a few sips, I felt fine. Paul said goodbye to Jake and Missy, who did not linger. Paul seemed overly worried, but he did not say anything one way or another. Aren was pacing the room until Missy and Jake left. Once they did leave, he stopped pacing and sat beside me on the loveseat. He took my hand and began to speak.

"Alva, I have something that I want to tell you, but I cannot start this story."

"Why not?" I asked.

"Because you have to start it in a way," said Aren.

"You mean make the first move?" I jested.

"Something like that, but I guess it's better to say that we both know the story, but you have to remember it and say it first," he said.

"Remember what, Aren?" I asked.

Aren took a deep breath and paused. He said, "Remember who you are."

My blood ran cold for a moment. I remembered that day in the Chinese restaurant with Hank. My fortune said the exact same thing. I had forgotten all about that silly moment. What else had I forgotten? I stared at Aren's pendant as I tried to remember. And then I did.

I reached out and touched the bronze circle.

"Where did you get this?" I asked.

"Do you not remember?" asked Aren.

"Yes, I do remember this, but it was clay." Suddenly, my dream from minutes ago came back to me. I remembered the rest of the story from that day. It was not a dream. It was a memory.

"I took it from you, and you came looking for me. The priests from the temple had put a price on my head, but you sought me out personally. They made that symbol up. It was worthless. It only had value to them," I said.

Aren's eyes became wide and he said, "Go on."

"You told me that part about the priests. You also told me that when you saw me that night, you did not kill me."

"And why was that?" Aren asked.

"Because you fell in love with me." I spoke as in a trance of memories. They came from a place so deep in me that I spoke without knowing what word I would utter next.

"You came to take the charm from me. You let me get my lover out first, but I gave it to you because I thought it was all over. I didn't know that my people expected me to keep it until I died."

"You led me to believe you were a priest from the temple. I gave it to you to keep from being killed for the bounty on my life. That night when the elders demanded to see it under the full moon, they found out what had happened. I think they knew all along that I would die along with my lover. They killed him that night. He was the only person in the world that loved me, and they killed him."

Tears welled in my eyes as I continued, "I wanted to die with him, but you stopped it. You offered me immortality that night. You said I had to be near death to shun it, but I never believed you. I still don't. I think you made an excuse. When the time came for them to kill me, I was so afraid to face the unknown that I accepted your offer in my heart. That was all it took, even though I did not realize it at the time."

The tears were completely streaming down my face by this point.

"You saved me from the physical death that could have taken me. I did not realize that immortality was different for humans. I did not know it would mean immortality of spirit and memories and not body. I was not like you. I was no longer human and not divine. I knew who you were when you saved me, even when you didn't say your name."

I rubbed my fingers over the intricate designs of Aren's bronze pendant.

"The moment you touched it; it turned from clay to bronze. That was when I knew that you were Ares."

I stopped talking and covered my mouth in shock. It came back flooding to me.

"All these dreams were my many lives with you. I was so mad at you for a while after you turned me. I even tried to run away, but I fell in love with you. I chose to be with you. I chose you repeatedly. And I have died repeatedly. All of this I suffered to be with you."

I sobbed as I heard Aren respond.

"And I have watched you die repeatedly. I suffer as well for I am always aware. You forget things while I remember every second of your pain. I remember every disease. I remember every death. It has been so long this last time. Your spirit took so long to pass through the womb of the earth. I thought I had lost you. You have been gone since the 1930s."

"Yes, thanks for that last World War, by the way." Paul interrupted when he said this to Aren, but it felt like a dagger to me.

"You know I gave up warring as a god the day I fell in love with Alva," Aren said.

"Well, could've fooled me. Every time the girl dies, we have another big war. It's not like you don't know it will happen, Aren. Alva, did you know that the Confederacy was doing fine until you got a fever?" asked Paul.

"Shut up, Paul. That is not her fault," said Aren.

"Of course it is not her fault, but she needs to know what pattern she has failed to escape for most of her lives," said Paul.

Before either Aren or I could say a word, Paul continued.

"You keep on dying early, girl. It's a mystery to us why, but it is true. If you do make it past a certain age, you end up not meeting him until later in life. But as soon as you two meet, you die. At least it seems that way."

I ignored what Paul said for some reason. He seemed to have bitterness in his voice that made me remember something about him. I looked at him and spoke boldly.

"Apollo, it was you in the temple that day. You gave me the emblem. You started this whole thing. You were there before Ares ever was. You were even there the night Ares made me what I am today."

Paul wanted to react, but his phone rang in his pocket. He picked it up and answered it. He looked at Aren and spoke.

"Aren, it's her. She won't allow our visit until you ask her personally." When Aren did not respond quickly enough, Paul said, "She will not wait."

Aren said, "Fine," and left the room abruptly.

Paul looked stricken as he asked, "Do you remember everything yet, Alva?"

"No, I don't remember much more than scatters of things here and there. It's like when you dreamed all night, but you can't remember it until something reminds you of the dream. You won't recall it until it's triggered, but even then, it is foggy and in fragments."

I stared at Paul for agreement, but he was silent. Of course he did not know that. I remembered that they did not sleep. I wanted to know one detail that I could not recall. I asked, "Why is it that you were gods and now you are not?"

"When the Age of Reason came, all gods and goddesses of our kind lost their standing. We were no longer worshipped. The kind that was drawn to our court was always the superstitious type. All major superstition lost its power when the Enlightenment came. It wasn't just us Greeks. It was many gods and goddesses of old. So, we became immortals like we are now. We could no longer procreate with humans as we did before we lost our divinity. We're now barren. We might as well be called superheroes. Some limited powers, but always a fatal flaw."

"But you can't die?" I asked.

"No, we cannot die." Paul said.

"I can die though."

"Yes, you can and have many times."

"Does it hurt when I die, Paul?"

Paul had tears in his eyes when he spoke.

"I do not know, but I imagine it does hurt for only a moment. Then it goes away. In death, the pain is always greatest for those left behind." He cleared his throat. I pretended not to notice the tears.

"Is making us humans this way a god thing?"

"No, we can do it even now as mere immortals."

"How many have you changed into hybrids?"

"None, actually."

"And Aren?"

"Only you. You are enough." Paul smiled at me dryly, but I could feel he meant what he was saying.

"What about the other gods from different cultures and throughout time?"

"They are like us. Once our influence is gone, we all become like this. That is why people believe in vampires and other supernatural beings. We are all there is. There are some gods who used to accept blood sacrifices who have developed a longing for it. That is where the vampire folklore came from originally. Of course, the god that loved blood who started the first vampire myth was from an extremely old civilization and is now thankfully gone, though others have acted similarly for similar reasons."

"How is he gone?"

"He is gone because no human remembers him. When a deity loses his influence, he loses his divine nature and becomes immortal like we are. However, that is only as long as he is remembered by at least one human. When the last human that remembers him is gone, the god goes to the next level of existence."

"Where is that, heaven?"

"Yes, basically. He goes to the great oneness of all beings before, to which he was deprived of for millennia. He can once again be with those that he loved so much—those that worshiped him and those that he chose to be reborn as his lovers. It is the place where we all finally become equals."

"Sounds more like to me that these are his children. I guess you can still procreate after all."

"Well, in a way, but you don't make love with your offspring."

"Yes, but I took mythology. I know the stories of incestuous relationships between you brother and sister gods."

"That is just human rubbish. Humans made up every story about us in what you read in mythology class. We just had functions as certain gods, but even that took a while for the humans to not screw up in their stories. We are not related. We have no father or mother. We were not created or made."

"What are you then?"

"We just are what we are. None of us really know."

"So, you gods and goddesses ever date one another?"

"Yes, we have, but we never have anything too serious. We always prefer human mates. I don't know why, but it is more fun to us. There is always more passion with humans than with each other, at least in the long run."

"So that's why ya'll mated with humans—for eternal passion?"

"Well, it is an eternal marriage in many ways. You want to make it last if possible."

"But there can be more than one?"

"Yes, but you can have multiple marriages. Your culture does well on that lesson."

"This doesn't make sense to me. If you keep bringing back people again, then how can there not be at least one who remembers you?"

Paul's face grew stern as he said, "It's not so simple. Each migration of the soul to a new body costs a little bit of energy for us. After a while, that reserve becomes empty and we can no longer do it. There is a chance that they may not come back again. Each time you bring them back there is a risk for both. When we are no longer gods, we have limits."

"So why would anyone want to do it?" I asked.

"They do not have to do anything."

"What do you mean?" I asked.

"They must choose to come back. It is a mutual decision for both parties."

"Oh," I said. That was a solemn statement. I needed a moment.

"Anything else?" Paul asked.

"I do remember that Ares chose me, but you did not. Why is it that I am thinking of that, Apollo?"

Paul's face began to change. I saw him as he truly was. He was Apollo, the Greek God of Light and Wisdom. He was beautiful. He realized that I could see him. He was surprised in his expression but remained silently beautiful.

Aren walked into the room and handed the phone to Paul. His face began to melt away from the middle-aged man into the eternally youthful face that I had dreamed about again. This was the man from the train. This was the man from the bathtub. I was not dreaming all those times but remembering.

This was the face of my eternal husband. Though the memories were there, the feelings were encased in memories and not active in my heart.

I did not ache for him the way that I had in my other lives. Something was missing. Aren searched my face, and I knew that he knew. He knew I could see them as they truly were. He also knew that I no longer loved him.

I changed the subject and asked, "Can we go now?"

"Yes," Aren said and we loaded into Aren's car while Paul closed the cabin and locked it.

"Okay, let's go," I said. Aren and I waited in the car while Paul gathered his things.

When Paul finally came out to the car, he climbed in the back and said, "I should have sent my luggage with Jake." He placed a small briefcase on the seat beside him in the backseat where he sat. A piece of brightly colored paper fell out.

I grabbed it and opened it out of curiosity. It was a small poster of Paul. However, it said Apollo the Great instead of Paul Light. Aren glanced at it and said, "That's very subtle, Paul."

Paul snapped, "At least I go by a pseudonym—you know that I hate it. It doesn't matter anyway. No one takes me seriously. It's not like they think I'm me." Paul had a look of dismay in his eyes. He really missed being a feared deity.

"As if you have a choice, Paul. You know what will happen if you didn't."

"What would happen?" I asked.

Paul mumbled, "I would lose the limited powers that I have left."

"And what powers are those?" I asked.

Aren glanced at me for a moment and then glanced at Paul in the rearview mirror. He said, "Let's not speak of that."

"Why not? I thought we were going to be all honest with one another now."

Aren sighed, "Because it is very bad manners amongst us to ask about our powers. We do not disclose that very often because we do not want others to know our current limitations."

"Others? What others?" I asked.

"Each other, actually," Paul interjected. "We are our worst enemies in the times that we knew what one another can do. After the Age of

Reason, when we moved from deity to immortality, we retained certain gifts. Though we are no longer limitless, we still have a diluted version of our divine powers."

"When we were gods, we fought one another for power because we craved more worshipers than the other. Now we no longer have the power to receive worship or to influence humans against their will. That is the one thing we all have in common. Otherwise, we do not know what supernatural abilities that we each retain, and we wish to keep it so. It keeps the peace more than anything else."

I thought about Missy.

"So why the oracle act? If you can see things about people, why pretend Missy is the psychic?" I asked.

"I cannot prophesy anymore. I must speak through an oracle. Though I can see, I cannot utter one word about it to anyone. She is the way I can keep using my power of prophecy." He glanced at Aren competitively and said, "But I have more tricks in my bag than that. Aren already knew that is how I roll, so it's no big deal to disclose that much."

Another thought occurred to me. I asked, "What woman is it that we are going to see in Nashville?"

Aren said, "Her name is Helen Case. She owns a ranch right outside of Nashville."

I leaned back in my seat and said, "Oh, we're going to see Hera. How nice."

CHAPTER 11

The drive was many hours, which meant many hours of time to fill. At first, it was mostly awkward silence. Aren looked depressed. Paul looked bitter. I probably looked confused, but when I looked in the mirror, I only saw that my lip-gloss needed a touchup.

Of course, Paul took great interest in watching me apply fresh coats of gloss on my lips. Aren pretended to watch the road, but I saw him squirm a little in the seat next to me when I puckered to check for smudges.

When we were halfway there, Paul spoke up first. His tone was quite feisty, "I remember you asking me about gods dating goddesses, Alva. Do you know why Helen did not want to see Aren?"

I giggled and looked at Aren. I said, "No, you didn't! Should I be jealous since you and I were so hot and heavy as well?"

I slipped up and both noticed it. I accidentally used the past tense for my relationship with Aren. I knew he realized it, but it must hurt to hear it. This was only fuel for Paul, as he had a wild look of pleasure in his eyes as he continued, "Oh, yes, they were together until he saw you. He gave up being a god for you, which really made her mad. Of course, she shortly recovered when she found her own lover."

"I thought he was a god until the Enlightenment, right?" I asked.

"I was deity until then. I gave up warring and functioning as the god of war after I met you," Aren said softly.

"Why?" I asked.

"Because it did not seem worth it anymore. I saw how it ruined your life, and for the first time, it mattered to me. When you joined me, I stopped receiving sacrifices of war."

Paul interjected, "Yes, and that is why Helen is so mad. She blames Aren for the fall of the gods and goddesses. She believes that Aren's refusal to perform his divine duties allowed humans to evolve beyond us."

Aren said, "I will not apologize for being in love. I doubt that I caused our reign to end. However, man is better now without us controlling their lives. Modern society was inevitable. If it was not born from our wards, it would have come from some other god's servants."

I felt a small tinge of jealousy for Helen Case. I decided it was my anger at her ignorance instead of jealousy of her former fling with Aren. I asked, "So she's over the past love affair?"

"Oh, yes. She is quite over him. It's a surprise, because Helen was the kind that mated for eternity. I thought that surely, they would stay together forever, but both found that humans did it for them better than either one could do for each other."

"You mean she's still with her human lover?"

"No, he left her. She's very heartbroken over it and refuses to move on."

"Is he dead then?"

Aren and Paul glanced at one another. Aren said, "No, he's not. In fact, we think he's involved with the Cooper murder in some way. That's why we had to go and see her. We need to find out where he is. She is the only one that would know."

"So, you knew where I was my whole life?"

"No, I had to touch you to realize who you were. But even then, I could not tell you who you were. You had to remember on your own. It's a law of our universe."

I remembered that. I remembered the day in the library when Aren first touched my hand inadvertently and the look on his face. He looked relieved. He was relieved to have finally found me.

"What if she doesn't know?" I asked.

"Then we're in trouble in more ways than one. Only she can really tell who he is. We sometimes can tell others belong to someone, but rarely can we tell which one it is. That is reserved for the one who made them to know upon physical contact."

"How long have they been apart?" I asked.

"For a very long time now," Paul answered.

I asked, "How can that be if it has to be a mutual decision?"

Paul replied, "It doesn't take much. Something must be bringing him back. He must want to come back each life, even if it isn't for the love of Helen. The smallest grain of desire to return is all it takes. Don't you remember?"

"Oh, right," I said. I did remember how it was the will to live that kept me alive and bonded me to Ares for eternity.

Helen still loved her man so that was why she brought him back. Why he allowed her to bring him was a different story. Maybe it was the key to the Cooper murder. Someone was killing off icons. It had to stop, so I would bite the bullet and meet my ex's ex.

I asked, "What kind of farm is this? A vegetable farm?"

Aren said, "No, it's an animal farm. She has some livestock, but her specialty is peacocks."

when we arrived at helen case's farm, I was unimpressed. There was a definite peacock theme. The front gate had peacock feathers made of wrought iron painted black. The metal was in the shape of the feathers. Even though there was no color, I could tell what it was meant to be.

After we drove half a mile through cow pastures, we found the horse stables. This was where Helen Case was. She had just finished brushing one of her many horses when we found her. Aren pulled up to the spot where she was with her horse. When the horse saw the car, it startled until she placed her hand on its neck. It immediately went placid, which was fine with me. Although I was country, I was afraid of all animals bigger than a kitten.

Helen knew who I was immediately. Paul had probably told her on the phone when he had called her hours ago. She did not waste any time when she asked, "So, you are Alva?"

I answered in unison with Aren and Paul, "Yes."

Helen laughed and said, "Nothing has changed. It never does after an eternity of inspection."

I did not understand her comment, but I did not like her already. I remembered vaguely that she always had been a real jerk to me. Why would this life be any different?

Aren did not waste any time. He asked, "Where is he, Helen?"

"I told you on the phone the same thing I will tell you now. I do not know where he is. He has refused me."

"How do you know that he just does not remember you yet?" I asked meekly.

Helen gave me a smirk and said, "My love was always resourceful. He never forgets for very long like *others* do."

I knew that was directed at me. However, I played dumb and asked, "Are you sure he isn't dead?"

This made her angry and she said, "I would feel it because I know when he is on earth. I know when he remembers. He has remembered for at least fifteen years now. He is not much older than you. Maybe he is younger. It is always hard to tell now that girls wear so much makeup."

She was rude. She tried to get under my skin. This would have been just like old times if I could remember any with detail. I did not care because it was easy to make cracks at human flaws such as wrinkles when you look like a goddess. However, she was no longer a goddess, so I did not care what she thought. I stood my ground and waited for someone to get something out of her.

Paul tried next. He said, "Helen, cut the crap. Just tell us what you do know. I know you know something about him. How close is he?"

"I am in the South like the rest of you. It seems this bunch was born here again. I hope they hurry up and find a new region if not a new country."

Paul was impatient. He said, "We don't have time for this."

Helen snapped, "Time is all we have, Paul."

Aren hissed, "June," which made her angry for some unknown reason. I saw it flash in her eyes. She successfully hid it quickly, though.

Helen sighed loudly and said, "I will tell you what, Paul. Give me a few moments alone with the girl, and I will tell her all that I know."

"Do you actually know anything?" I asked in a smart aleck tone.

Aren interrupted, "Better yet why are you asking Paul's permission?"

"Oh, she's yours?"

"She is her own. Ask her yourself!" Aren growled.

"Fine, will you come with me?" Helen asked in a pretend demure fashion.

"Yes," I answered.

I could tell that Aren and Paul did not like it, but I went anyway. I had to get answers. Helen led me to a large area fenced in with chicken wire. It was a beautiful flower garden, and it was full of peacocks.

Since the moment I met Helen, she kept a distance from me. Now was no different. She motioned for me to sit on a bench while she walked around and petted her peacocks. They seemed calm around her in the same way that the horse had been. Helen had a way with animals. That was for sure.

As Helen attended her pets, I looked around. The flower garden was enclosed in a tall fence of chicken wire. There were colorful decorative streamers and flags stuck at the top of the fence. It looked like some type of Renaissance celebration. Of course, Helen had lived through that era. So, she would know what it looked like.

The rest of the garden was just as colorful. There were so many beautiful flowers in bloom, which confused me because of the time of year. She must have found flowers that bloomed in the cooler climate.

Someone had taken care to keep all the changing autumn leaves off the ground in the flower garden. However, there was color all over the ground. It was the petals and full blooms from the flowers. They were strewn about the grass like organic confetti.

Helen noticed what I was looking at and said, "Yes, I love my peacocks. They are such intelligent creatures. They do not eat the flowers because they crave the meat of the bugs that hide inside of the bloom.

They are willing to sacrifice the beauty of nature to get what they want. Of course, sometimes they are just bored and do it for fun."

"Sounds like you have something in common with those birds of yours," I said before I realized how inflammatory I was being.

Helen stopped petting her birds and stood up straight. She looked me directly in the eyes and said, "I can tell that you don't remember much, Alva. Otherwise, you'd not be in my presence so blindly."

"How am I blind?"

"You are trusting Paul again. You are speaking to Aren. I thought your last life would have been the end of it. You are back, but neither you nor I know why you chose to be here. It's not like you love him anymore."

"Would you rather rekindle? Be my guest," I snapped.

Helen opened her mouth in surprise. She cocked her head back and laughed loudly. She exclaimed, "Of whom do you think I'm speaking?"

With that statement, I was left confused, and Helen was left intrigued. She marched over to me and plopped down beside me. She grabbed my hand, lifted it to her face and sniffed me from fingers to shoulder. It was kind of creepy.

Her eyes went wild as she said, "You have been with him. His essence is all over you!"

"Who?" I asked timidly.

"My lover," Helen said. "You have been so close to him that he is in your pores. You have known him for long?"

"I don't know who it is you speak about," I said nervously confused.

Helen snapped her fingers, and a peacock came running over to us. I was startled from the sudden movement of an animal that size, but Helen's grip kept me from moving. She plucked a feather from the peacock. The peacock stood in attention at our feet. She rubbed the feather on my right wrist first. Nothing happened. Then she rubbed it on my left wrist. The peacock began to go crazy with its wild call.

It sent chills through me as I heard Helen announce, "He's not a family member. He's a lover."

I said, "I do not have a lover right now."

Helen rolled her eyes and said, "That's just a term, dear. I mean it's someone you are dating or having sex with currently. Who is that?"

I was offended as I snapped, "I am not sleeping with anyone." I paused and then realized that I was dating Hank. I then remembered the oracle's crazy reaction to the keychain that held the key that Hank had given me. Even though the keychain was an old one that Aunt Dawn had used for years that Craig had given her, it was now Hank's key that was on it.

I whispered hoarsely, "Hank is yours?"

Helen's eyes grew wide as she asked, "That's his name? What is his last name?"

"Rowling," I uttered. "Hank Rowling. He is from Birmingham, but he now stays in Guntersville, Alabama."

Helen looked exuberant as she stood up quickly and marched away. She stopped for a moment, glanced over her shoulder and said, "Thank you so much, dear. You may go. You should really focus on Ares. Hank is mine." She walked off abruptly after that. I was alone in the garden.

I made my way back to Aren's car. Aren and Paul were waiting for me. They looked nervous and impatient. When they saw me, both had a look of relief on their faces. Paul asked, "Well?"

"It's a guy that I'm dating named Hank Rowling that belongs to Helen," I said.

"You're dating the murderer? One like you—I knew it!" Paul mused.

"You're dating *him*?" Aren inquired. That was a loaded reference perhaps. Or it may have been jealousy of me dating at all.

A few moments into our conversation, a man appeared. He was dressed in a cowboy outfit, though for a farmhand, that was just the uniform. He waited for a pause in our conversation, which came now, to say, "Miss Case thanks you for your visit, but your welcome is worn. Please leave now and nothing will happen."

I made a face because I was irritated at how dramatic her rudeness had become. Aren intercepted my rude comment before I could make it by grabbing my arm gently and saying, "Let's go, Alva. We have what we came for, so let it be."

With that, we loaded into the car and left the ranch. Helen was probably on her way to see Hank. Hank was hers. One like me was the killer, according to the oracle, and Hank was the only one in my life. At least, that I knew of currently.

Once we were near the Tennessee border, Aren said we needed to stop for gas. Paul suggested that we stop for something to eat as well. I remembered that they did not have to eat, but they liked it. I did, however, and I was hungry.

We pulled off the interstate into a small town. There was nothing but a gas station it seemed, but a sign indicated there was a little bar and grille off the beaten path. We followed the signs until we finally found it.

It was the kind of place that was so good because it was completely innutritious but delicious. The fries were too greasy, and the sweet tea was too sweet, but that was what made it good. Paul had even talked me into getting a cocktail to calm me down. It was strong enough to take the edge off my nerves. I felt better for the moment.

When we finished our meal, we needed to get back on the road. We had already gassed up before we ate, so it was time to return to the interstate and get back to Alabama. Aren did not have a navigation system in his car. I feared we would get lost. Then I remembered that one of Aren's gifts was that he could never get lost.

However, I began to doubt my memory when it seemed we were most definitely lost. It seemed strange since we were in such a small town. How could anyone get lost in such a small place?

Finally, after thirty minutes of driving through blank farmland, Paul asked Aren, "How is it that *you* are lost?"

Aren said, "I don't know. It's like something is scrambling my compass." He smacked his left ear and said, "There's some kind of interference there. I can feel it."

Paul asked, "Why didn't you say so?" He reached out and touched Aren's forehead. It must have worked because Aren said, "Thank you," and made a U-turn.

We were on our way out of the city when we saw a four-way stop blockade by local cops. This was on the way to the chicken plant that we had passed earlier, and traffic was quite backed up. There must have been a shift change because there were cars everywhere.

We waited a few minutes in line behind five cars until it was our turn. The cops kept pulling people out of the cars and searching the cars. My lawyer within was getting upset at the constitutional violations running amuck, but I would bite my tongue to get out of here.

However, we did not fare any better. When it came our turn, the cop shined his light on our faces repeatedly. He said to Aren and Paul, "You boys look a little tan. Why don't you step out of the vehicle, senores?" He looked at me and ordered, "You too, little lady."

The cop that ordered us out of the car then escorted us over to stand with the other people that had been forced out of their vehicles. We all had to watch helplessly while our cars were illegally searched. There were a couple of cops guarding us with guns, so we did not move.

I was in a crowd of at least ten other people, and most of the people looked Hispanic. I realized that not only was I the victim of an illegal search, but I was also part of a racist motivated harassment by local authorities. I sighed as I leaned against a pine tree. I knew that this was going to get worse.

It did not take long to get worse, as the cop that had been searching our vehicle came over to us with a small cardboard box. He looked at Aren, who had been driving the vehicle and claimed ownership earlier and asked, "Is this yours, son?"

"Yes," Aren said.

"So, you admit to owning and transporting the contraband?" the cop asked.

"I admit that it is my wine, yes." Aren spoke calmly. Paul looked bored.

"Don't take that tone with me, boy!" the cop ordered loudly. With that, he took all three of us into custody. I was in one car, and Aren and Paul were in another. I wondered why they did not fight. I kept silent and played along for their sake.

As a lawyer, I knew a truth that keeps the taser away: fight it in court instead of at the time of arrest. That would also keep the charge of resisting arrest away from your doorstep.

I rode silently with a cop that was about my age. He was not bad looking, but he was redneck cute. When I did not speak or cause a scene of any kind from the backseat, the cop decided to debrief me.

He spoke loudly as most Southern men tend to do without realizing it, "Your friend brought alcohol into a dry county. Did you know that?"

"No," I answered. I knew silence would make him angry, so I went with it.

"It's true. Most people don't realize it because the county line is just past the stop sign. That county is wet, but we're dry." The cop turned into the station. We arrived. He still had not told me what I was charged with or why Paul was also arrested for what Aren had admitted was his.

The cop took me to the back into a segregated waiting room. I was handcuffed the entire time, but the cop decided to remove my handcuffs in what should have been the booking phase of this fiasco. However, he put me in the interrogation room and sat down across from me.

He said, "I guess you're wondering why we brought you in as well?"

"Yes, I did wonder that, officer," I said with as much respect as I could fake.

"Your dark friend had a higher amount of wine than statutorily allowed in a dry county in Tennessee. Your other less dark friend resisted arrest."

"What was the original charge for my less dark friend, officer?" I was still polite and he seemed fooled.

"Disorderly conduct, of course, counselor," the cop said slyly. He knew that I was an attorney. He had not even taken my identification from me yet. He had only patted me down and took my purse with us.

He had enjoyed the pat down too much it seemed, but how did he know I was an attorney?

He saw my reaction and said, "Yes, I know you're an attorney. I recognize you." I did not know how that was possible. I never practiced in Tennessee in any capacity. Something was terribly wrong here, so I decided to drop the coy act.

"If you know that I'm an attorney, then you know all the lawsuits that are coming your way. We have illegal Terry stops, illegal searches, racial profiling, false arrest, not to mention false imprisonment."

The cop leaned forward and said, "You smell awful funny, counselor. Have you been drinking?" I remembered the one cocktail that Paul had talked me into with our meal. Uh oh. He knew that I knew the moment I stepped out of that car, that he could bust me for public intoxication. Even if I did fail a breathalyzer test, which was unlikely, I would have the charge over me.

The cop finished my thought, "An alcohol-based offense for an attorney could mean severe disciplinary actions."

"It's not illegal to drink," I said.

"Yes, but it is illegal to do it out in public. You are an attorney. You are held to a higher standard." It seemed the cop was not so simple anymore. He was quite calculating. However, he had yet to arrest me. He wanted something else.

"What do you want?" I asked. There was no point dragging this out.

"Well, funny you should ask. There's a lock on this door. We can be in here undisturbed all we want. Why don't we just kiss and make up, and I'll let you and your friends go?" The cop grinned as he waited for my response. He had done this before today.

So, there was at least one cop who would help him in this game. The cop who had Aren and Paul must be his buddy. Of course, all the cops were male, so they may all be in on it. I wanted to know what I faced, so I asked, "Just you?"

The cop looked ecstatic because he thought we were negotiating, which meant I might be game. He said, "Of course, my dear. It's my turn. Don't worry your little head. I won't force you to share. I promise it will be just you and me."

I wanted a minute to think, but a minute was not what I had. I decided to use the only trick I could think of when I said, "Okay, but let me freshen up first. I've been on the road all day."

The cop reached into his pocket and handed me a breath mint. He said, "That is fine dear. I don't like the taste of rum anyway." He handed me my purse, which he had kept hostage the entire time. He had already gone through it, so he knew there were no weapons in it, only girlie stuff to make me prettier.

The cop stood up and stretched for a moment before he pulled me up by my arm. When he did this, I noticed something. I noticed he had the same belt buckle as the farmhand on Helen's ranch had. It was a pewter rectangle with two peacock feathers that made an "x" symbol. Now I knew why he knew me. Helen had put them up to this. Did she cause us to get lost as well? I did not know her secret powers, but I knew she was the cause of this.

He took me to a one-person restroom and said, "Five minutes," before he closed the door. I had to think. Where was my phone? I remembered that I had dropped it somewhere. I think it was in Aren's house. I dropped it when he had startled me in the hallway of portraits. I could not call anyone, but whom would I call—the cops?

I could not get any ideas at all, but I decided finally to quickly try to remember what I could about Aren. Maybe there was something he could do. Helen had powers, and so did Aren. He must be good for something other than navigation. I tried to think about it for a moment.

My mind went blank as I tried to focus on remembering. Then something came to me. I remembered that Aren could hear anything that was uttered, even the smallest sound. If breath was involved, he could hear it. I also remembered that he was unnaturally strong, but all of them were.

They were playing along for some reason, but I did not know why. Something was holding them here. I remembered that they could not risk being discovered for what they were in the public eye. In this age of media frenzy, it was a possibility that any act could be recorded and distributed to the masses. Exposure on such a large scale was a bad thing for immortals. It was another way that they could forfeit what little power they had left.

However, if Aren knew I was in danger, he would risk it. I would tell Aren what was going on so he could come and save me from this creep. If he knew Helen was behind it, he would realize that his secret was safe with her underlings. However, Aren could not hear through walls. I had to be in the same room, no matter how long, for it to work. I had to wait until I was in the hallway and hope that there were no walls between us when I called for him.

I heard a tap on the door. It was time for me to deliver the ransom for us. I stepped out of the bathroom and pretended to clear my throat. I covered my mouth with my hand and whispered as quietly as I could, "Aren, these are Helen's boys. One is about to make me have sex with him. Please come now."

Within seconds, I heard a whoosh. The lover cop was now on the floor unconscious. Aren looked down and said, "Don't worry, he's just asleep."

Paul was behind him. He had not heard what I said like Aren did, but he looked concerned. He must have followed Aren blindly. He was just as fast as Aren, but Aren was always the better fighter. Aren was also stronger physically. I remembered that much.

Aren said, "Paul, it's time to use what you got. All the guys in here have the same belt buckle, which means they're linked in battle. It's a smaller version of a coat in arms. Immortals use it, but I did not notice it until Alva said they were all Helen's boys."

Paul sighed and said, "Okay, fine," as we went back out to the main room. Paul snapped his fingers, and everything stopped. Paul could stop time it seemed. Paul noticed me looking around in amazement and said, "No, it's just slow. No one can stop time. We are just moving faster than the rest of them. They will not see us. It's not like they got our names anyway. They just impounded the car."

Paul grabbed the keys from a table and threw them at Aren. With that, we walked out and got in his car. Nothing was missing. The cops had wanted to detain us, but for what reason?

We drove for a while in peace. No one followed us. Either they did not know where to look for us, or they did not care. I imagined that the crooked cops that worked for Helen had done what they intended to do for the most part—stall us.

After we had made it into the boundaries of Alabama, Paul said, "Helen is behind this so hardcore that I don't even know what to say. I guess she's not over it yet."

"No, this isn't about us. This is about Alva. She wanted to punish Alva. It seems that Alva is dating Helen's mate," Aren said.

"Oh," Paul said. "That's heavy. Well, good thing that she's softened up because she would have had her tortured in the old days."

"She wouldn't dare with us near her." Aren looked at me and answered my concern with, "Don't worry, Alva, she can't kill you. She would forfeit her powers if she directly ordered your killing or did it herself. We can't kill each other's mates, even when they forsake us. She's too fond of what power she has left to waste it on something as silly as revenge."

"She could manipulate the situation to make sure you died, though," Paul said as if he was thinking out loud instead of commenting.

Aren looked angry and said, "That would not happen. She knows better than that."

"Is that why I die so early every life?" I asked.

"No, that can't be it," Aren answered. "She hasn't been involved with us in hundreds of years. She wouldn't know where you were. I wouldn't see her for a thousand years until today."

"So does this mean that Hank is the killer?" I asked.

"Not necessarily," Paul answered. "He's involved by knowing you, and you are the next probable target. It's not so unusual that he's in your life, though."

Aren looked angrily at Paul for a moment as I asked, "What does that mean?"

"Oh, just that you guys are all drawn to one another. You tend to be born in groups. It's something about the patterns of life. You are close as we are close to our mates. Even before we find them, we will know what area of the world to be in so that we can run into them and begin our life anew once you remember." Paul seemed to speak of it as if he had done it before, even though he never had taken a human mate.

"Helen stalled us for a reason. Does this mean that Helen is on her way to meet Hank?" I asked Aren.

"Probably, as she fled the place after speaking to you. Odds are good she's off to Guntersville to see him. Even though he doesn't want her, it won't stop her."

"Why not?" I inquired.

"Because when Helen made him, she said that he would be her first and last. On the day she made him, she told me, 'May he live forever.' I knew that she meant it. She will try to make at least a little contact with him. All she needs to do is to trigger whatever it is in him that makes him want to live at least one more life. She believes that eventually he will wear down and return to her. So, she makes sure he passes to the next life for another chance at love."

I asked, "That is why Helen is going through all this trouble to be with Hank when he left her so long ago? Whatever could she say that makes him live again?"

"I don't know, but it must be something good. Whatever it is, she's successfully brought him back thousands of years. They did not stay together very long. In fact, he left her during his very first life. She will not give up. She is persistent."

"Well," I said, "we need to get to Hank and see what all the fuss is about. And we need to find out how he's involved with these murders."

Because we were closer to Huntsville than Gadsden, we went to Aren's house first to get my car. I had to go inside and get my phone, and frankly, I needed to use the restroom. So, we all went inside together into Aren's house.

After I used the restroom, I found my phone in the hallway. It was on the floor in the corner by the window where Aren had proved that he could tolerate sunlight. Aren turned the light on for me so that I could find it easier. I still could not see where the light switch was. He did it before I could pay attention to its location.

Paul had followed us out of curiosity. Either that or he was chaperoning us for some reason. Whatever the reason, all three of us were walking down the hallway when we heard someone speak to us.

"Hello, again," the voice said.

Aren tensed up, "You have a lot of nerve coming here."

CHAPTER 12

I stared at the intruder. It was obviously another immortal, but I did not know his name. He stood there in all his perfect glory—platinum blonde hair and pale, silvery blue eyes. He was tall and muscular. He was beefier than Aren or Paul was, but he was not as big as a modern body builder. His skin was the color of caramel. He was all in all quite striking.

The man walked closer to us as he answered Aren, "I am here because an old friend asked me to intervene, Aren."

"Helen," Paul said under his breath.

"You always were her sniveling puppy dog," Aren sneered. "Whenever she said jump, you'd jump right up them skirts. You always made a fool of yourself for her."

"How is being in love foolish?" the man asked Aren. "I see you still love your mate."

"It's only foolish when the love is one-sided."

He stared at me and said, "Oh, please, Aren. You're not fooling me. You can't have them both, Aren. You cannot have Helen and the human."

"I don't want Helen, Zeke," Aren said. "Is that what she told you?"

"She told me that you were trying to keep us apart because you wanted to have her all to yourself but keep the human as well. You're humiliating her. It doesn't matter, though, because she doesn't want your back. She finally wants to be with me. So, stand down, Aren."

"Zeke, I don't want her. I haven't wanted her since I took Alva to be mine. She is just pulling your strings. She wants you to stall us while she goes to her human."

Zeke became furious as he yelled, "That's not true! She finally chose me!" The foundation of the house must have shook a little because I felt a tremble and saw a little dust fall from the ceiling. I grabbed onto Paul, who stood behind Aren.

Aren was in Zeke's face as he spoke, "You always did think she would come around. Believe me, she hasn't changed."

"It's destiny that we be together. Remember all the stories of old? We are to be married. It's inevitable," Zeke said.

Aren replied, "Now, Zeke, we both know that those stories were made up by humans. It is neither truth nor prophecy. Face it and quit being her fool."

I realized this was Zeus and then I remembered how he was Helen's perpetual stalker. She would manipulate him to do whatever she wanted him to do but would never be with him. She always led him on, and she seemed to have done it again.

"Is this what this is all about?" Paul mused. "Helen has made promises to you again, and again you believe her, Zeke? Last time in India, she told you that she would quit it all if you did her bidding. Do you remember what happened?"

Zeke's face went dark, as he was becoming agitated. He screamed, "That was not my fault! It was Aren's fault that all those people had to die."

"But you caused the earthquake when she dumped you, Zeke," Paul said very calmly. It seemed he was a third-party neutral in this strange love triangle. Zeke was responding to him without too much anger. He seemed to be calming down as Paul continued to reason with him, "So, she asked you to come here for what purpose—to do her bidding yet once again? It's not fair to you, Zeke."

Even though Paul's reasoning seemed to reach him on some level, Zeke shut Paul down. He said, "Paul, this is between Aren and me. Stay out of it. You can go. Take the girl with you."

I remembered that Aren was strategically strong and Zeke was brutally strong. They would be a stalemate for one another. They could not physically fight it out without causing a scene that would bring the press and unwanted attention. Aren was stuck with Zeke for the moment.

Aren walked over to the end of the hallway to talk to us two. Zeke waited on the other end of the hallway. He blocked the only way out, so we were not going anywhere. Aren spoke, "This is getting strange. Helen is calling Zeke in, which means only a few hours until some of our other friends may show up for this party."

"Why would Helen do this? This is extreme even for her," Paul whispered.

"I don't know what is going on, but it must be something bigger than we think. Either that, or she's just growing impatient without her mate," Aren said.

"Do you think it's possible she's running out of time with him?" Paul asked.

"I doubt it, as everything is still okay with us," Aren said uncomfortably. I realized the "us" in that statement meant him and me. I did not follow what he meant, but to me, there was no "us."

Aren said, "He won't let me go, Paul. This means you need to go with Alva and protect her."

I snapped, "Wait, don't I get a say in this?"

Aren said, "Normally, I would be very sensitive and politically correct with you but now is not the time for feelings. Helen may have called in other favors. If she has convinced them that I ended our reign all those years ago because of you, you may be in danger."

"I thought you said they couldn't hurt me?" I asked.

"They cannot kill you, that is all. There are many things worse than death, Alva," Aren answered.

"So, it is settled," Paul said. "I'll go with Alva. You stay here and try to wait for Helen to call Zeke off to another errand." Paul glanced at Zeke's foreboding appearance and commented, "Good luck with that."

With those words, we parted ways with Aren. Zeke let us pass without incident. I was driving the god Apollo to my apartment in Guntersville, Alabama. But first, we needed to find Hank.

There is a large dead spot for phone reception between Guntersville and Huntsville. The angles of the cliffs around the road seem to block all viable phone communications. My phone was in and out of service for a period of about fifteen minutes during the hour-long drive. When we finally got out of the dead zone, my phone buzzed. I had a message.

I listened to it and heard Hank's voice, "Hey, Alva. It's me. I just wanted to let you know that I am tied up with family stuff for a few days. I might be done by tomorrow. Otherwise, I'll be in Birmingham for a few. I'll call you later."

I wanted to call him back immediately. Even though it was quite late, Hank had called me. I checked the details on the message, but it said that he had called at ten last night. It was now four in the morning. Why was my phone service so flimsy?

I did not care what Hank thought about the late hour. I dialed his number. However, the phone dropped the call and flashed a message about the network being busy. I tried again, but nothing went through. I tried to text him, but the message failed to send each time.

I glanced at the various gas stations that we passed before we reached my apartment. I did not see any payphones at all. What had happened to all the payphones? I had almost given up when I saw one at the last gas station outside of Guntersville. I pulled in and used the phone.

I called Hank's phone but got nothing but some automated message that said the network was down. This time, it was a voice saying that the caller was not receiving calls at this time. I was unable to leave a voicemail or anything. I went inside the gas station and asked to use their phone. The same thing happened again.

I resolved to go home and change clothes before going to his place to see if it was possible that he was there. If nothing else, Helen may be there. My place was on the way anyway, and I desperately needed a shower and something to drink and eat. I resolved to spend a few minutes there before going to Hank's place.

Paul could stay or go, but I was not going to worry about him. I needed to see Hank. I wanted to know what was going on, but more importantly, I wanted to know if he was all right.

When we got to my apartment, Paul silently followed me up to my place. He seemed surprisingly nervous, which was odd. However, I was too tired to give much thought to it.

Paul silently sat in the den while I stripped down and took a shower in the bathroom. When I finished, I came out to the kitchen. To my surprise, Paul had made me a scrambled egg and cheese sandwich with bacon. I sat down and devoured the sandwich. I drank a large glass of chocolate milk that he had mixed up for me.

After I ate, my head began to swim a little. Paul seemed to sense it, and he helped me to my bedroom. He said, "Lie down for a while."

I argued, "I need to check on Hank."

Paul handed me the phone in my apartment and said, "Call him."

When the same crazy message came on the phone, I hung up. I was still unable to get through or to leave a message. I checked my cell phone, but it was totally dead. Paul plugged it in for me.

Paul said, "Just rest until the sun rises."

I agreed and felt Paul brush my hair out of my eyes. That was the last thing I remembered. I was completely gone and deeply asleep.

I felt Paul touching my face again. This time, he bothered me, so I swatted his hand. Instead of dodging my hand, he grabbed my hand and held it tightly. When he refused to let go, I opened my eyes and said, "Stop it, Paul."

However, it was not Paul. It was Aren. I jumped up and pulled the blanket to my chin with my free hand. I asked, "What are you doing here?"

"I'm not here. You're asleep, Alva." Aren refused to let go of my hand. Though he was not hurting me, I wanted it back. However, he held onto it while he spoke to me.

He asked, "Why don't you love me anymore?"

"I don't know. I just don't have feelings for you other than memories that are very foggy. I can only remember a few things in bits and pieces. It's like trying to recall a book I half-paid attention to while reading."

"Why don't you remember me?"

"I don't know."

Aren released my hand. He asked, "Do you remember this?" He kissed me deeply. I felt the universe whirl past me like it was so insignificant.

I pulled away and said, "Stop it."

This time Aren pulled me to him with a passion that felt bordering on violence. It was not the violence of a man who wanted to harm a woman. It was the violence against those that would come between us. It was territorial. It was primal.

Aren's kiss felt so right. It felt like home. I felt lust so strongly for him. Lust was not love, however, and I pulled away again.

I had to keep him from making another move on me because I did not know how much longer I could resist. Though I was asleep, I was not dreaming. This was how Aren had been communicating with me all these years. He could dream-walk.

To distract, I said, "I do remember bits and pieces of our lives together. I thought all these years that I was just a creative dreamer. The last life we had together was in the 1930s in America. I was from the South, but you moved us up to New York City."

Aren's eyes lit up with joy as he said, "Yes, I found you and took you away from the horrible life you had. The South was destitute as it was, but the Great Depression made it worse."

As I spoke, it all came back to me, "Yes, but you didn't realize that we were so poor already that we couldn't really tell that the economy had crashed. I don't think we needed saving."

I did not say what I wanted to say. I wanted to say the fact that Aren took pride in saving me was his arrogance. He had always struggled with being too arrogant. He had thought that he had to save a pauper. This was typical of his mindset. I sighed and said, "I only went with you because I was a widow with two kids who needed a roof over our head."

Without a moment of pain, Aren countered, "Yes, but you grew to love me when you finally remembered who you were...are. Remember who you are."

I closed my eyes and tried to wish Aren away. However, he was still there. I could feel him breathing on me. My mind began to clear. I began to remember the wonderful lives we had together. I remembered a few pieces of the larger puzzle. I remembered the first time we had went to bed in our last life together. My cheeks flushed. I remembered what an amazing lover he was.

Aren must have sensed my thoughts because he pulled me closer and kissed me again. I kept my eyes shut for a few minutes in the hope that it would make it less tempting. However, it seemed to make it worse, and finally I opened my eyes. Aren's appearance had become even more like I had remembered him being on that first day we met and he had been Ares, God of War. I sighed as I gave in to Aren.

Aren kissed me on the lips once more before moving down my shoulders, to my breasts, stomach, and finally my thighs. He gave each thigh a loving kiss before going to my sex. I moaned as he took his time down there. I climaxed quickly but that wasn't enough for him. I had two more before he moved up and kissed my lips. I felt his swell against my pelvis. He kissed me on the neck and breathed, "I love you."

I was breathless and wanted to say it back, but I just let my actions show my feelings. I took him and placed him where he needed to be inside of me. He groaned as I slowly took him inside of my body. We were one. We were connected.

After a few moments of slowly grinding into me, I grabbed his ass and pushed him to indicate that he should pick up the pace. He was all too ready, and I was a little surprised about how deep he went. It felt amazing and I could feel myself beginning the climb to another orgasm. This time it was his pelvis working on the outside of me while his manhood worked on the inside of me. He found the magic button's internal root, and I was bracing myself because I could barely handle the intensity of the pleasure.

I tried to squirm away out of instinct, but he would not let me move an inch. He held me firmly in place with his hands gently on my sides at my ribs. This was the war god showing me his favorite instrument of war, and I was losing my mind in pleasure. Then it happened, I had a full body orgasm. The first one this life. The only one who could do this for me was Aren. It was as if the room grew bright with the stars of the universe around us as I begged him to not stop fucking me. He complied and we went on for hours like this. When he finished inside of me, he held my face and kissed me softly. I could feel dawn was coming. I tried to tell myself that this was only a dream, but I knew what we were doing was real.

the next thing i knew, I woke up to my favorite smell in the world—coffee. I could also smell food cooking, but the coffee was what brought me from my deep slumber.

I stretched underneath the quilt that Paul must have pulled up over me. I fell asleep before I had the chance to cover up. I kicked the quilt off and got out of bed reluctantly. My mind was willing, but my body was resisting. I ached in muscles that I did not know that I had until this moment.

Paul must have heard me groan because he came into my bedroom and asked, "Are you sore from the stress?"

"I think it's the trip more than anything."

Paul disagreed, "No, stress does more harm to the body than any amount of traveling or exercise could ever do. I can sense the pain originates from stress. Let me help you."

Paul reached over and took my hand. Warmth spread from the point of contact in my hand all the way throughout my body. It was like I dipped myself in a warm bath. Immediately, all the pain and fatigue left me. Something flashed in Paul's eyes, a knowing of the source of some of the soreness came from less scrupulous activities. He never said a word, though.

I looked at my hands and the rest of my newly healed body. I cried, "That's amazing, Paul!" I looked up at Paul, who looked pleased at my praise and said to him, "I remember that is one of your gifts. You can heal people."

"Yes, that is one of my many talents. I can also correct things that ail immortals as well. Although we cannot die, we can get other symptoms." I remembered how Paul had touched Aren's forehead and it corrected the interfering signals. That made me ask, "So you did this for Aren when we were lost?"

"Yes, but he was not ill. It was one of the immortals that did that to him. I'm not sure which one it is, but I would guess it is Zeke who can block the gifts. That is a dangerous power indeed. If he could stop Aren from finding his way, he could stop me from healing you if you got hurt. For that reason, we need to hide."

"They'll just find me again, Paul." I thought of the implications of what Paul had just said. He needed to keep me from dying. I could sense that was what he felt with such urgency, though he hid it well.

"Alva, they know where you live now, but they cannot find you. If it were so easy, Aren would have been around you much sooner. We cannot sense that strongly, even to the ones to whom we mated."

"So where do we go, Paul?"

"We need to go to a place where you can learn to fight Helen. She's coming for you. She may send others to do some of her dirty work, but ultimately, she wants to confront you directly. I know her style."

"But why now, after so many years?"

Paul sat on the bed beside me and said somberly, "Because she never confronted you since you took Aren away from her."

"I thought she was over Aren."

"She is. I can feel her emotions. She is over Aren. However, there is something else there. There is another reason why she is angry with you—not Aren, but you. There is more there. I cannot get a good read on it without touching her, and she'd never let me do that. When an immortal is secretive about something, I must touch them to get an accurate reading. And believe me, Helen's keeping this hidden for good reasons."

"Is it really my fault that the Greek gods fell?"

"No, and that is not what she's mad about. She blamed Aren for that for a while. However, she is over it for the most part. She's too focused on this Hank fellow. I really don't know why she's going through all this trouble over a broken heart."

"That must be it, Paul. She's mad because I was dating Hank."

"No, Alva, that's not it. I can sense it is something more established than that. She just learned of you knowing Hank in this life. Yet before she knew anything about your current life, she had these feelings in her heart. I felt them when she laid eyes upon you."

I sighed and Paul said, "Come eat something already. I made you some pancakes."

We went into the kitchen together and had a meal. The coffee was nice, but it did not give me enough energy. Paul reached out and caressed my face. I felt the warmth come from his hands once more and I was no longer tired. I felt relaxed instead of energized, however. I think Paul wanted it that way.

After I ate, I noticed that the heater was on a high setting. I was surprised, as it was not that cold yet. I usually kept the air on until it was cold, which never happened until around Christmas. I could smell the dust burning in the vents, as it was the first time it was on all season it was abused this much.

"Why is the heat on?" I asked.

"Because it was so cold that you were shivering under your quilt. So, I turned it on for you. The temperature had gotten low in here. According to the thermostat, it was fifty degrees in here. I remember that human bodies don't like the cold."

"That's strange," I said as I stood up and walked to the closest window. I looked outside and saw something that was completely unexpected. The entire landscape was completely covered in a thin sheet of ice. Icicles half the length of my two-story apartment building hung suspended above the street below.

"What in the world?" I asked as Paul rushed to my side to see what surprised me.

"Is this seasonably normal?" Paul asked.

"No, this is not normal at all. In fact, this is never normal for any time of year here in the Tennessee Valley." I reached out and touched the windowpane that the frost had almost made opaque. If it were not for the heating system, my windows would not have thawed out at all for any visibility.

Paul said, "Well, I guess it has begun. Helen called in another one. It seems that Don's in town. Of course, you probably know him by his other name."

"Poseidon," I said. I remembered him. He had manipulated the lake into the unseasonable frost. He had power over water. It was such a strong power that he could still cause storms and hurricanes at sea. What most people did not know about him was that he could work with any form of water. He could do anything to it that was inside of natural law, including freezing it. Poseidon had manipulated the lake into a rain and then froze it.

I reached over and turned on the television. The weatherman was discussing the frost that had covered our town. Poseidon was smart enough to hit up all the local areas with the lake nearby. It was cold enough to keep the ice from thawing. The weatherman expected a possibility of more ice storms.

Paul said, "Good move, Helen, but you're not the only one with a friend of the water." He grabbed my phone and dialed a number. He said, "Cletus, Don has frozen us in Guntersville. Can you clear us a path to Abby's place? We're across the street from the courthouse in an apartment. Great, see you in a few. Yeah, I figured you were nearby. That explains why there was no ice there. Yeah, I saw it on the weather report. Okay, thanks and see you then."

After he hung up my phone, I grabbed it and called Hank. I was still unable to get through to him. I was still defeated, so I gave up and turned my attention to the ice storm. I looked at Paul and asked, "What was that about?"

Paul said, "Oceanus is now Cletus Blue. He lives in Grant, actually. He is on his way to clear a path."

I searched my mind for a moment but did not remember him. Paul took my blank face as an indication to elaborate. "He is one of the titans. He is the ocean titan. He can manipulate water just as much as Poseidon can, so he's going to melt us a way to get to Aphrodite's—Abby's house."

"Why are we going to Abby's house?" I faintly remembered her. She had used Abby Smith in my last life. "What is her current name?" I asked Paul.

"Abby Stephens," Paul replied. "We're going to see her because she can teach you how to fight Helen."

"The ex-goddess of love is going to teach me about fighting. Are you crazy? I cannot take an immortal on with my bare hands. No amount of training will help me overpower her."

Paul corrected, "No, you cannot fight her with your hands. You're going to fight her with your mouth. You must learn how to psyche her out. Since she's hopelessly in love, you're going to have to hit her where it hurts. That is where Abby comes into play. She will teach you all about females. Immortal or not, Helen is still female. So are you, so you can beat her."

"Oh," I said. "When does Cletus get here and how will we know it when he does?"

CHAPTER 13

It was not too long when I heard a loud honk that sounded like the horn of a transfer truck. I looked out the window and saw that it was one, without the cargo bed attached. "I think he's here," I said.

Paul wasted no time while we waited for Cletus to arrive. He had made me pack a week's worth of stuff in a small duffel bag that I usually used for the gym. He told me that we had to be as inconspicuous as possible. He also told me we may be gone longer than a week, but I could always wash my clothes at Abby's place.

When we got to Cletus' truck, I climbed in the center between Paul and Cletus. It was cold outside, and I was glad that Cletus had the heat running. I assumed it was for my benefit. He drove here, but there was no cleared pathway on the dead, frozen street. In fact, we were in the only vehicle I saw as we made our way down the street.

"Why isn't the water melted for the path you cleared?" I asked Cletus after a brief introduction.

"I must hide my powers, dear. I froze it back after I passed through." Cletus spoke very articulately. He was not quite what I had expected from a being named Cletus, but that was the point. He wanted to hide, and he was doing a good job.

"How come no one is out here salting the roads?" I asked Paul.

"The ice has shut everything down. Don was thorough. He froze the water in the cars as well. Antifreeze won't save them when he's involved."

"So, everyone in the frozen area is basically stuck at home?" I asked.

"Appears so," Cletus said as he drove us south on the highway.

As we got near the road to take to get to Hank's house, I begged Paul and Cletus to let me check on him. Paul did not want to do it, but Cletus had mercy on me. He followed my directions until we made it to Hank's home.

The minute we took the solitary road that led to Hank's place, I knew something was wrong. There was no ice or frost anywhere.

When we got to Hank's house, I saw that all the lights were illuminated inside the small residence. However, Hank's vehicle was not there. I got out of the truck and went to the front door. I knocked but no answer. I looked through the windows and saw a seemingly empty house.

I decided to walk around to the back to see if anyone was there. Hank had a chain on the front door, so my key was useless. I had to go to the back to get inside, which was what I intended to do.

Paul rushed in front of me before I could step off the front porch. He said, "At least let me go with you in case Helen's here." I nodded and we walked together around the small pathway of flagstone that led to the back porch.

Since it was the right temperature at Hank's, it made sense when Paul found a small snake lying on one of the stones. He grabbed it and slung it out of the way. He said, "Probably trying to use the rock to stay warm. It's lucky it didn't get in Don's way, or it would be a poison Popsicle."

"That's not a poisonous kind of snake," I said to Paul. Paul shrugged and said, "Well, they used to all be poisonous before evolution made them boring. They also used to be wider in body and flatter like little turtles without the shell or legs."

"Thanks for the science lesson, but let's go," I said impatiently.

Paul followed me. We made it to the back porch without further incident. I knocked for good measure, peered in the window, and then unlocked the door. As I had figured, no one was there. However, someone had been there, as the entire bed in Hank's bedroom was covered in figs.

I knew it was Helen. She had been in here. Hank must still be gone, as she left the figs on his bed as some kind of message. Helen knew he would understand it. She also knew that I would be there as well, for she left me a note on the floor of the hallway. Paul said it was probably some kind of insult and to leave it where it was—in the entryway of the door of the hall leading to the kitchen. I read it anyway.

"Soon." That was the only word written. I knew it was for me because my name was on the envelope that held a card with a peacock emblem on the front of the card.

I handed the envelope to Paul, who read it. He said, "No one is here. Let's go before someone shows up and makes it difficult."

I followed him outside. I took the card with me so that Hank would not know I was involved. He may remember Helen, but he did not know me for what I really was. I preferred anonymity with Hank. I hoped that he did not know even though it was inevitable that he would find out.

I locked the door and left Hank's place. As we drove to Abby's, I took a nap. I did not want to know what was next. Even though humans made up the stories of mythology, the Greek gods were proving to be as dramatic and catty as the myths depicted them to be. The nap was a welcome escape as we drove to Atlanta to see Abby Stephens, former goddess of love, and my soon-to-be trainer.

After my nap, I woke up to find that we were in a small town outside of Atlanta. We were at some country club. I waited in the car while Paul went to summon Abby. Abby was working on her game of golf when we disturbed her. She was not pleased, but she allowed us to go to her house, which was nearby, as the golf course was her backyard.

Cletus dropped us off and left after a silent nod goodbye. Paul and I went inside of Abby's house. A severely handsome young man let us inside. He was the butler. There were many more men, all young and all handsome, inside the luscious mansion. Some had formal titles, such as cook or gardener. Others seemed to be there for other unnamed jobs, which all the men probably shared.

The cook made us lunch because Abby called and told him to do so. The butler showed us to our room, which had only one large bed. When

I demanded my own room, the butler told us that Abby instructed that we share. He said that with a wink, which made me wonder what else Abby had said about us.

After we had eaten and settled into our room, we had time to talk. However, I did not feel like talking. Paul seemed to have something that he wanted to say or do in my presence, but he never did anything other than sit quietly on a chair. He stared outside and watched someone play golf.

A few hours passed us by when Paul said, "I see her coming." I panicked momentarily because I thought he meant Helen. When I looked outside and saw a pink golf cart with purple hearts on it coming our way, I knew he meant Abby.

Another two hours passed before we were finally summoned to speak with Abby. She had showered and changed clothes. She was wearing a pink dress with a matching pink bow. I liked her commitment to color coordinating. Her lips and fingernails also matched, along with a chunky necklace and earring set made of pink plastic. She was quite striking, however. In fact, she was the most beautiful female I had ever laid eyes upon. Though immortal, she appeared to be nineteen. I suspected that if she removed the makeup, she would look more like the fifteen-year-old looking girl I had met long ago, though I could not remember much more than her face.

Abby's long black hair curled into thick ringlets that went down to her waist. She flipped it a few times and batted her eyelashes at her male servants as they waited on us. The butler was missing, which made me think he was recovering from other duties. That might be the reason why we had to wait for her for an additional hour or so after she had time to shower.

The cook brought in several plates of sweets: cupcakes, pies, candies, and chocolates. Abby's eyes grew round, and she took a large chocolate truffle from a plate and waved him away. The cook offered us some, but we refused.

Abby pouted after she took a nibble of her candy. She asked, "What's the matter, Paul? Don't you love the bounty of life?"

Paul said, "Of course, but I lose my taste for food sometimes. It grows boring."

Abby said, "Well, you should try my chef's food. He is the best in the world. He would change your mind." She winked at her chef, who grinned enough to show his cute dimples.

Paul replied dryly, "Oh, Abby, every chef you bless is the best in the world. That's your gift to them. How else would there be a high ratio of culinary skill to muscles and pretty faces in your employ?"

Abby giggled as if she had been caught doing something she wanted to get caught doing. She laughed, "Oh, Paul," as she ate another chocolate.

Paul got to the point, "Abby, we're here because..."

Abby interrupted, "Oh, honey, I know all about it. Gossip is my thing, after all."

I thought of how appropriate that one of her gifts was gossip. I held back a giggle.

Paul continued, "Well, you should know why we're here then. We need your help preparing Alva to stand against Helen if she should catch her alone."

Abby stretched and shooed out all the servants. She looked at Paul and said, "You too, Paul. This is for girls only. I will tell her what she needs to know."

Paul reluctantly left. Once the doors were closed and we were completely alone, Abby said, "You must realize that female is more powerful than male. We set forth the universe. However, we're not talking man versus woman. We are talking two women, which is an equal fight. The only thing that will save you from falling into your early death this life and at Helen's hands, no less, will be to realize you are the alpha female."

Abby stared down at her perfectly manicured pink nails as if they hid claws and continued, "If men are dogs, women are wolves. You must realize that not only did you take Aren from her, but you also took Hank.

She's wounded, so you must pounce. Never back down and always remember you are stronger. You are a mere mortal, yet you beat a goddess at stealing what should be hers—everything."

Abby sat back in her chair to indicate that she was done. I was completely confused. I said, "That doesn't make sense. You are telling me philosophical points that do not make sense in the situation."

Abby replied, "It is all a game of the mind with us. We cannot physically kill you."

"But you just said she could cause me to die young again."
"Yes, she can start a chain reaction to bring your early death. I doubt it's difficult since you have died young every life you ever led."

A thought occurred to me about Abby. She knew everything that had happened. I could ask her about my lives. I felt that her advice with Helen was a waste of my time, so I would get information from her while she felt like sharing. I asked, "Why is it that I die early each life?"

Abby smiled and said, "Well, the same person keeps causing it, time and time again."

"Who?" I asked anxiously.

Before Abby could answer, there was an explosion that knocked me across the room and on my back. Abby was not affected as much, and she ran off to another room. I could not move well because I felt a little numb. It had felt like a rush of air had pushed me back. The same air was holding me down.

When I felt the floor vibrating under me, I realized that it was probably Zeke. It was confirmed when I heard Zeke's distinct scream. He was screaming for Paul, who was now standing over me. Paul scooped me up in his arms and carried me out of the house, which was shaking. When we made it outside to leave, Zeke caught up with us.

Zeke screamed, "Paul, you will not take her. My Love commands that she stays where she is."

Abby stepped out behind Zeke and said, "I am mistress of this house and land. She will not command anything in my stead."

Zeke turned around and said, "I apologize, but she requests that you keep them here. You will be rewarded for your favor."

Abby cocked one eyebrow and said, "I know all about it, dear one. I know that Helen was angry with you for letting them go. I also know that your blind rage and jealousy for Aren distracted you from completing her orders. But why does she order you? If you are to be her king, then she should be attending you, and not the other way around."

Abby had hit the right nerve with Zeke, as he said, "Yes, you're right." Abby walked over to Zeke and wrapped her arms around him. She petted his face and said, "There, there, now. Why don't you come in and eat?"

Zeke paused for a moment to look back to us. When Abby reached up and kissed his ear lightly, he turned back to her with a wild look in his eye. He picked her up and toted her into the house. Abby waved us away before Zeke shut the door behind them. Abby still had it.

From above us, a male voice called, "Heads up!" I looked up to see that one of the male servants had opened the window and was throwing our bags down. Paul caught them effortlessly. The servant said, "Take the black SUV." He threw down a set of keys to Paul before shutting the window abruptly. Paul smiled and said, "Let's go."

Paul did not have to tell me twice, as I wanted to leave. I did not know if Zeke had given up on Helen, or if he would snap out of it and come looking for us. It was unfortunate that I could not get the information that I wanted from Abby, but I felt that I would come to know what I needed to know when I needed to know it.

We drove for about an hour toward Alabama when my phone rang. It was Aren. I was surprised to hear his voice, but there was some relief in me as well.

Aren asked, "Where are you?"

"We're on our way to Alabama from Abby's house."

"Did you see Zeke?"

"Yes."

"And?"

"He confronted us and tried to keep us from leaving, but Abby seduced him. We left."

"Good. Are you coming to Guntersville?"

"Yes."

"Don't do that. It's not safe for you here. I've checked your apartment, and it seems untouched, but you can never be sure."

My blood began to boil as I demanded, "You did what? Did you just say that you broke into my apartment without my permission?"

"Yes, I did. I don't need your permission to protect you."
"You need my permission to get into my house. That's illegal."

"Human laws change. They are as stable as the weather. I am not bound to them."

Aren's audacity was making me ill. I was constantly reminded of his arrogant streak. I said, "I am human, so respect me."

"You are not human."

"Oh, really? Then what am I, Mr. Know-it-all?"

"You are mine." Aren said this flatly in the same way mortals said the sky was blue. My anger peaked, and I hung up the phone. I mumbled under my breath, "Who says divinity is perfection?"

Paul bit his lip to hide his smile. His phone rang as he said, "On cue," and flipped it open. "Hello, Aren. Yes, I understand. Uh-huh." Paul looked at me with a guilty look and said, "You don't say? Well, these things happen." He returned his gaze to the road and said, "I'll work on it. Alright then, thanks."

Paul hung up his phone and said, "Aren wants me to keep you away. But unlike him, I revel in the mystery that is free will. So, we will do what you want to do." Before I could open my mouth to tell him to drive me home, he said, "But I will protect you from everything—including yourself."

I knew he meant that he would not drive me into trouble willingly. This must have something to do with what Aren had told him. It was probably something that Aren might have told me, but I had hung up on him. I flipped my phone over in my hand to see if I still had reception. I did, and yet he had not called me back.

I felt conflicted, but I ignored that feeling and said, "Drive me home, Paul."

Paul said, "Okay, I will drive you there if that is really what you want to do."

I did not take the bait, as Paul wanted to hash around why I wanted it, and I felt that was a sure way for him to attempt to talk me out of it. I looked at him and said, "You must not remember how stubborn I am."

Paul laughed and said, "I remember that plus much more." There was sadness in his face. He said, "Alva, I do not want to see you die again. I don't think I can bear it."

"Paul, it is inevitable that I will die. I must die. I am in a mortal body."

Paul squeezed the steering wheel tightly and said, "I mean you, not your body. The last death made you lose something. You don't remember anything. You don't remember...us."

"Sorry, Paul, I don't remember much of any of you crazy Greek gods."

Before I could utter another word, Paul violently jerked the car off the road and pulled the parking brake. I tried to ask him what he was doing, but he grabbed me and kissed me. Unlike Aren's kiss, his was not violent. It was gentle and reassuring.

Paul said, "Not us gods, but us—you and me. Don't you remember that you were supposed to be mine?"

In all the craziness that had happened to me lately, I just wanted to let go of reality. His kiss felt like a good way to achieve my escape. I grabbed him and kissed him back. We kissed again, until finally it seemed the next move in the lovers' game was inevitable.

Paul looked around and said, "I think there's a road near here where a guy charges a hundred dollars to let you park. It's a good way for us to do this off the radar. The guy keeps cops and strangers away. We'd have some privacy. Then I'll need to get some food in you if you can walk when I'm done with you."

I smiled and said, "You heal, right?"

Paul grinned and said, "I know, but it sounds raunchier to say it like that." He pulled me closer to him and held me. He inhaled deeply as if trying to take my essence into himself. He said, "Oh, how I have missed your touch, my love! It's been ages since you let me hold you."

His declaration of love hit me the wrong way just as Aren's had. Unlike with Aren, I felt a need to not wound Paul. I pulled away and said, "You know, Paul, I think dinner sounds good. I don't feel so great. All that stress released in my body, and now I am finally feeling hungry. Can we just wait until I can figure some things out before we continue with what we started?"

Paul felt the rejection and went cold on me. He said, "Fine, let's get you a burger." We went to a place where you ordered at a window and sat on picnic tables to eat. The food was amazing, and I devoured everything that Paul had bought me.

After we finished, we returned to the road. It would not be long until we were back in Guntersville, and I wanted a captive audience with Paul so that I could get some answers.

I began, "Paul, Abby was about to tell me who caused me to die early before Zeke came in and attacked. Do you have any idea what name she was going to say?"

Paul had a blank look on his face. He demanded, "What exactly did she say?"

"She said that the same person caused me to die early each life."

"But she didn't say who it was?" Paul asked.

"No, she was about to say who it was when Zeke arrived." I took my hair and twisted it in my fingers.

Paul grabbed his phone and said, "I did not realize someone caused your death. I thought it was fate. I read it so." He trailed off as if he wanted to keep a secret. He cleared his throat and said, "I never thought to ask her about you. Let me call her now."

He grabbed his phone and tried to call her. There was no answer. He must have tried thirty times before he gave up and slung the phone across the seat. He slicked his hair back behind his ear in a nervous tick. He said, "I will check with her later. Maybe it was hidden from me because I have yet to touch the one who does this."

"Or maybe," I interrupted, "you can't see who it is because it's another god."

When I said that, I thought I saw fire flash in Paul's eyes. He said, "That is a possibility that I have yet to consider."

I added, "Of course, you didn't know until now. How could you?"

"I should have known," he said.

I could tell that he was about to shut down on me, so I changed the subject slightly. I said, "Well, Paul, if you don't want to talk about my death, let's talk about my life. I assume it counts as one since my soul is eternal."

"I suppose," Paul mumbled. "What do you want to know?"

"I honestly don't remember much. I just remember things only in fragments. It's mostly feelings and things like personality traits of you guys. I also remember patterns of behavior, but that's about it." I began to tear up as I said, "I mean, I do remember my last life more than I care to remember. I remember that I had kids."

Paul sighed. His guard went down and he said, "I remember them as well. Delilah and Gustavo were so amazing."

Just hearing their names seized something painful in me. I felt a fist in my stomach. I had to gasp for air. I said, "Paul, are they still alive?"

Paul's face showed his guilt. He said, "You made me promise to keep you away from them. You said it would only hurt them worse if they knew the truth."

Fear gripped me and the first became a chill that went from my stomach to my extremities. I yelled, "Paul, tell me."

Paul knew the threat was valid. He did not even fight me. He said, "Gus still lives. Delilah died shortly after you died in a horrible accident. She was never a strong swimmer." He did not have to finish. I instinctively knew the rest. I waited for him to continue, which he did, "Gus had one child, a girl, but she was never healthy. She died before you were ever born again. Her name was Delilah, just like his sister. Gus's wife is gone. He's all that is left."

"Paul, where is he?"

"He's being taken care of by the best nurses."

"Paul, tell me now."

"He's at one of Aren's estates. Where Aren lived full-time until shortly after you were born."

"Where is it?" My blood was boiling again because it was something else that Aren had hidden from me.

"It's in Florida near the Alabama border."

"Drive me there now," I demanded.

Paul sighed and said, "Okay." He did not bother to reset the GPS. He instinctively knew where it was. I sat back with tears in my eyes as I realized that we were heading for where Paul was living now. Paul had been watching over my child.

CHAPTER 14

Paul drove me down to Perdido Key, Florida. The drive was about five hours. I was too antsy to be sleepy, at first. After a while, I began to feel hypnotized by the sound of the vehicle driving over the bumps of the interstate. I began to zone out. There, I entered a place between awake and asleep.

I could hear myself speaking a narrative to someone. I realized that someone must be me. It was a part of me that was telling my true story. Though my story was quite long, I only remembered hearing the part about my last life.

The First World War came and went. When it was over, you were a child widow. You were eighteen with two small children. Gus was still in your belly when the war ended. Your husband had visited you briefly before returning to war. He died in that war, and you were alone. You had married him when you were fifteen. His name was Nathaniel. You had Delilah when you were sixteen. You married him because you wanted out of your aunt and uncle's house. You were an orphan and an only child. He was twenty-one and you were fifteen. You met him when he tried to sell soap to your aunt. Her name was Maria.

Nathaniel was not a cruel man. His only betrayal was dying and leaving you alone. He was also an orphan, so you had no one to go to for money when he died. You lived off the money that was paid for his death from the government and rented a room in your aunt's house. She charged you for everything, even water from the creek. You began to hate Nathaniel for leaving you alone. You hated him for binding you to the world. You had begun to remember who you were by that time, but it was too late. You had already made ties that were difficult to sever.

When Aren came for you, you went with him reluctantly. He took you away from poverty. He raised your kids as his own. They never knew that he was not like them. They never knew that you were not like them. You had finally fallen in love with Aren when a chill came to your bones. You never could warm up again. One day, everything went black.

I screamed, "No!" My scream echoed so loudly that I could now hear myself screaming as if I was outside of my own body listening to my screams. I felt someone shaking me. It was Paul, and he said, "Alva, wake up. It's just a bad dream."

It took me a minute to process what he was saying. I was still asleep. He said, "Are you okay?"

I rubbed my face and said, "Yes, I'm fine." I did not realize that I had fallen asleep, but the slobber running down my chin let me know. I saw a smudge spot on the window where I had rested my face. I rubbed it with my sleeve and then rubbed my sore cheek.

I looked in the mirror to see that my cheek was bright red. Paul said, "Don't worry. It will go away."

We were only a few miles away from our destination, according to Paul. He said, "Are you sure that you want to do this, Alva?"

When I silently nodded, we continued the drive in mutual silence. Within minutes, we pulled up to a beautiful mansion that had a gate with a speaker and keypad. Paul pushed in a code on the keypad, and the gate opened automatically.

After we parked in the garage that opened automatically for Paul, Paul looked at me and said, "Before we go in, you must know that Aren kept everything from the last life you had together for Gus' comfort. So don't be shocked if you get overwhelmed or choked up."

"Okay," I said. The fist in my stomach had returned.

An attendant came out and escorted us into the house. He offered us food and drink, but we turned him down. At first, nothing was familiar, but once we made it past the foyer, I gasped at what I saw. It was a replica of our New York apartment contained within this mansion.

Tears welled up in my eyes as I whispered, "I thought this place wasn't real. I dreamed about it my whole life."

Then I saw it. I saw what Paul must have not wanted me to see. I saw the face that I used to have when I was Clara Greg, mother of two, wife of Aren Steele. I crumbled to the floor. Paul did not catch me but instead let me fall. He wrapped around me and held me. He began to rock me and said, "Let it out," as I cried bitterly.

On the adjacent wall was a picture of my family of four, including Aren. Aren's face appeared to be the perfected face of the former god that he was. I was confused and asked, "Why does Aren photograph like the way he really looks?"

Paul answered, "He doesn't, but you will always see him for what he truly is once you realize he is a god. Two years ago, you would have seen the face others saw when he lived that life. It's not even the same face you saw when you first met him weeks ago."

I smiled as I looked at the children. I remembered their faces without having to look. Gus looked just like me, while Delilah had looked like her father. It had never bothered Aren that I had kids. He seemed thrilled since we could not have any of our own. Once the gods had lost their divinity, they lost their ability to procreate. Aren had a few children when he was Ares, but we never spoke of them.

I heard a voice calling me from the other room. A voice so soft that it had to be that of a child, but it had the timbre of an old man. It was Gus. He called, "Momma, is that you?"

Tears streaked down my face as I approached the room from where it came. I knew he was in there, my child, and I was afraid to see him. I walked into a room to see a man sitting in a chair. He was wearing silk pajamas and was covered in a blanket. There was a male attendant with him sitting in the other chair. The attendant nodded at Paul and left the room.

Gus was staring out of the window. When he heard us come in, he turned around and said, "Momma?" but when he saw me, he turned away. He said, "Oh, Paul, I thought you and your lady friend was Momma."

Paul smiled and said, "I brought someone else to see you. Do you want to meet her?"

Gus said, "Sure, but I'm waiting for Momma. You can't stay too long because you know she doesn't like it when Daddy catches you alone with her."

My face burned bright red. Paul and I indeed had a past, but I would deal with him later. I sat in the chair beside Gus and said, "Hello, Gus, I am a friend of your Momma's."

Gus began to smile, but something changed as he said, "No, Momma is dead. Why are you talking about my dead mother?"

Paul reached out and touched his forehead and said, "There, Gus, you should feel better."

Gus' eyes became clearer as if he had awoken up from a dream. He said, "Paul, you're older than me. You should be dead." I could only imagine what old man Gus saw when he stared at Paul, even though I could see past the glamour that concealed Paul's true nature.

Gus looked at me and said, "Hello, young lady, nice to meet you. Are you Paul's granddaughter?"

Paul laughed and said, "No, she's, my great-granddaughter."

Gus smiled and asked, "Could you tell Lane that I am ready for bed?"

The attendant returned, presumably named Lane, and put Gus to rest. It was eight in the evening when I stood over my little boys' bed for the last time. I looked at Paul and asked, "Why isn't the healing working?"

"It only fills in the holes that are there in the brain tissue. It does not prevent new ones from forming. It's very rapid and mystical, it seems. He keeps falling away quicker each time."

"Paul, he's quite old to be alive still. You must quit healing him and let nature takes its course. This is cruel."

Paul had tears in his eyes as he said, "I can't ignore my gift. It's the one good thing I can still do for people."

"Paul, this is different. Nature is what it is. You are not helping his suffering. You are increasing it. That is why it is no longer working like it should. You are not meant to bend the laws of nature—not anymore. You are no longer a god. You are just immortal."

Gus' breathing began to change. Nature was intuitive, as it knew the moment when Paul had finally given up on healing Gus. Gus exhaled loudly, and we both knew it was over. I was not sad, but relieved. I knew that one day, I would see him again, even if it took a million years. That gave me comfort.

As we left the mansion, Lane informed us that Aren was called about Gus' passing. I knew that he would be as relieved as I was. I wondered if he knew that Paul had been sneaking over here all these years and healing him. I doubted that he knew because I was sure that Aren would not have allowed it for Gus' sake. Although Paul meant well, it was wrong. However, I was not angry with Aren or Paul. I was just happy to have been a mother. In all my years, this was the only time I had ever had children come from my own body. I knew it would be my one and only time, yet I had peace.

I expected to be sadder than I was. However, I was beginning to feel like my old self—a person who understood eternal time. That person lived for thousands of years and came to know loss. That person could appreciate humans without falling apart when they left. That person understood the cycle of life and had peace with it.

Paul's house was nearby, so he took me there. I was too tired to do anything but shower, eat, and sleep. I knew that Paul did not require sleep but could mimic it. After I showered, Paul fed me, and I crawled into his bed. He wrapped his arms around me, and I felt at home.

i woke up two days later. Paul was still holding me. I was not sore or hung over feeling, which was from Paul's continual healing touch. I felt a small kiss on the back of my ear as he said, "Morning."

"What a night," I groaned as I sat up and stretched.

"Nights," Paul said.

"What do you mean?" I asked.

"You slept for two days."

"Really?"

"Yes."

"You let me?"

"Yes, you needed it."

"I won't fight you on this, but it kind of makes me mad."

"Why?" Paul asked with a look of amusement on his face.

"Because it's wasted time."

Paul began to laugh as he said, "Oh, I think you got nothing but time, my girl."

"Not in this life, Paul."

"Well, then in the next one we'll make it up." Paul rolled over and jumped out of bed. He asked, "You want to shower first or should I, lazy bones?"

"Very funny, Paul. I know you used your healing mumbo jumbo on me to make me sleep so long."

Paul said, "Well, it is a method of healing—sleep."

"I knew it!" I screamed as I pushed past him and jumped in the shower.

When I got out, Paul had made us some breakfast. He was a great cook. After we ate, he jumped in the shower. I took a cup of coffee outside to watch the ocean. Paul had managed to get a house that was on the beach. I sat on the balcony and watched the clouds float past the sun. It was a beautiful November day. Thanksgiving would be soon.

My sunbathing did not last long, as my phone rang from inside my pocket. I knew I should not have brought it outside with me. It was Craig, and he sounded emotional for once in his life.

"Alva, you finally answered your phone! I have been trying to call you for days. I called Larry and Ernest, but they told me you had called in for a week for a personal family emergency. I acted like I knew what they meant, but is something wrong that I don't know about?"

I clenched because I had forgotten to get in touch with Craig. I had called in that excuse without telling him. In between running from Helen and dodging her shady cronies, I had forgotten to call him. It was not as if we talked often, so it slipped my mind. Surprisingly, I was not too worried what my job consequences would be, which was a new feeling of freedom for me. I did not know what to tell Craig, so I lied.

"Craig, I just was about to have a nervous breakdown from all of the stress of work lately, so I just bailed down to Gulf Shores for a mental health holiday."

Craig answered slowly, "Oh, okay. Well, I just wanted to know what was up with you. Hank has been all over town looking for you. He's gotten people to start worrying. If you two had been more serious, I think he would have been able to get the cops looking for you."

I did not understand what the big deal was about. I asked, "What does it matter to Hank? I've been trying to call him for days." I had been worried about Hank, but when Zeke showed up at Abby's house, I assumed it was because Helen had found him and needed me out of the way. Hank had never called me or checked on me. I felt that meant he was with Helen.

Craig interrupted my fuming thoughts, "Alva, Hank had been calling you and calling you. He can't get through ever. He said he left you tons of messages, emails, and text messages, but you never got back to him. He was only gone a few days to take care of some family stuff in Birmingham. During that time, you disappeared. It scared him."

A little light went off in my mind as I asked, "Is he there with you?"

"Yes, that's right." Craig was being smooth so that I could ask questions without Hank knowing that I was speaking about him.

"Were you with him when he called and texted me?"

"Several of them, yes."

"Well, I don't know what happened. My phone has been working fine."

"I did the same too, but nothing," Craig said.

"So, you called me as well."

"Yes, several times."

"Alright, I'm sorry. I guess I need a better provider. I'll fix it when I get home."

"When will that be?" Craig sounded anxious.

"Soon, I guess." I did not want to come home. I did not want to work. Just knowing that Hank was okay had made me want to avoid the subject all together. However, I needed to warn him. I was afraid that if I tried, Helen would come around. I did not want to face her. She would not harm him, so he could deal with her. I was the one in danger. There was also a killer somewhere on the loose, though that had been far from my mind. I felt guilty because I did not want to let Cliff Marcel down.

"Is there something you're not telling me, Craig?" I asked suddenly.

"Well, I have court tomorrow, and I wanted you to be there," Craig said.

"You have court? Who's your lawyer?" I asked.

"I was hoping it was you," Craig said.

"Craig, you can't just show up for court. I must put a notice of appearance in and there's the discovery and all that." I began to panic as I thought of the possibility of Craig going alone to court.

"You know, I can just show up there and explain my side of the story." Craig had unrealistic expectations in justice, it seemed.

"No way, Craig. I will call up there and decide. I'll call you back." I hung up the phone and immediately dialed the clerk's office. There was no answer, so I freaked out. I tried about ten minutes later, and the line was now busy. I finally jumped up and went inside to find Paul, who was out of the shower and finishing getting dressed.

Paul pointed me in the direction of the computer. I used it to draw up and email a notice to the court. I also sent a discovery package. Craig had a copy of the police report, so I would get one from him. I did not have time to subpoena one from the police department. I finally got through to the clerk's office to confirm that they received the documents. When I requested a continuance, they asked me to try to make it because the victim and a witness had been subpoenaed and had already decided to take off work.

I knew that I had a right to a continuance, but I decided to not push it because I wanted things to go well for my brother. I could always get the prosecutor to agree to a continuance at court tomorrow. In a small town, it pays to be patient as a criminal attorney. I agreed to be there tomorrow with Craig.

I called Craig and told him to email me a copy of the police report. I waited for the email to come in and once it did, I read it thoroughly. Paul gave me privacy and when it was time for lunch, he made us some grilled cheese sandwiches.

As we ate, I broke the news to him, "Paul, we must go back to Guntersville. My brother needs me."

"Really, what happened?" Paul asked as he bit down on a crunchy pickle.

"He was attacked, but the attacker had my brother arrested instead." I was still mad about the injustice of it all.

"Wow, that is strange. Was the man wealthier than him?" Paul asked.

"No, I think it's quite the opposite, but the police believe the man because he had his woman with him. She lied and backed his story. Craig had no chance."

"Justice never prevails. No matter what century," Paul said in a nonchalant fashion as he chugged his grape soda.

"That's true, but I am fighting to change that. When can we leave?"

"Anytime you wish."

"How about now?"

CHAPTER 15

When I got to Guntersville almost eight hours later, I went to bed. Court would not be until the afternoon, which was a blessing in this case. I would also have to tell Ernest and Larry that I was back in case they saw me. Ernest rarely did city court, but it could happen. I did not want to seem like a liar to my possible future boss. I decided to stop by Ernest's office before court. I would call Larry as soon as I woke up that morning.

The next morning went quickly, and when it was almost time to go to court with Craig, I looked at my phone before I put it on silent. I felt strange that Aren had not yet contacted me. Paul told me that it was Gus' wish to be cremated. Paul went back down to see that the ashes were put in the ocean, as Gus had wanted. Aren would be there. I decided not to go because I did not want to stir up any dormant emotions. My peace was unreasonable, but it was there. I was fine with it because it felt like the loss was never mine. It was Clara's life, and I was now Alva. I did not hesitate in that feeling.

There were only ten minutes before court began, and Craig went outside to smoke. I had never seen him smoke, but I did not know much about my brother. He had spent many years away from here, living with our father. When he was around, he never spoke about nor showed any of his emotions. If he were not my brother, I would have believed the false testimony found on the arrest report from the alleged victim.

I always got nervous before court, but this time it hit me hard. I also felt angry that I had to defend my own innocent brother. It should never have come this far. I went to find the prosecutor and see why he had decided to pursue the charges in the first place.

The prosecutor was a round woman with black, curly hair. She was very fair advocate, so I thought that it would be all right. I approached her and asked, "Do you got a minute for me?"

She smiled and said, "Sure, what do you got for me today?"

I said, "I have this." I handed her the case summary the clerk had given me.

After she read it, she said, "Oh, and this is your brother, right?" I tried to conceal my cocked eyebrow reaction. She knew something I never said. Craig was not well known, but it had gotten out that we were related. People had been gossiping about this case.

I replied, "Yes."

The prosecutor said, "Well, I'm going to have to recuse myself."

If she did that, the case would drag on and on. I wanted a dismissal or a not guilty verdict. It would take months to get a special judge and prosecutor coordinated together. If the prosecutor bailed, the judge would also. The pain of a small town is that there cannot be any appearance of favoritism. When it happened, it was always without the appearance and very hush-hush.

I politely demanded, "On what grounds?"

She knew that she could not say, "Because you're a lawyer." That would not fly. She had to come up with a specific reason to remove herself from his case. She had no problems with him. She had no connection with him. She was stuck.

She asked, "Didn't I do a case for him before? A contract or will or something?"

"No, he's just recently come back here. He didn't spend his adulthood here."

"Oh, well, just give me a minute." She disappeared into another room. I suspected that she wanted to check with the judge to see if she would recuse herself as well. Both ladies did not have a chance of getting out of it, it seemed, because the prosecutor returned twenty minutes later and said, "Let me talk to the witnesses and see what they say."

She was in the mood to deal, it seemed. Maybe it was a lucky day after all.

I went outside to wait. Craig came up and said, "You really scared me. I called you, and you didn't answer—again. If I hadn't seen that your car was still here, I would've killed you."

I reached into my pocket and pulled out my phone. It was silent, but there showed ten missed calls from Craig. There was also a text message from Hank. It said, "Love you," which made me feel weird. I wanted to process it, but unfortunately, there was Hank, sitting in one of the waiting chairs a few feet away. When he saw that I noticed him, he waved.

Craig looked guilty and said, "Sorry, about that, but he was worried. He came for moral support."

I said, "Fine. I can't talk now, but I'm working on getting this dismissed. I've been back there with the prosecutor working on it since the minute I got inside."

Craig said, "Fine, I'm here," and went to sit beside Hank. I could only imagine that Hank had been following Craig around like a puppy dog for days. I doubt he ever left his side since yesterday when we spoke.

The prosecutor came back and said, "One of the witnesses is not here. I need a continuance."

I asked, "Which one?"

The prosecutor named someone I never knew about. It was a man named Dennis Seabridge. Supposedly, he saw the whole thing. However, the other two witnesses were there. I said, "Sorry, but you have your victim and his girl. You have enough for your case. I think we should try it or you dismiss."

The prosecutor was annoyed that I had not agreed. I was usually very patient and played fair. This time was different. I was fed up with the system that had failed to protect my family. It was the same system that had not only failed to protect him but was also falsely prosecuting him. I was going to fight.

I looked at the prosecutor and said, "Let's go talk to the judge. We'll see what she says."

After the judge heard about the mystery witness, she told the prosecutor to put on her case without him. When I saw the look on the prosecutor's face, I knew there must be a crack in her armor somewhere. This case had a large flaw. I was very good at finding flaws.

When we began the trial, it was very informal. In rural city court, there is no jury. It is a bench trial, which means the judge decides the verdict. There is no stand to sit at and testify. Everything is done standing in front of the judge's bench. The only formality that most would recognize is the rule that forces the witnesses to stay outside while the trial is going. Of course, I had to exercise that rule by making a motion that it be observed. Otherwise, it was quite informal.

This left Craig standing beside me while we listened to the witnesses lying about him. He said nothing. Hank was sitting in the seats in the courtroom with other people that were waiting for their turn for their trial. When it came time for Craig to testify, he did well. I was never so thankful that my brother was stoic. The prosecutor tried to get him riled up, but it did not work. He was calm, which thankfully appeared to be the peace of the innocent, rather than the coldness of a criminal.

In the end, Craig's verdict was not guilty. I was so happy that I wanted to scream for joy. However, I had to have candor as the lawyer. As a sister, I was jumping up and down on the inside. I was glad that we had gone ahead and tried the case because it turned out that the chink in the case was that the complaint was not properly filed. I had noticed it, but knew that if I gave that away, the city would have dismissed it and then perfected it, just to arrest him once more. The moment the trial began, jeopardy attached. It was much better this way.

After that was over, Craig hugged me. I had never seen him so happy. Behind his hug came Hank's hug. I knew that I would have to speak with Hank about many things, but being in Guntersville made me almost forget that any of that was real. I pushed it in the back of my mind for a time when I could think about it privately. Now, I just wanted to celebrate. We decided to go to a bar. The trial had stretched on until nearly six o'clock in the evening. We were ready to unwind.

The bar we were going to was about fifteen minutes away from the courthouse. Luckily for me, Hank did not try to ride with me. He never approached me. I wondered if he was a little gun shy because I had not immediately reciprocated his declaration of love. I may be old fashioned, but it seemed strange to take such a large step of saying "love" via electronic means. I wanted something like that to happen in person and face-to-face.

Hank had said it twice. The first time was on a voicemail, and the second was on a text message. After brief reflection, I decided he did not deserve a response because he was being cowardly by not saying it to my face. Sneaking it into the relationship is not good enough for me.

When I got in my Jeep, I fumbled to see if Aren had called me. There were no missed calls or voice messages on my phone. It was puzzling that Paul had not even called me. I knew that Paul must be busy and would eventually call me. However, Aren's brush off was starting to make me feel very insecure. I had gotten accustomed to Aren waiting in the background for me. I could feel him pulling on me my whole life. Now that I knew it was not my imagination, I could now see that he had always been patiently waiting for me. I could no longer feel his pull, which made me wonder if he had given up on me. Surprisingly, I felt empty without it.

I sighed loudly as I stared at my dormant phone. When it began to vibrate and ring loudly, I jumped and nearly dropped it. I looked at the screen and saw that it was Johann Sockeye that was calling me. Johann was Craig's employer. Johann was also the reason that Craig got arrested in the first place. Although not legally Johann's fault, I imagined that he felt a little responsible.

I answered, and Johann said, "Alva, I have good news. I found out that the security camera was on battery power when that man attacked Craig. Do you need me to get a copy to you for his trial?"

"No, that's okay, Johann. We just left court, and Craig was found not guilty. What did the tape show? I never knew there was a tape in the first place."

"Craig didn't know about it either. He assumed since the electricity was out, the camera did not catch the action. I thought the same, until I inquired with the company about an upgrade for future outages. The guy from the security company told me that the back-up battery would last twenty-four hours. I asked him to produce a tape for the timeframe of the tornado, and he sent it to me."

"You didn't have the tape in the camera?"

"No, that would be a waste of space and energy. This company records it by sending it to an online storage. That way, it is only placed on a disc when requested."

I was so behind on technology. I said, "Oh, okay. So, what was on the tape?"

Johann laughed and said, "Oh, I haven't watched it yet! I just got the disc over-night mailed to me. I called you as soon as I got it. Sorry that I didn't make in time for court. I am just glad that everything worked out. Do you need me to send it to you?"

"No, that's okay. Just keep it for future reference. You may be able to use it to prosecute anyone who stole from you."

"Good idea, Alva. I will watch it when I get a chance. I am still very busy with my work. I'm sure Craig has told you that we're pushing for an early deadline."

I was too embarrassed to admit that Craig barely told me anything. I said, "Oh, yeah. Good luck."

I hung up and drove to Ray's Pub. It was nice and quiet, for a bar at least. It was close to the waterside of the county courthouse in Guntersville. I parked and locked my Jeep. Somehow, I had beat Craig and Hank there. I decided to go inside and talk to the owner, who was my classmate from high school.

Before I could get inside, I saw a figure coming out from the alley between Ray's and a window cleaning business named Sparky's. The walk seemed familiar, but I could not figure out who it was. My blood ran cold when I heard a familiar voice saying my name. It was Cliff Marcel, and I was starting to wonder if maybe he did kill Morgan. I had always trusted in his innocence, but that was in daylight and when other people were around. I was too nervous to be alone with him, especially in the dark. I began to feel guilty at how quickly my faith in him waivered.

I forced a smile because if he was indeed a killer, he probably fed off fear. If he was not the killer, I wanted to show him that I was not afraid of an innocent man. I tried to silently clear my throat when my voice seized up, and I could not get the words out of my mouth.

I finally was able to speak, and asked, "Cliff, how are you?"

Cliff pouted and said, "Not too well, Miss Alva. I was worried about you. You ran off for a while, and I started to wonder if you didn't like me watching you anymore."

A chill shot through my abdomen when the thought of Cliff watching me made me nervous. He had caught me twice in odd places where he should not have been. Both of those times, he was in an alley. He must have been following me and watching me. My fear for my safety grew in this moment.

Cliff saw my fear and said, "Oh, Miss Alva, please do not be afraid of me. I see that you don't remember me like you remember the others. I know you remember something of your old lives because you seem changed since the last time I saw you."

I could not believe what I was hearing. I said, "What do you mean, Cliff?" I had decided to play dumb. I had yet to reconcile my past with my present.

"You are like me. I can see in your eyes that you know what I mean. Don't lie to me. I won't hurt you. I want to protect you. I want to keep you from becoming like Helen."

"What do you mean when you say like Helen?" I asked Cliff.

Cliff mumbled, "A goddess."

I was terrified. Cliff knew of the pattern of staging the women to look like goddesses. Abby had said that the person who caused my death was immortal. Cliff was some kind of immortal, but he must be damaged somehow. A damaged immortal may be dangerous enough to murder. I did not want to die tonight. I was so terrified that my face was going numb. It was difficult to speak, but I tried.

"Cliff, I don't understand."

"Do you not remember me?" Cliff looked angry and frustrated. I had to act quickly to diffuse the situation. Before I could speak, Cliff said, "So many years ago, you were kind to me when I lost my brother. He was half of me, yet we were only half like you. In those days, I was called Zethus. My brother was called Amphion. Do you remember us?"

I abruptly remembered. Cliff was half human and half god. He was what is now called a demigod. Demigods were reborn again like humans made immortal, but they always remembered. There was never a time of amnesia for them. Because of this, there were not many lefts since they grew restless and would commit suicide eventually.

Suicide was the only way that a demigod could prevent his rebirth. Cliff's twin brother, Amphion, had committed suicide when his child died. Cliff was left alone, and as a twin, he was now incomplete. This was why he came across as simple. He was, in fact, damaged.

I remembered Cliff after his twin had died. I had found him crying in the temple of Zeus, his father. In those days, my family worshipped Zeus. That was before I knew how the gods really were. Before the gods went to being only immortals, they could produce a child with a human. They could never produce children with one another. Despite what the stories said, none of them were related to one another by blood.

When I found Cliff, he had wondered why Zeus had let it happen. Zeus, now Zeke, was always self-centered. He ignored his child's pleas. This was before I ever met Aren. Cliff showed me the way to the temple of Ares. It was as if Cliff introduced me to Aren. Cliff had been a large part of my fate.

Cliff was also a large part of my immortality. I remembered that clearly now. When I died, my spirit would move from one body to another. I would find a new soul after I crossed the abyss between life and death. Modern terminology for my experience is transmigration. However, Cliff reincarnated each life. His spirit and soul remained fused, and when his human body died, he would reincarnate again as a complete person poured into a human body like water into a glass. Because my soul was not the same, I had to reconnect with my spirit each life to remember. It was a subtle difference, but that was why he always remembered; yet I had to remember slowly.

Another difference between Cliff and I was that his fate was in his hands entirely. If he wished to not live again, he could simply take his own life. I had only a part in my eternity. If Aren did not wish to let me live, I would not live the next life.

Cliff's mother was Antiope, and his father was Zeus. For some reason, Antiope did not embrace eternal life. I was not sure if Zeke ever offered it to her. Cliff had attached all his family affections to me. He took this connection seriously. He tried to protect me each life. Even though I died early each time, he was nothing more than a failed protector. He was not the killer. I felt relieved that my memory had not fallen short in this instance.

"I remember you, Cliff. I'm sorry that I forgot." I reached out to hug him. He rested his face on my shoulder. Even his scent was familiar now that I was so close.

I wanted to take this opportunity to get some answers about the holes in my memory. Though I remembered Cliff, the fullness of my story was confusing. I needed to connect the dots. I wanted to understand why I died early each life and who was responsible. I wanted to avoid it, even if it meant that I had to avoid Aren and Paul entirely.

I asked, "Cliff, can we talk about my past?"

"You want to talk about Aren and Paul?"

"Yes."

"You want to know why they fight over you?"

"Yes."

"Paul was mad because he wanted you. He wanted to change you from human to immortal, but Aren made it there first. Paul wanted to take you, but Aren was already in love. Since Aren changed you, he had the right to keep you."

"Do you mean that even though Aren changed me, Paul could have taken over and kept me immortal?"

"Yes, but only because of Paul. He's different. He has a secret." Cliff kicked the gravel in the parking lot and asked, "So you don't think I'm a killer anymore?"

"No, Cliff. I know you're innocent. What is Paul's secret?" I felt nervous again. I was fed up with secrets.

"I'm so glad that you know that I didn't do it. When you went away, I thought that maybe you quit because of that DNA stuff. They said it was all over the place, but I can explain that. My blood was there because I cut my hand the day before that. Miss Morgan let me inside to wash it. Then we had relations. I know I shouldn't have, but it was her idea. I just cut my hand, but she made me take off my clothes and shower. She got in there with me. It made me see how much I loved her. I never would hurt her. Our loving got my germs all over her. The DNA is what they called it."

I wanted to make Cliff answer the question I had asked him about Paul. I also wanted more answers about my lives. I did not have time for confessions and alibis. However, as if Cliff had read my mind, he continued.

"I know that you believe me about Miss Morgan. I just left her early that morning to do a job before coming back to have lunch with her and finish the job that I started when cut my hand. When I took too long, she got mad at me and told me that she didn't wait on any man. She told me not to come back, but I felt bad because she had already paid me to fix up her yard. So, I was going to sneak and do it. That was when I saw you and your lover there. Then we found Miss Morgan, dead."

Cliff began to sob again. I felt insensitive to push the point of my unanswered questions. I put my arm around him and patted him on the shoulder while he cried. He began to shake as he said, "All of this over poisoned bread in her sandwich."

I pulled back and asked, "How did you know that?" I knew that Ernest would not disclose that to Cliff because he feared Cliff would blurt it out and seem guilty because of his simplicity. Cliff should not know the cause of death for Morgan. Ernest made a point of telling me that repeatedly as a strategy for Cliff Marcel's successful defense.

Cliff looked truly guilty for the first time since I met him. He said, "Don't pull away, Miss Alva. You really remind me of Miss Morgan. I loved her so." He reached for me and pulled me near to him once again. I heard him sniff my hair. This made me feel strange, so I tried to pull away, but Cliff would not let go of me.

I said, "Cliff, I can't breathe. Please give me some space." Cliff ignored me and squeezed me tighter. He began to rub the hair that he had just sniffed. I tried to jerk away from him, but he held onto me. It began to hurt.

I pled, "Cliff, let go."

"No, I can't let you get away from me like Miss Morgan did. She had another lover. She betrayed me. Just like you're betraying your lover. You have three. You shouldn't really do that."

Anger flashed in Cliff's eyes. I did not know if I should scream for help because I did not want to have the cops bring in Cliff. I was supposed to be something like his attorney. I was at least working with his attorney for his benefit. I decided to call for help, but no one heard me over the noise of the pub. Cliff became more incensed as he screamed, "Why are you scared? I won't hurt you. Let me protect you. I just need to protect you like I did for Miss Morgan!"

I heard the screech of wheels stopping quickly behind us. The next noise was the door slamming. I prayed for help, which came when I heard Hank scream, "Take your hands off of her, you killer!"

Cliff shoved me toward Hank. Hank caught me, which prevented him from chasing Cliff down the alley from which he came. Before Cliff disappeared, he shouted, "I'll see you later, Miss Alva. I will always protect you from that killer."

Hank said, "Likely excuse. It's so obvious that he's the killer."

Craig came up from his truck. Hank had been in the passenger seat, so he was able to get to me first. However, Craig seemed to be taking his sweet time. He asked, "You, okay?"

I said, "Yes."

Craig had a strange look on his face. He looked angry. Hank, however, looked guilty. I felt strange at both of their reactions. Hank would not look me in the eye. He let go of me abruptly and in such a fashion that I almost fell. Craig caught me. He looked me in the eye and said, "You got to quit being alone. You need to stay with Hank until all this blows over."

"I don't think I am in any danger behind the lock and key of my apartment."

"It's not up for discussion, Alva. That loony is dangerous. He needs to be locked up and euthanized."

I jerked back and said, "I have you know that the loony you speak of has rights. That's what I'm trying to protect here. It's not the Old South. You can't just get a lynch mob up or perform vigilante law."

Hank, who had been facing the door instead of me, turned around quickly and demanded, "You mean that you are his attorney?"

I was busted. I knew that Hank would know of the possible ethics violation because of his journalism research resources. He also knew that I was a witness because he was my co-witness. I tried to think of a diplomatic way to answer him. I said, "No, I'm not his attorney."

Hank would not back down. He asked, "I know that Ernest is." His face changed as he persisted, "Is that why he hired you? To tamper with a witness?"

It felt like the blood drained from my head. I could not think straight. I said, "No, that's not it. I'm just the next young attorney in town without a stable foundation. He's mentoring me."

Hank asked, "But why now?"

"It was just a matter of bad timing." I was not going to let Hank persecute me, considering that he had written an article about a similar killing in New Jersey. He had his own secrets, it seemed.

"I'm not dealing with this right now," I said. I wanted to say more, but Craig interrupted me.

Craig whined, "I thought this was my celebration party. That creep is gone. You two just kiss and make up already."

Hank took Craig's cue because he leaned in and kissed me before I could realize what was happening. Out of instinct, I kissed back. It felt good, which was another problem that I had to think about later. I was not in the mood to solve anything, so I just decided to let it go for now. We went inside of Ray's, and that was the last thing that I remembered.

CHAPTER 16

"Not him, Alva. Not him," a voice whispered to me again. One word sounded like Paul, but the next sounded like Aren.

I opened my eyes and saw that I was in my bedroom in my apartment. I was completely dressed, apart from my heels. Normally I would have been thrilled to know that no one undressed me, but I was quite physically uncomfortable. It is not very comfortable to wear a suit and pantyhose, let alone sleep in them.

I rolled over to look at the time. It was four o'clock in the afternoon. I did not remember coming home. I hoped that no one had let me drive. I could have walked home from Ray's Pub, but that could land me with a public intoxication charge. Since I was home and not in jail, I must have not done those things.

I heard someone coughing from my den. I reluctantly got out of bed to see who it was. It was Hank, and he was in his underwear. When he saw me, he did not make any effort to cover up or get dressed.

He smiled clumsily. It was obvious that he had just awoken as well. The couch had a pillow and blanket on it. This must be where he slept it off. He did not seem as hung over as I was feeling. I asked, "What happened last night?"

"We got extremely drunk. Craig didn't drink much, so he drove us here."

"Why didn't he take you to your house?"

"I didn't ask him," Hank said sheepishly.

I knew that nothing had happened between us because I was fully dressed. As I became increasingly conscious, I could feel how itchy my skin was from sleeping in so many layers. I did not know what to say to Hank, but I needed a bath and a cup of coffee first. I went into the kitchen and started my coffee maker before silently going into the bathroom for a hot bath.

It was probably the wrong thing to do for my hangover, but I needed to relax a little bit. The room was only slightly spinning, and there was not any nausea yet. It was enough for me to tell myself that a nice, long soak in a tub was just what I needed. I poured essential oil into the filling tub to help soothe my itchy skin. Once it was full enough, I got into it and tried to relax.

I was in the tub for a long time. Hank never bothered me. When I was finished, I got out and got dressed. When I came into the kitchen for my long-awaited coffee, I felt a wave of nausea hit me. I also felt very lightheaded. I almost lost my balance, but Hank came behind me and steadied me.

He helped me to the couch. He smiled and said, "See, you just need someone to watch over you—to protect you."

I reclined on the couch and closed my eyes. I was too sick to have an argument about modern woman's needs. I hated to admit it, though. A part of me did want to be protected. I was always independent, but it was only because of necessity. It would be nice to be lazy and let someone else take care of things for once. I was having quite the vulnerable moment, it seemed.

Hank reached over and brushed the hair from my forehead. He did not try to kiss me, which may have been his fear of my nausea. I did not tell him that I felt it, but the look on my face must have given it away. He went into the kitchen and poured me a glass of cold water. He came back and handed it to me. He had even put a little straw in it for me.

He said, "Here you go. You just need to rehydrate. You'll feel better in no time. Do you want some crackers or something?"

"No, water is fine." I took a sip. The first sip did not want to go down, but once I took a second sip, I felt the greatness of my unknown thirst. I gulped down the whole glass quickly.

Hank said, "Slow down or it will come back up. I should know. I was quite the frat boy."

"I can imagine," I said and I choked on my last sip. Hank took the glass and refilled it but told me to slow down.

I did slow down somewhat, but that was only after three more glasses. The process of rehydration had made me feel better, but I was now more tired than I was when I first woke up. Hank helped me into my bedroom. I was now wearing comfortable clothes that were sleep-friendly, so I climbed into my bed for some more rest.

Hank grabbed a bucket from the utility closet and placed it on the floor beside my bed. He said, "Just in case you need this, but I will stay with you until you fall asleep."

"Where are you going without a car?" I asked.

"My father is in town, so I will ask him to come by and get me. My car is at my home since I had gotten a ride with Craig to court."

"And yet he didn't think to return you there? My brother just doesn't think sometimes," I said under my yawn.

"Well, it's not a problem. I would have insisted that I be here to watch over you. I know you do not want to admit it, but I know you want my protection. That is what I can truly offer you. I can offer you a stable life. It would be free from drama, and you could quit working two jobs. In fact, you could choose whether to work at all. And we could have kids. That must be special that I would and could give that to you."

I hesitated to ask what he meant by that last part. It seemed like he was saying that he could give me kids, while he knew that Aren and Paul could not. It could not be that he meant that since he never once mentioned Helen. I doubted that he remembered, no matter what delusions that Helen had concocted in her obsession driven mind. I barely remembered anything, even though many people had tried to jog my memory. Hank probably just meant that he could offer me stability, which was very rare to have between two people of our age in this current generation.

Hank could also be referring to protection that I needed because there was still a killer on the loose. I had believed so strongly that Cliff was innocent, but after he had acted out last night at the end of our conversation, I began to doubt myself. He was damaged, which meant he could not be fully accountable for his heinous crimes. It was possible that he did not remember or did not understand that he had murdered.

Hank was not completely out of the suspect pool either. I never believed that he was even a suspect, but with doubt in my heart, I did have to remind myself that although Hank seemed to be ready to propose at any moment, we had barely known one another for around a month or so. In that time, we have not spent very much time together. He was a stranger. I felt a little uncomfortable, but my fatigue won as I fell asleep.

"Not him, Alva. Not your lover," the same voice whispered to me again. Once again, it brought me out of my deep sleep. I sat straight up in bed and saw that it was dark outside. I had slept the whole day away. I did not regret it at all.

The apartment smelt of stale coffee. I went to see if the coffee maker was still on, but Hank must have turned it off and poured out the coffee. I had to turn all the lights on because it was completely dark in my empty apartment. Hank was gone. I looked at the clock and saw that I had slept another six hours. Of course he was gone.

I went to sit on the couch and watch some television when I noticed something was out of place. My briefcase, which I kept my legal papers, was moved. It was a very slight move, but I was very meticulous where I kept it. I had a theory that if I placed it a certain way in a certain spot, I would know if someone had messed with it. Someone had messed with it. The person who moved it had forgotten which way it faced because it was now facing the opposite direction.

I went over and opened it. All my papers were in the correct order. It seemed that nothing had been touched. It was possible that in my drunken state, I had knocked it over. I could not imagine what Hank or anyone else would want out of there. Then dread washed over me as I remembered that I had that briefcase with me in my car at the bar. I had gone by that afternoon before Craig's trial to tell Ernest that I was back in town. He was not there, so I left a message with his secretary and grabbed my files. He had left a note on them for me to do some reviewing of his notes that he had made while I was gone.

I reluctantly took them with me, but I had always made it a rule to not put them in my apartment in case Hank or anyone else could accidentally stumble onto privileged information. If anyone read any of this, I could be in some serious ethical trouble. I did not know how the briefcase got there, but I just prayed that Hank had not read them. It was possible that I brought them with me because it would be a problem to leave them overnight in a car at a pub. I hoped that was the case.

I decided to put my mind at ease and call Hank to ask. Hank answered on the first ring. He sounded anxious. I asked, "Hank, how did my briefcase get in my apartment? I remember it being in my Jeep, but now it's here."

"What, that purse? Craig brought it in because you wouldn't go home without it."

"It's not a purse. How could you think something that large is a purse?"

"I don't know. I just assume that everything a girl carries with a handle is a purse."

That put my mind at ease. I did not have the audacity to ask him if he went through it. Considering that he thought it was a purse, he had proved his innocence. I agreed to call him later. I was unable to sleep, so I watched some more television.

It was almost dawn when I heard a knock at my door. Somehow, the person got into my building without a key. I looked through the peephole and saw it was Paul. I was not sure if I wanted to see him, but I let him inside anyway.

"Good morning, or is it yet to be good night?" Paul asked while he looked me over. He reached to touch me, but I pulled back. He did not argue but instead took a seat on the couch.

"What do you want, Paul?" I asked impatiently.

"Well, I didn't realize we had left it so cold between us? I thought I was supposed to come back as soon as I finished my business," Paul said as he adjusted his collar.

Paul was correct, but I was not in the mood to play-house with him. I did not even know what it was between us, though I seemed to think of Paul the most of the three men in my life. However, Hank had been making me feel like a normal life was the way to go. I did not know what to do. But I had made passionate love with Aren. I did not know how I could return to my normal life after all this knowledge was inside of my head.

I plopped down on the couch next to Paul and apologized. He wrapped his arms around me. His touch removed the last traces of my hangover. He seemed to smile as he felt the healing energy leave his body and go into mine. He gave me the look, which only meant one thing in such a situation. He wanted to kiss me, and I wanted to kiss him back. So, we kissed, and it was nice. In the back of my mind, I wondered if Paul's healing energy went through my body and into my soul because with every kiss and touch, I felt better. I felt safe and confident. I felt warm and loved.

I hoped that this gift of his did not cause me to love him as if I was under a magic spell. Then I remembered what Cliff Marcel had said about Paul. I pulled back and asked, "Paul, do you know Cliff Marcel?"

"No, who is that?" Paul asked dreamily as he went back in to deliver another gentle kiss.

I dodged him, but he landed on my cheek instead of my mouth. This did not deter him, as he took inspiration from his miscalculation and began to kiss me on the forehead and even the tip of my nose. When he was finished kissing the rest of my face, he returned to my lips.

After one more kiss, I pulled away and said, "He's the man who is accused of being a murderer. The same man that people believe may come for me next."

"People, what people?" Paul asked flatly. He paused and inquired, "Do you mean Aren?"

"I don't know, maybe. He was working on the case with me. That is how I met him. That is also how I met you."

"Met? Don't you mean found?" Paul asked with another kiss to follow-up his question.

I pulled away entirely and stood up so that Paul could not kiss me again. I wanted to know what Cliff had meant when he said Paul had a secret. I told him, "Maybe you will remember him better by his true name—Zethus."

"Oh, him. Yes, I remember him." Paul sounded unenthusiastic about it.

"Is that it?" I demanded. "There's nothing about him that you have to say?"

"What is there to say? The half breed never liked me."

"I cannot believe you sound so ... racist!" I yelled.

"Racist? How can I be racist? The color of his skin has changed throughout the ages. Bodies mean nothing to me. They are interchangeable, and I can wear a disguise of any which one that I choose!" Paul yelled back.

"I mean you think you're better because he's half god or something. I got a news flash for you, Buddy! You're not a god anymore! We're all just the same. We're all stuck here for eternity until people forget ya'll. And since the creation of something they like to call the written word, no one will ever forget you! I know you can do your parlor tricks, but séances and hoodoo are no reason to be snobby!"

Paul looked hurt. He asked, "Why are you fighting with me like this? Are you trying to avoid being intimate with me? I got a news flash for you, princess. You're not dipped in gold."

"Then why don't you leave me alone? Life after life, you were there. You have always been there. You are the reason why I am doomed to this eternal existence. Please feel free to go away."

Paul shook his head and said, "Your existence is eternal whether I am involved. All life is eternal. We're just stuck in a form that your limited mind can understand. And I can't leave you because I love you. I am selfish. I admit it. I want you and I want you to be mine alone."

"What is this secret that Cliff said you had?" I asked in a defensive tone.

"Why should I tell you? I have told you each life, and yet, in each life, you reject me for Aren."

"What does Aren have to do with your secret?"

"It's nothing to do with him. It's just a gift of mine. After Aren changed you, I offered to take you and keep you."

"I'm not property, Paul."

"That's not what I meant. I mean that I could change you back to a mortal."

"Why ask Aren? Why don't you just do it already?"

"Because you have to agree to it, and you never have."

"Why is that?"

"If I turn you back to a mortal, I will also become mortal. We could be together for real. We could be normal. We could even have kids."

"Then why have I always turned you down?"

"Because I would die like a mortal. It made you feel guilty. Besides, you always died too young to give it serious consideration. You have always been so in love with Aren. But that is no longer a problem. You don't even care for him now. I can tell by the way you look at him. Please accept my offer. We can leave this place and start a new life."

I sat down on the couch beside Paul. I was stupefied. I was speechless. I sat there in silence too long for Paul's liking because he demanded an immediate answer.

He said, "Come on, Alva, what are you thinking about? This is what we always wanted. This life is free of attachments or commitments for you. You and I could just leave. Forget Aren. He has no power over you."

I looked at Paul and asked, "You and I have been having an on-again-off-again affair forever. Why haven't we already done this? What are you not telling me?"

Paul looks down and said, "Aren must release you."

"Oh, he'll never do that. Why did you tell me all of this if nothing could be done?"

Paul demanded, "Why are you so certain that he won't?" The wheels of his mind began turning, and he asked, "You two haven't been together yet, have you?"

"No, not really," I said.

"Either you have or you haven't. Which one is it?" Paul asked in an irritated tone.

"I haven't physically been with him, but I have dreamt about us making love over the years," I was a little embarrassed to admit what I was saying to Paul.

"Yes, but that was before you knew he was real, and that he could dream walk?"

"There was one time a few days ago that I dreamt it again," I said in a quiet voice with the hopes that I said it quietly, it would make it less true.

"When exactly?" Paul asked.

"The day before we went to Atlanta."

"But you knew by then what you were doing was real?" Paul inquired.

"I guess. I mean yes, but it felt like I could not resist. It didn't feel real."

"Oh, you didn't enjoy it? Or are you saying he is lousy in bed?" Paul snapped.

"I can't believe you're getting mad at me for something that I did during a dream. Dreams are not real, Paul!"

"You know better. You knew it was real. I can even tell that you liked it!" Paul yelled at me. He could tell whether I was lying, which was an unfortunate gift of his, at least when used against me.

"Paul, it was before you and I ever kissed," I said to defend myself.

Paul cooled down somewhat, but he said, "Yes, but now Aren won't let you go. That explains why he acted so strangely at Gus' memorial."

"In what way did he act strange?"

"He told me to stay away from you. He said that he had given your life, and it was his to keep or take away. He told me that he would rather see you dead than be with me."

My mouth felt open. I knew that men said crazy things in the heat of jealousy, but that was ridiculous. I did not know if Paul was lying, but I knew he had a good cause to tell me a lie. He also had a good cause to always be honest with me. I was fed up with all the drama. I craved a normal life. Death would come early to me if I chose to be with one of them. Which one, if not both, I did not know. My only solution was to abandon both Aren and Paul. Hank's offer at a normal life was looking more appealing than ever.

I looked at Paul and asked him to leave. Paul did not say a word but left graciously. We left it in a strange place. There were no promises to call later. There was not even a promise to see one another again. I knew if I needed Paul, he would come for me. I just hoped that I would never have to call upon him for such a need. At this moment, I was not sure if I ever wanted to see Paul or Aren again.

I finally fell asleep. It was early Sunday morning, and I would have to go to work at Ernest's office first thing Monday morning. I called Larry, but he told me that he had enough people to spread out the hours through the holiday season. It was his nice way of telling me that I should not call him back until after Christmas. I knew that the holiday season was a slower time for him, so he had to cut down on hours.

It was a relief, so I told him that I would call him in January to see if things were busy again. I needed to not burn a bridge with Larry. Though I needed the money, my instability as a worker would be tough on any employer, especially lately. I just hoped that Ernest would decide to hire me for real soon enough. Working for free was not cutting it, and my court appointments had slimmed down for the upcoming winter season.

As I slept, Aren came to me once more. I had just dismissed Paul, and here was Aren to pester me. I buffed his advances. However, I did not have more autonomy than that. I wanted to ask him if he had really said that to Paul, but my mind and my mouth did not line up in the dream. I felt like a prisoner in my own body. I had to sit and listen to Aren speak to me.

He only said the same things about love and our life together. He tried to initiate sex with me a few times, but I refused. After a while, it took all my concentration, but I was able to finally speak up to him.

I said, "Aren, stay away from me. I choose Hank, and not you."

He asked, "What is wrong with me that makes you choose him over me?"

I realized in this moment that I could only speak from my true heart. I wanted to say so many things, but instead I heard myself say, "The only thing that is wrong with you is that you are not Hank."

Aren looked furious, and said, "If only you knew what he had done!"

Before I could ask what, he meant, I heard my alarm. I had slept through the entire day. It was now Monday morning and time for work.

CHAPTER 17

I went to work at Ernest's office. I knew something was wrong when I arrived, but no one would tell me why everyone all looked like someone had died. For some reason, Ernest was not in the office. He was usually the first to get there and the last to leave. However, he was missing. I did not feel privileged enough to ask the others in the office what was wrong. I barely knew them. I also did not feel comfortable enough with Ernest to call his cell phone to see where he was.

I made myself as busy as I could, but there was little that I could do because the ice storm a few weeks ago, courtesy of Don, had messed up the phone lines. There was no email or online research for me because of this. I waited patiently to hear that the technician, who had been working on it all day, was done. It was the fifth time he had been out there to service the system. It kept failing repeatedly, despite his best work.

I silently cursed Don and Helen under my breath as I drank coffee and flipped through Cliff's file for the tenth time that day. I hoped that something new would jump out at me, but it did not. I looked around for a newspaper, but there were none to read. That was odd because there were usually multiple newspapers spread throughout the firm's building. It was another oddity to an already weird day.

My phone was also eerily silent. No one had called me, which was unusual. I at least would receive one or two calls by lunch from potential client's price shopping. When I was not in my own little office down the street, I would forward my office phone to my cell phone. Today it did not seem that either one of my lines were busy. I remembered that the lines were down all over and decided that was why my phone was not ringing, at least in part.

I finally got my answer as to what was wrong right before lunch, when Ernest came bustling into the office. I heard quiet talking in the hallway, but I could only make out one sentence coming from Ernest, "She must not know yet. No, let me tell her."

A sense of dread hit me, as Ernest came into the vacant office that I had made my temporary home. He had yet to remove his trench coat. He was in full suit and tie underneath. He must have been in court all morning. He sat his briefcase on the floor with his right hand. In his left hand, there was a stack of newspapers.

He said in a gentle voice, "Alva, the cops have found out about an unsolved murder in New Jersey. They believe another girl was ritualistically killed in a manner that is consistent with the way Morgan died. This case has now become a serial murder case. They have named him the Icon Killer. Cliff was charged this morning and went into custody. We had a hearing about his bail. It was set very high, but at least it was set."

My mouth dropped open. I never disclosed to Ernest about the girl in New Jersey. Ernest handed me a newspaper. It was the same case that Aren had discovered. It had made the front page of five different newspapers. Some were local, while others were national. I searched out to see who wrote each article. Luckily, Hank's name was not on any of them. The thought of Hank made me wonder if he had in fact gone through my briefcase after all and tipped off the cops. I then remembered Aren's warning about Hank.

I suddenly felt nauseated. After the nausea faded, I felt rage. I began to throw all the newspapers in the air and scream, "Why do we bother? The guy is a mental case! He has been following me around. Did you know that? He probably did it after all."

Ernest's face seized up for a moment as he processed what I was saying. He remarked, "I had no idea that he was following you around. Trust me, Alva. He did not do it. I don't know who did, but we will find out. I just need more time to find another suspect. If I do not, there is too much circumstantial evidence and physical evidence."

Ernest's mind began to wonder, and he then looked guilty. He said, "We both know that I was wrong to put you on this case. I am so sorry, Alva. You are no longer to work on this case. I will speak to Cliff and tell him to stay away from you."

"I don't know if that would make it better or worse," I said.

"Well, I will tell him that you are a witness and that if he bothers you, it could make him look guilty. That should work. But in the meantime, I am sending you to a CLE on criminal procedure. It starts tomorrow, so you need to go home and pack. It will be for three days, so I will pay for you to stay down there for five days. It is in a resort, so all the food, drinks, and entertainment are provided. I will send you with some spending money as well. You will need to drive there unless I can get my secretary to arrange an evening flight for you."

All of this was happening very fast. I was confused. I said, "Wait, why are you sending me to a CLE all expenses paid like this?"

"Because" Ernest said, "you are now a paid employee of this law firm. Welcome to the family. Now go home and pack. Come back at five to see get your information on the CLE. I'll have everything arranged for you by then."

I still never found out where I was going. I called Mary, Ernest's secretary an hour later to ask how I should pack. She informed me that I was to pack for Miami. I should bring bathing suits because the resort I was going to had indoor and outdoor pools. Though it was November, it was still warm down there. She also informed me that I was to leave on a flight at eight o'clock in the evening. She had arranged for a taxi to drive me to the airport.

Mary emailed me the itinerary and details of the conference. Although it was a conference on criminal procedure, there was more spa time, elaborate meals, and evening entertainment than there were classes. However, the conference fulfilled my entire continuing legal education, or CLE credits for the entire year. I was glad to know that, as I had yet to go to a single class this year due to lack of money. I cringed because it was Thanksgiving next week, and if not for Ernest's intervention, I would have had to attend two classes by the end of the year. Those classes are not cheap, let alone something like this, which was more of a vacation than a learning seminar.

I finished packing and decided to call Craig to tell him where I was going. He never answered, so I left a message. I remembered how much work he had with Johann, so I did not give it a second thought. I called Hank but got his voicemail as well. I left a message for him with fewer details. I did not know if he had been the one to tip off the cops, but it did not make sense for him to do that and lose the scoop of a lifetime. A quick online search for his name pulled up multiple entries, but I had only a few minutes to look, so I refined the search to see if he had posted anything about Cliff Marcel. When nothing came back, I was satisfied enough to let it go.

One of the runners for the law firm brought me a packet from Ernest. It included all the information I needed for the CLE and the roundtrip air travel. There was also one thousand dollars of spending money inside of the packet. I cringed because that seemed like a lot of money for souvenirs. I began to wonder if I was being bribed into being quiet concerning Ernest's ethical breach. However, since he never said anything about this being a bribe, I decided to ignore my guilt.

A few minutes later, the taxi arrived for me. I went to the airport, and by that evening, I was in Miami to get massages and learn about proper criminal procedure. When I got to the hotel, I found that there was only one message on my phone. I checked it. It was a voice message from Cliff Marcel.

He said, "Alva, I made bail. I need to talk to you. I will come to your house if I must. There is something very important that I must tell you. I found something when I was working on a yard yesterday. I didn't tell anybody because you are the only one, I can trust."

The message ended abruptly as if Cliff had timed out. However, he did not call back with more information. I did not know Cliff's number. He did not have a listed phone number anymore because Ernest had it disconnected after Cliff was initially charged. My phone had been off during the flight, so there was no missed call that would show his number. I knew better than to call Ernest and ask him. Cliff would simply have to call me back or wait. I wished that he would just tell Ernest what he had found. It would make my life much easier. I would call Ernest in the morning and tell him to contact Cliff and make him tell him what he had found.

The next day was boring. I had six hours of classes to sit through. I found it difficult to stay awake, so I frequently left class to stretch my legs in the hallway. We had a wonderful breakfast and lunch. At the end of the day, there was an optional keynote speaker on forensics. I knew that I should go but decided against it because I was no longer on Cliff's case.

That evening, I opted to attend some kind of circus performance held in an attached theater. There were seven different restaurants to choose from, so I went to the one that sounded the most appealing to me. It was the one with the buffet, which was rarely found outside of the South in my experience. At the end of the evening, I went to bed. No one had called me, and I had forgotten to call Ernest. I would try to remember to call him the next morning after breakfast.

The next day went the same, and again I forgot to call Ernest. On the third day, I did the same exact thing. I was very frustrated. I vowed to call him the next morning before my flight left. After breakfast, I called him and told him. Ernest said, "I will call him. I haven't seen him since he made bail, but that's not unusual. I know that tomorrow is Friday, but I want you to take off until Monday, okay?"

I agreed and then got ready to leave. By six in the evening, I was standing at the doorstep of my apartment building. I had just tipped the taxi driver when I heard a voice offering me help with my bags. It was Blue Stevens, my extremely private neighbor.

"Hey, Alva, I got those for you. I am glad to see you because that makes what I am about to tell you more important. If you go out of town, you need to not let your friends housesit. I know you are a single woman and all, but I don't like strangers going in and out of the building. And I take extra exception to you hanging out with Cliff Marcel, the town's serial killer. I know you're a lawyer and all, but you need to have a little more sense about that guilty until proven innocent theory."

I was surprised as I said, "Who was it that was in the building besides Cliff Marcel?"

"Three fellows beside Cliff Marcel were roaming these halls," Blue was saying as we made it to the top of the stairs. We were standing in front of my apartment door when I noticed a small piece of paper sticking halfway out of the door. It was shoved under the door and must have gotten caught on the carpet. Blue reached down and grabbed it quickly and reluctantly handed to me.

I opened it because I was curious to see what it was. I knew Blue expected for me to read it to him. Once I saw Cliff's name signed at the bottom, I flipped it over and asked Blue, "So what did these guys look like?"

"One of them was that guy I seen you with a lot. I think you're dating him. He introduced himself to me once before, but I don't remember his name."

"Hank Rowling?" I asked. My mind was focused on the letter, so I was half listening to Blue's reply.

"Yes, that's it. He's a good-looking fellow. I see why you keep him around. The other two were strangers. One of them looked Mexican or something, but he was tall. Maybe he was Puerto Rican."

"Okay, and the other?" I asked half-heartedly.

"The other one I didn't see. He had his back to me."

"What color was his hair?"

"Don't know because he was wearing a coat and a hat."

"Can you tell me his build? Or anything about him?"

"Not really. It was from the bottom of the stairs. I couldn't tell you if he was fat or skinny, short or tall, since he was wearing quite a bulky jacket and from the bottom of the stairs, everyone looks the same height to me."

"Oh, well I apologize. I will make sure that I will not have any more house sitters." I did not want to tell Blue that no one had a key. I did not want to alarm him. I especially did not want him to call the cops on Cliff. My lawyer within made me protective over Cliff. I felt I could get Ernest to handle him.

Blue was standing there waiting for something, and I said, "Okay, see you later then." He finally took the hint and went to his own apartment. I waited for him to shut his own door before I flipped over Cliff's letter.

It said, "Alva, please do not avoid me. I know you're in there. Why won't you answer your door? I am coming back tomorrow night at midnight to bring you what I found. I know that you're here because your Jeep is outside. I've seen the light on from the street. I will break in if I must, Cliff."

I was extremely scared for my safety. I quickly unlocked the door. I decided to slowly open it in case Cliff was waiting for me inside of the apartment. As I opened the door, I noticed that someone had left the lights on, which was not how I left the apartment. I had failed to even look up to check from the street outside because Blue had distracted me.

I wanted to be brave, so I pushed the door open quickly. I knew that if there was trouble, Blue would hear me scream if I stayed in the hallway. As I had feared, Cliff was indeed inside of my apartment. However, he was dead.

CHAPTER 18

There was blood everywhere in my apartment. It soaked the carpets and was splashed on the walls. That was quite a mystery since from what I could tell, Cliff had been strangled with my favorite pink scarf. I did not scream. It was difficult to control my urge to vomit. The smell was surprisingly strong. It smelled more metallic than I ever imagined it would be. It also smelled a little rancid to be so fresh.

I did not enter the apartment but instead walked over to Blue's door and knocked. He opened it quickly, which made me realize he was listening at the door for trouble. I told him to call the police. I did not stop him at his gawking from the hallway while he called on his phone. He never tried to enter, as I suppose that he knew better than to do that.

The only thing that Blue said to me was, "Why does the blood look so gunky?" I did not answer him. Instead, I went outside and sat on the curb until the police arrived. I left my bags in front of my door. Blue hollered down the staircase that he would put them in his apartment. My silence must have been an affirmation to him because he never said another word.

The cops were there in a few minutes. It seemed like seconds to me. They questioned me, but when I showed them my multiple receipts from my trip, they let me leave. I gave them the letter Cliff had left me and told them about the phone calls and strange visitors while I was gone. They went to question Blue about my visitors. At that time, they released me.

It was not as if I had anywhere to go. I tried to call Craig and Hank, but neither answered. I knew that the cops would soon question Hank. I refused to call Aren. I was certain that he had been the visitor that Blue had described as a Mexican. It might have been Paul, but Aren was my key suspect. I did not tell the police about him. I pretended not to know whom it was that Blue had seen. I acknowledged that he thought he saw Hank, but that was because Blue now knew his name.

I finally decided to call my rock, my cousin Kim. We had not talked much lately, but she was very busy with her new man, while I was busy with my crazy new life. It was a life that I wanted to forsake, now more than ever. She came and got me immediately. Fortunately, she was alone, as her boyfriend was out of town for the upcoming Thanksgiving holiday.

Kim informed me that I was to have Thanksgiving lunch with her and her parents. She went and grabbed my bags from Blue's apartment. The cops had already searched them. I laughed because most of my clothes were warm weather friendly. The laughter felt good, yet borderline hysterical. Kim smiled and said, "I know, go ahead and let it all out."

I tried to cry, but instead laughter came. I imagine that is what is called hysterical laughter, though we use the term improperly in daily vernacular. I laughed all the way to Kim's house. I finally stopped, which was good considering Kim lived with her parents. Kim's parents were my aunt and uncle from my mother's side. They never spoke of my mother to me. They even managed to keep up a civil relationship with my father, which was more than I ever did. It was not as if he was to blame for her suicide. Our problems were unrelated to my mother's demise.

Kim called my doctor for me. He came by for a house call. He left me with a bottle of sleeping pills. He told me to take them and sleep it off. I took one and fell asleep. For almost a week, I stayed in a zombie-like state. I took the pills to sleep, and dreamless sleep was so sweet.

I never heard from anyone because Kim was screening my calls. She told me that Ernest gave me as much time off as needed. Craig had been working but would see me soon. Hank wanted to see me, but Kim made him stay away. She also informed me that a couple of clients had called me but did not leave more than their name. One was Paul, and the other was Aren. I pretended that I would call them later but knew that I would not.

Kim also arranged for my apartment to be professionally cleaned since the cops were now done with it. She never told me any of the details of the crime scene that she heard from local gossip and limited news coverage. The cops were keeping evidence information hush-hush, but a few details probably had leaked out. It did not matter, as Kim kept everything shielded from me. I was not allowed to watch the news or read the newspapers. I did not ask for them either. I mainly slept and barely ate.

One morning, I awoke to the smell of food and coffee brewing. The smell was so strong that it pulled me out of my deep sleep. I got up and went into the kitchen to find something to eat. For the first time in a week, I was ravenously hungry. I saw that the oven light was on, and when I opened the oven, I saw a giant turkey.

"Hey, girl, let me get you some cinnamon rolls for your Thanksgiving breakfast," Aunt Tama said. Tama was Kim's mother and my mother's sister. She was married to Gary. Their two girls were my first cousins. Kim was my best friend cousin. At least that was what we called ourselves.

I scratched my bed head and asked, "Thanksgiving is today?"

"Yes, silly. Do you want to watch the parade on television while you eat?" Tama asked.

I felt normal enough, so I plopped down in front of the television and watched the parade while I ate a breakfast of coffee and cinnamon rolls. When I was done, I realized that I should probably shower and make myself presentable for dinner.

It was quite cool outside, and I borrowed some of Kim's clothes to wear. I found a nice dark purple sweater and jeans to wear. I even borrowed a pair of her brown leather boots to make the outfit complete. I fixed my hair and put on my makeup. I borrowed some of her jewelry to make my outfit look complete. The last thing to do was to paint my fingernails, which did not take too long. I was back to my old self, or as close as I could get to it.

Kim came and found me just as I was finishing getting ready. She had been strangely absent all morning, and she had a suspicious look on her face.

She said, "Don't be mad at me, but."

"But what?" I asked. I was still too cheerful to jump on her. The lifting of the fog from my life felt wonderful.

"My mom made me pick up your dad from the airport. She sprang it on me at the last minute. I didn't know until this morning. You were asleep. I didn't want to upset you anymore than necessary. I know you don't like him. I hoped in vain that he would miss his flight, but he's here."

"And where is Craig?" I asked.

"He's not here. He went out of town with his girlfriend for the holiday. They went to some place in Georgia where it's snowy. Your dad showed up to surprise him but found out too late that Craig was gone. He called my parents last night to ask if he could eat with us instead. He didn't know you'd be here."

"Does he know now?"

"Yes, my parents told him what happened to you. He said Craig didn't say anything about it, but he hadn't spoken to Craig in a while. He was missing Craig. That was why he was coming. He knew you wouldn't see him. Now that he knows what happened to you, he is upset and wants to talk to you about it. He's genuinely worried about you."

Kim sat on the bed beside me. The look on her face worsened. I asked, "What else?"

Kim bit her cheek inside of her mouth and said out of the other side quite casually, "He thinks you should be on suicide watch. He demanded we take all pills away from you. He doesn't want you to end up like your mother."

"Oh, that is rich!" I exclaimed. I stood up and said, "Believe me, that thought had never crossed my mind during all of this craziness." I checked myself in the mirror and adjusted my clothes. I said, "Okay, I will have a family moment with him for Thanksgiving, but only for your parents' sakes. As soon as it's over, I am going to Craig's house to stay. I know where he hides his key."

"You don't have to leave," Kim said.

"When is he leaving?" I asked.

Kim stuttered, "Next Monday morning."

"Well, I am not staying in the same house as him. I will not deal with him right now. I have enough on my mind. There really isn't anything between us. I am not letting him use my tragedy as an excuse to talk about how he feels. For once, I will be selfish and not let people force me to comfort them amid my tragedy."

Kim nodded for she knew of this pattern in my life, especially with my father. She knew that he strained our relationship years ago when he tried to make me move away with him. He had told me that I should do this to comfort him, the widower. He had gotten deeply manipulative about the whole matter, but I had already gotten him to pay for law school, so he could not control me any further. Craig followed him because he had worked a while before he decided to go to school. Craig claimed it was because he wanted a new start and to stay close to our father, but I doubted it.

It was almost noon, and before we went out to have dinner, Kim handed me my phone. She said, "I think you can have this back now. You have very persistent clients, especially those two, Paul and Adam."

"It's Aren," I said flatly.

"Well, never mind them. Hank called you this morning. I had the phone in my purse, so I wanted to tell you to call him back."

I took the phone in my hand and called Hank. He answered on the first ring. He must have been scolded by Kim not to speak to me about Cliff's murder because he did not mention it. Instead, he invited me to supper with his parents. He was staying at the State Park. His parents rented two chalets, and they had reservations for Thanksgiving supper that night at the restaurant in the Lodge. He offered me a place to stay with him through the weekend, but I informed him that I was going to stay at Craig's house instead.

I hung up after I agreed to eat supper with him. I wanted to see him, and the thought of being alone on a holiday evening was too depressing for even me. I grabbed my bags for Craig's and placed my phone in my purse. I left everything in the guest bedroom where I had been staying. I put on a fake smile and went to eat Thanksgiving with my dysfunctional family, minus Craig, who was probably having a much better time than me.

I went to join the family, which consisted of Kim, Betty, Aunt Tama, Uncle Gary, and my father. I fought the urge to sigh as I took my seat next to Kim. Father had taken his spot across from me. Aunt Tama took her seat after she placed some rolls and butter on the table. We began our family pass around, which started with the dressing and ended with the rolls.

I was not sure if I had an appetite left because being around my father made me nervous more than anything. I always felt the eyes of judgment when he was around me. I noticed that my hand was a little shaky when I tried to sip my sweet tea. I sat my tea down as smoothly as possible and hoped that no one noticed. Everyone was too involved with their food to pay attention to me, which was a relief. We began to eat, but after a while, everyone left the table to watch the football game in the den. I was alone with my father, who meticulously creamed and sugared his coffee.

I was about to get up from the table when he said, "Alva, wait." I stayed put and waited for him to speak. It surprised me that after all these years, I still responded to his parental authority. I silently waited for him to speak.

"Honey, I am just so glad to see you. It has been a few years. I remember the last time that I was in town you were busy doing some out of town business."

I remembered that as well. I had lied and said I was out of town to avoid him. Craig must have not told him that I lied.

My father removed the spoon from his coffee after he had stirred it enough for his liking. He took a sip and asked, "How have you been?"

"Fine."

"Have you been busy?"

"Yes."

"Is business doing well?"

"It's fine."

"Any boyfriends?"

"Not really."

"Anything else new?"

"No, that's about it."

"That's wonderful to hear. I hate that your brother could not be here. It would be a rare moment to have the two of you together in one room with me."

"Well, he's been dating Sandy. The two have been getting serious. It's proper that they have a romantic getaway. Craig has been working hard lately." I dared not speak of his arrest. That was his business to tell, not mine. I did not, however, think it a problem to tell our father about Craig's love life for some reason. It was probably to get the heat off me.

"Yes, your brother told me all about her, but I thought her name was Lisa. Isn't she an accountant?"

"No, Sandy isn't an accountant. You must be mistaken."

My father leaned back and said, "Well, I remember meeting some girl named Lisa from Huntsville. She was an accountant for the college that Dr. Johann Sockeye works at."

"I didn't realize you knew Johann," I said.

"Yes, I am the one who introduced your brother to him. I got him that job. In fact, I am quite sure the girl was named Lisa. She was all that Craig talked about." He rubbed his chin and said, "Oh, wait, now I remember. That was the girl that disappeared while hiking in Utah or someplace like that. The group of girls that were with her said she wondered off one night. The family confirmed that she slept walked. They believe that a wild animal ate her. I can't believe that I forgot that. I am glad that I didn't slip up in front of Craig. He was very upset about it."

I was shocked. I had never heard of this whole ordeal. I remembered hearing about that in the local news but never heard anything about it from Craig. I never knew that he was dating her, let alone connected to her in any way. It bothered me that he was so secretive. Sandy was the only girlfriend that I had ever met. It made me think that Craig must be very serious about her to let me meet her.

My father seemed be too able to read my last thought. He said, "I don't think your brother should ever get married. He's like me. Loomis men are not quite cut out for commitment. You are much better than us. You're like your mother in that way. You should find someone and settle down. It suits you."

He began to laugh as he said, "It's almost like you're not really related to us! If you didn't have your mothers' eyes and my chin, I would think that you weren't ours at all."

I halfheartedly smiled. If he only knew that my spirit just chose a body to inhabit, he would realize that I am anything but related to him. I might as well be an alien or a pod person.

Things were going okay, but like always, my father had to spoil them. He changed his tone and said, "I hope you are not too like your mother. She was kind but weak. That weakness is why she is not here with us today. Would you have turned out better if she had not left you?"

"I didn't realize that there was something wrong with me," I snapped.

"You're just not going anywhere. By the time I was your age, I had two kids and a mortgage. You don't even own anything other than your Jeep and some clothes. What kind of life is that? And your biological clock must be ticking. If you were a man, you could wait and build a career first. A man can marry a younger woman when he is in his prime, but a woman must conceive younger. Her prime is much earlier than man's prime."

"What is your problem?" I demanded.

"My problem is that Craig will never conceive. Did you know he had himself fixed that way on purpose? They say it's reversible, but I doubt it! You are my only chance to carry on the family line. You need to hurry up before you dry up."

I jumped up and stormed out of the dining room. I grabbed my things and left without another word. I now remembered why I could not stand to be in my father's presence. He was a jerk. No wonder he remained single. No one would ever have him. My mother must have been a fool or a saint to put up with him.

I drove to Craig's house. My phone rang. It was Kim. I answered but regretted it when I heard my father's voice. He said, "You can't just run off like that. I still didn't get to talk to you about what happened to you. You are in danger. You don't need to be running around by yourself. Someone needs to watch you."

"I am going to be with friends. I won't be alone," I argued.

"I heard that you went to Craig's house. He's not even there," my dad argued back.

"He will be soon enough. He'll keep me safe," I said defensively.

"Your brother's house is the last place you need to be. Why don't you come back here? I'll give you your distance."

"No, thanks," I said.

"At least promise me that you won't take any nerve pills or sleeping pills. I don't want you to end up like your mother," my father said in a sarcastic sounding tone. It made me wonder how genuine his concern for me was. It seemed like he just wanted me to be a captive audience to his criticism.

I cut him off before he could say another word by saying, "Gotta go." He relented and said goodbye to me. I hung up and pressed the gas down. I wanted to get to Craig's place and calm down before I had to go and see Hank. I wanted to cancel, but I knew that I should not be alone too long.

When I got to Craig's house, I was upset to find that he had removed his spare key. I searched in all possible and known hiding spots, but it was gone. I assumed he did it because he knew he was out of town. I tried to call him to see if he had hidden the key in a well-concealed spot, but he never answered. I left a voice message but never said what I wanted. I was worried that he might shoot me down if he knew I wanted to crash in his place. He was very private, and he did not like anyone to stay in his house while he was not in town.

I reluctantly called Hank. He was staying in his own rented chalet next to his parents at the State Park, so I knew he would have a place for me to stay until I could get in touch with Craig. Hank was thrilled to let me stay with him, and when I arrived, he met me at my Jeep to help me with my bags. I wanted to keep them in the car, but I did not want to offend him, so I let him bring them inside. I had swapped out my Miami friendly clothes for some of Kim's fall friendly wear. I had enough for a week and a half without having to wash my clothes. I needed to check with Kim about when my apartment would be ready for me to return. I would probably move out, but I needed to get inside to get access to my own things.

I tucked those thoughts into a things-to-think-about-later space in my mind as I went inside with Hank. He had a nice fire roaring, and it was a welcome feeling. We were on the cliff of the mountain that over-looked Lake Guntersville. There was quite a breeze outside. The day, though cool, was quite clear. The brilliant blue sky reflected in the water, and I realized that I truly loved living here.

Hank and I settled down into a couch in front of the fireplace. He did not pressure me for affection but offered to rub my feet. I had been in heels all day, so I took him up on his offer. He was very good at it, and I slightly let my guard down.

I asked, "Who do you think killed Cliff?"

Hank answered too quickly, "It was probably someone who wanted revenge for Cliff killing Morgan."

"I assumed that since he is now dead, he is no longer a suspect," I said in a matter-of-fact manner.

"If that were the case, the person would have situated him in the pattern of the others," Hank lazily argued.

"That is not necessarily true. The others were women. That is if they were done by the same person," I said with a little bit of lawyer flare.

"Or maybe he has one pattern for men and another for women," Hank offered.

"What makes you think it was a man?" I asked rhetorically.

"The person who strangled Cliff must have been strong. A man alone has that strength," Hank replied.

I shuddered because I knew quite a few women, or rather yet female immortals, who could handle Cliff. I did not know why Cliff did not fight back. He was half-god at one time. He had supernatural strength in comparison to a human. My mind wandered to the realization that my neighbor had seen someone who fit Aren's description at my place around the time that Cliff had been there. It was possible that Aren had killed Cliff, but I doubted it.

Hank followed up with, "You never know. Maybe someone was coming to kill you, and he got in the way. It may just be that he did not mean you harm. Or the person caught him lying in wait, and with great love and devotion, they killed him."

I felt struck with terror at Hank's last statement. I knew my neighbor saw him snooping around my place as well, but I did not have the courage to ask him about it. Before I could move another muscle, Hank's parents came in through the front door. They were bearing gifts. I quickly sat my feet on the ground and put my heels back on my feet. Even though Hank had freaked me out, I was safe in his presence while his parents were around.

Hank smiled and said, "This is a Rowling family tradition. We like to do two things for Thanksgiving. One is we always eat our Thanksgiving meal at night, and the other is that we give out presents to herald in the holiday season." He took four packages from his father and said, "These are for you from all of us."

I opened them to find that all these gifts individually cost more than one month of rent for me. There was a designer handbag, a watch of gold and diamonds, a fancy cell phone, and a sweater. I smiled and was speechless. I felt bad that I did not have any gifts for them, but I was assured that it was quite all right.

After Hank and his family finished exchanging gifts, we all went to the lounge to listen to a piano player that had a good voice for nightclubs. The Rowlings sipped on spiked eggnog and the occasional cider. I enjoyed a cup of coffee, which was alcohol free, but only after I had to make sure that the bartender understood I did not want it with a kick. I felt like I was the only person not drinking alcohol, but I wanted to keep a clear head for when I needed to sneak away to Craig's house.

The second Thanksgiving meal that I had that day was quite a feast. I felt like I was about to pop from all the food that I ate. I noticed that Hank did not really eat much. He mostly pushed his food around on his plate. He would let the server take away his old plate just to fill up another untouched one. This gave the illusion of partaking that must have satisfied his parents, for they did not inquire as to what was wrong with him.

When we finished our meal, Hank's parents invited us to their chalet for drinks. I could not say no after the lavish gifts they had given me, so I accepted. Before we made our way there, Hank pulled me aside in a corner and spoke to me.

He said, "I wanted to give this to you when we were alone." It was a small box that looked just like a ring box. My heart jumped as Hank dropped to one knee. I calmed down when I saw that he was only picking up the small bow that had fallen off the velvet box. He stood up and handed me the mended package. I opened it to see two diamond earrings. They were beautiful, and I was grateful. No one had ever given me such a present, at least not in this lifetime. I gave him a kiss.

Hank said, "You can try them on later if you like." He paused for a moment and then said, "Alva, I'm sorry that I sounded like a creep while ago. I guess I just am glad that Cliff is gone. I really believe he did it. I have it on good authority that he did, but we'll talk about that later. I imagine that it sounded like I was the killer for a second. I had been there looking for you the day that Cliff was killed. The cops asked me about it, but I was in Birmingham at a meeting when it happened. I have proof that I can show you later if you are worried."

Hank began to laugh as he said, "It's like one of those old murder mysteries of who did it, isn't it? But I don't want to harp on that. I really believe that the killer is gone." I did not want to remind him that there was still another killer out there. Someone had killed Cliff, and I was relieved to know that it probably was not Hank.

We spent several hours with Hank's parents before we returned to Hank's chalet. As soon as we got back, he asked me to try on the earrings. I did. They were lovely. The earrings seemed to sparkle intensely in the dim light of the chalet. Hank threw another log on the fire, and he poured us some wine.

In the back of my mind, I remembered my father's words. I decided to forego the sleeping pill tonight. I took the glass of wine from Hank. The other things that my father said about me basically being an old maid made me want to embrace what was happening between Hank and myself.

Hank casually grabbed his laptop and sat it on his lap. He logged in, and I was surprised to see that his password was my name. I pretended that I had not been watching, as it was rude to stare at people as they typed in such private things. I had accidentally noticed it. There was nothing more devious about it.

Hank proceeded to pull up the log from his meeting with the board of directors from some company that his family owned. It turned out that he was at the meeting from ten until four. There were not only the minutes of the meeting, but there were also numerous emails and even a video with a timestamp on it. I recognized the software and knew that it could not be tampered with at all. The timestamp was accurate. Hank was innocent.

Cliff had been killed at around two in the afternoon. Hank had been at my apartment around seven in the morning. He did not know I was out of town. We had left it in a strange place, and he had become insecure when I would not return his phone calls. I felt a wave of relief come over me. If I chose, I could indeed have a normal life with Hank Rowling.

At such moments in one's life, certain things collide. I like to call them a moment of truth. That was the best way to put what happened next. Hank and I began kissing, and when we were partially undressed, Helen showed up. We had moved things into the bedroom, and between kisses, I looked up and saw her standing at the foot of the bed. She had her arms crossed. I was relieved that she was alone. She did not bring any of her goons with her.

"How precious yet expected," Helen sneered. Helen was a beautiful woman, and she had worn her best to come to see Hank.

I expected Hank to ask me who this woman was or to demand that she leave, but instead he said, "I see you cannot take a hint. How many times will I say no before you get it through your immortal mind that I do not want you? I have not wanted you since you stole me from Alva thousands of years ago!"

Hank jumped out of bed and put his shirt back on so that Helen did not get any pleasure from seeing his bare flesh. I still had my bra and panties on, so I felt vulnerable. I grabbed the sheet and pulled it to my chin. I was too shocked to speak.

Helen ignored Hank and zoned in on me. She hissed, "What's the matter, little girl? Are you frightened?"

I remembered Abby's words about being an alpha female. I wanted to speak, but she had me intimidated. It was so bad that I could not even ask Hank what he meant. I did not remember him being in the past with me. I did not remember anyone other than the gods, except for Cliff and his twin brother, who were demigods.

Helen did not back down. She saw the confusion in my eyes. She desired to increase my fear when she said, "Do you not realize who Hank is? My dear, he is the cause of all your sorrow. He is the lover that your people swore to kill if you did not take the emblem of the Cursed One, your precious Aren. Did it seem that he was a victim like you to their superstition and ignorance? He was the very one that pledged your soul to Aren. He offered you as a tribute to Aren in exchange for victory in worldly battle. When Aren did not take you, he cursed him. That was when your village also became cursed. Your people then pledged to kill him if he did not take the emblem. When he refused, they sent you."

"That is not how it happened. I was tricked by Hades!" Hank screamed.

"Whatever you may say, say it as we leave, my love," Helen purred.

I began to find courage. I asked, "What is she saying, Hank?"

"Hades came to me and said he was Ares. I never knew the difference. I had been praying to keep the warmongers out of our village. I came from a village as an orphan since my family was killed. The rest of my people became slaves. If I had not been so tiny, I would have never been able to hide and flee."

Hank cleared his throat. He continued, "I prayed to Ares for the power to protect us if a battle came our way. A local mystic gave me something to burn, and when I did, a god showed up. I thought it was Ares, but it was Hades. The mystic had given me the wrong root! When I called him by the wrong name, he never corrected me. He then told me to pledge myself in completion to him. I had no idea that included my entire family. When we were betrothed, you became family. He came back on the evening your uncle agreed to let us marry. He told me that you were also his through my pledge. I thought he was Ares, so I cursed Ares."

Helen interrupted, "And to curse the Cursed One brings curses. No matter how it may have happened, it did. Your lover betrayed you. He did not even go to retrieve the emblem himself!"

Hank said, "I was afraid. I did not know that they would send you instead. I just wanted to let them kill me so that you would never belong to anyone but yourself."

Now it made sense why Hank was so familiar to me. He was the boy that I barely knew so many years ago. I had a different idea of love then, and I had given up my life for my lover. I asked in disbelief, "Why aren't you dead? I saw them kill you."

"That is where I come into the picture," Helen said with a smile. "I offered, and he chose me. He forsook you in that moment, if not way before then."

"She lies. My only desire was to protect you. I accepted her offer, but it was only because I wanted to save you. Apollo was there. He healed me. And the true Ares showed up. He and Hera made a deal. She got me, and he took you. I have spent an eternity avoiding her. I just want to be with you. That is all that I have ever wanted."

Helen laughed, "How sentimental! If only she remembered everything like you do. She would know to avoid others of her kind. Yet, she dies too quickly to remember much. Maybe that is why she is an incomplete person—she never really had a chance to awaken before the slate is wiped clean once again!"

I looked at Helen and demanded, "What do you mean?"

"We all know that you die young, girl. We also all know that someone causes that death repeatedly. I always thought it was Aren, but a few seem to think it's my sweet Hank. He always comes around right before you cross over. His timing is either good or bad. Of course, you always marry Aren at the same time as well. Such a mystery!"

"I have nothing to do with her early deaths! I wouldn't doubt if your hand was in it, or maybe that scoundrel Hades."

"He's not involved. I have settled your account with him. His claim on the girl is void once she became Aren's," Helen said as she smoothed her hair. She demanded, "So, will you come to me, my love? Or is it to be another life for us two?"

"I will not come. Do not return to me this life. I will kill myself and not accept another life if I see your face again this life," Hank said coldly.

This seemed to terrify Helen, and she backed down. She said, "I will wait for you. If it takes a thousand more lifetimes, I know you will return to me eventually."

Before Helen left, she said to me, "You should watch what company you keep, my dear. You may end up in the ground once again if you are not careful. Don't rely on Aren or Paul to take care of you. They have failed to keep you safe even once."

I said, "I don't know what I will do, but I don't think it's your business."

"I understand you don't trust me, and you shouldn't. I am your enemy. I fear my former love's wrath too much to harm you. So, it's not me to fear."

"I don't love Aren," I said defensively. I assumed she meant Aren, and I did not want Hank to think I was with him.

"I was speaking of Hank. I know you don't want Aren right now dear. You're too hung up on Paul this time to even notice him."

Hank snapped, "Apollo can focus on his own mate and leave mine alone."

Helen sneered, "He has never taken one because he is waiting on yours to come to him. After all, he can only have one mate. That is his limitation, or so I am told."

With that, Helen left. I was alone with Hank once more. I wanted to leave, but there was too much wine in me. I called Kim, but she never answered. I decided to take the other bedroom and spend the night thinking about everything I had just learned. Hank respected my decision. I just hoped he would respect it still if I did not choose to be with him.

Before we went to bed, I could tell that Hank wanted to talk to me. I decided to give him a moment to explain himself. We sat on the couch once more. The fire had died down to a few glowing embers. Hank offered to revive it, but I was warm enough.

He began to speak, "I can only imagine what you must think of me. I hope you believe that I did not do those horrible things. I only agreed to go with Hera because I wanted to save you."

"How long have you remembered?" I asked Hank.

"Since I was very young. It all came back to me at once. I remember everything. I don't know why you always have trouble remembering. The others of us do not, at least not for very long. Most of us know everything by puberty."

"So, you know more people like us?"

"Yes, but that is not the point. The point is that I want you to forsake immortality. Let this be our last life together. Let this be the life we were meant to have ages ago," Hank declared as he took my hand.

I let go and said, "I don't understand why you never let me know who you were."

"I was not sure you had remembered. In fact, I don't know how much you remember. Hera said a few things that let me know that you've already met Apollo and Ares."

"Why don't you use their common names?" I asked.

"Because I don't respect them. They don't like it and hurting them gives me pleasure."

"Hank, I understand that you want me to be with you. However, now that I know you are part of my past, I know we can't have that normal life you promised me."

Hank pled, "Please don't say that. You knew that I was like you. Hera told me the first time she found me. She told me everything you had said to her about me. How did you find her?"

"Paul and Aren took me. I am sorry to bring her to your doorstep like that, but I honestly did not know," I apologized.

"It's okay. I would rather you remember so that I can protect you. I want you to stay away from all of that. I think Ares is the reason that you die so young. It seems as soon as you choose him once again, you die."

"That doesn't seem right. I don't feel that he would harm me," I argued even though I wondered if he was the Icon Killer. As the war god Ares, he had killed many.

"I never said he harmed you. I am saying that he is the same cursed being that brought this upon us," Hank said coldly.

"Aren has been good to me. I just don't want him anymore. I don't know what it is that I want," I said.

"I hope that is enough to keep you alive," Hank said. "Unfortunately, Ares is already in your life. I fear the cycle that causes your death has already begun."

"What if it hasn't?" I asked with fear and hope in my voice.

"Then pledge to me that you will not stay alive another life. It only takes the desire to be born again to make it happen. I should know," Hank said in a serious tone.

"Hank, just don't live again. If you hate Helen so, it should be easy for you to have let go by now," I said kindly.

"You don't understand, Alva. You are the reason that I keep coming back. I cannot rest in peace until I know that you have not chosen to be born again."

"I know that you love me, but that is a little extreme, Hank."

"You don't understand what my intentions are. I do love you, but my motivation is not to spend a life together with you, or even an eternity alive on Earth with you."

"What is it then?" I asked.

"Ares can only bring you back so many times before he loses that ability. Once the power is gone, he can never bring anyone, not even you, back."

"So, what? I will go to the other side. What's the big deal?"

"If Ares fails to bring you back, your spirit won't know it. You will become an earthbound spirit without a body."

"You mean a ghost?" I asked.

"Yes, that is a word for it. There are other words, though. You become the tormented and the tormentor. You will stay on earth until the very end with Ares."

"But he will leave when he is forgotten," I said.

"How can a Greek god be forgotten now that history is written down? He will remain until men destroy one another, with or without you."

"You can't be serious, Hank," I jested.

"I am," Hank said.

"How long did you know it was me?" I asked.

"Not until I came into town looking at houses with my dad. I just accidentally met you. It is always that way. We are drawn to one another. We travel in packs from life to life. We always find one another," Hank said.

"So, you really did buy my Aunt Dawn's house to get to me?"

"Yes, my dad was going to bulldoze it. I talked him out of it," Hank said with a smile.

It lightened the mood somewhat, but I had much to think about. I did not believe Hank was correct about the fate of the lovers of the immortals. As I fell asleep, I soaked the pillow with tears of uncertainty.

CHAPTER 19

There was a crashing noise outside of my window that woke me up at two in the morning. I looked outside and saw that it was a fallen icicle. Apparently, the temperature had dropped, and we had our first natural freeze of the season. I did not count what Don had done as natural. I surveyed the wintery landscape under the illumination of the full moon. Everything was frozen over. I hoped that the road crews would come soon with the salt and gravel mixture they spread on the roads. Alabama shut down in the ice and snow, so I did not want to be stranded.

I had the problem that one gets when being awakened suddenly—I was shaking terribly. I was not very cold, but my nervous system was reacting to the sudden awakening from deep sleep. I thought that I might feel better near the smoldering fireplace. I walked into the den to see if there was any warmth left coming out of the fire, but there was not.

I stared at the beautiful sight of the frozen landscape once again. I wondered if it was cold enough to freeze the lake over. As I began to walk to the kitchen to get some water, I tripped over a cord on the floor. I bent over to inspect the source. It was coming from Hank's laptop. He must have had to charge it while we slept. I had heard him typing away after I went to bed alone. He must have worked to keep his mind at ease.

I decided to check my email. I typed in the password that I had learned by accident was my name. When the desktop opened, I saw a curious file named "Stuff." I opened it and found that it was a code for his journalism file. In that file, I found the article Hank had written about Cliff. In that article, Hank had written that Cliff was in fact the Icon Serial Killer. He also wrote that it seemed that the female defense attorney would be next. He described me down to my nail polish. He only left out my name.

He also included tons of information that was from my personal file on Cliff. There was stuff in there that Ernest had not even seen. That was pure work product and should be privileged and confidential. When I saw a saved email showing that Hank had sent the article to his editor tonight for Sunday's edition, I knew that I was ruined. I was responsible for that file, and I may lose my license to practice law for compromising it.

My heart sank. I had so wanted to give Hank the benefit of the doubt. I saw that he had written multiple articles about other killings. It seemed that Hank linked Cliff Marcel to at least ten unsolved murders, in different parts of the country. I was so traumatized that I knew I had to leave immediately. The roads were so iced over. I needed to think of a way to escape.

I called Kim, who answered. I knew she was already up and getting ready for the Black Friday sales after Thanksgiving. When I told her that I needed a ride, she told me that she would come and get me. It seemed that her boyfriend made it back in town earlier than planned. He had been up North, so he had the proper tires to come and get me out of here.

I silently went and gathered up my things. When Kim made it outside my door, she called me. I had forgotten to put my phone on silent, so the noise woke Hank. He came out of his room and saw me about to leave. He asked, "Where are you going?"

"I'm leaving with Kim."

"I mean why are you leaving?" Hank asked with frustration in his voice.

"The jig is up, Hank. I saw the article, or should I say articles. You painted quite the picture of me. Good to know that I was dead set to be the next victim of the Icon Killer. Good thing it wasn't Cliff, or I wouldn't have anything to look forward to."

"Alva, it's my job. I needed to provide for our future. I secured a book deal from this article. It should set us for life. We can be married. Besides, I know Cliff did it, but he's dead. Why does it matter?"

"Because you have probably ruined my legal career. I mean technically ruined it. I will probably be disbarred for this. I cannot believe you snooped in my files. I should have known that bit about 'isn't that a purse?' was a bunch of crap."

"Alva, don't overreact. They won't disbar you," Hank said gently.

"Even if they do not, my reputation is ruined. That was a national newspaper. And a book to follow! Every lawyer in the country will know me as the girl who let her boyfriend read her confidential files. I will never gain the trust of an employer or client ever again. And if the killer wasn't after me, he is going to get me now since you put a big target on my back. Nothing says, 'come on and kill her' like a detailed reason why I am the perfect victim."

I began to leave the chalet when Hank grabbed my arm and shouted, "Alva, wait!"

I said, "You seem to know so much about the killer, Hank. How do I know you're not him?"

"I only followed the killer around the country because I knew that he was looking for you. I could just tell he was leading to you. I used his patterns to try to find you. I promise that is the only reason I know so much about it," Hank pleaded.

"Just forget you ever knew me," I said coldly.

Hank finally let go of my arm. I said, "Don't worry, I left the gifts on the bed. Have a nice life, Hank." With that, I shut the door. Kim and her boyfriend were awaiting me. They drove away slowly as I choked back my tears.

By the time we were getting near the turn for my apartment, Kim informed me that we were not going that way. She said that she had wasted enough time driving out to the State Park. I would have to go with them for the sales. I wanted to sit in the car, but I found out that the heater did not work when the truck was in park. So, I reluctantly went inside for pure shopping chaos. We waited in line two hours for the sales to begin. I did not have any money to buy anything, but even if I did, I was not interested. I walked around the place like a zombie. Kim made me hold things and stand in line for her. I did not object. I just floated around until it was time to leave.

The truck was loaded down when we finished. It was daylight by then, and I asked Kim to take me to Craig's house. She dropped me off and drove off before she even checked to see if I made it inside. I knew there was no spare key, so I tried to call Craig again. He did not answer, so I decided to be a little creative. I checked all the windows until I found one that was unlocked. My luck was that the lock was broken. I told myself that I would tell Craig to fix it for his safety. In the meantime, I put a bell from an old cat collar on it so that if anyone else opened it, I would hear it.

I sat down to watch television for a while. The local station was showing a Christmas movie marathon, which helped lift my spirits. I wondered if Craig would decorate this year. He usually was not home enough to want to decorate, but now that he was dating Sandy, maybe he would at least put a wreath on the door. Since things were getting serious with Sandy, it was possible that she could convince him to put up a tree. I did not even know if she celebrated Christmas, however. I frowned and made a mental note to ask more questions about my potential sister-in-law.

I got hungry, so I went into the kitchen to find something. The one thing that Craig and I did have in common was a love of ice cream. He kept his freezer full of little pints of different varieties. True to form, when I looked, there was a freezer full of choices. I grabbed the chocolate mousse ice cream and sat down for another stretch of movies.

As I saw the couple hugging and kissing in a Christmas movie about redemption, I began to think about my love life. I did not lack for suitors, but I was not sure what to do. I knew that if I rebuffed Aren or Paul, they would follow me around and make me miserable. Paul would be more aggressive than Aren. Aren would wait patiently for me to break my heart or come to my senses. Paul would continuously try to kick my door down in hopes that he could drag me home.

I felt tears welling up in my eyes as I thought of Hank. He was the one that I had chosen unofficially in my heart. Yet, he was the one that betrayed me the most recently. I knew that there were some questions that he posed about Aren and Paul concerning my crossover into immortality. However, I just knew that it was not their fault that I was now immortal. I also knew in my heart of hearts that despite what Helen had said, Hank did not cause my demise. He was ignorant to the true consequences of his actions. He had said that Hades had tricked him. I had never met him. I did not even know his common name.

The temptation came to call Paul and ask him. However, neither Paul nor Aren had contacted me lately. I resisted and instead took another bite of ice cream. There was none left, but I was still hungry. In a moment of gluttony, I decided to turn the pint up and drink the melted remnants. I got what I deserved when the melted, sticky ice cream missed my mouth and poured all over my shirt. My nose had gotten more ice cream than my mouth, as I could feel the stickiness all over the tip of my nose. In frustration and embarrassment, I went to the bathroom to wash my face and try to clean the ice cream from my shirt.

Because I was still a little shaky about my personal safety, I took my cell phone with me to the bathroom. I sat it down and began to dab a wet washcloth on my shirt. It would have to do until I changed. It did not matter because I was completely alone. I could be a slob and considering that I was running out of clothes, I did not want to have to fool with washing just yet. When I finished cleaning my shirt, I washed my face.

It always seemed like my phone rang at the most inopportune moments. This was no exception. My phone began to ring and vibrate against the porcelain of the sink countertop. I had soap in my eyes, but I squinted to make sure it was not someone I really needed to talk to at that moment. When I saw that it was Johann Sockeye, Craig's boss, I decided to let it roll over to voicemail.

A few minutes later, I was finished with washing my face. I always enjoyed scrubbing it vigorously. I had slept in my makeup, so I needed a good face scrub. I was probably too enthusiastic, though, because my face was now bright red and a little tingly. I shrugged it off as I grabbed my phone. I hated accumulating voicemail, so I went ahead and listened to Johann's message while I wiped down the bathroom sink counter that I had made wet.

"Alva, this is Johann. I just wanted to call you because you are your brother's attorney, and I needed advice. I finally watched the footage from the tornado, and it turned out that Craig did beat that man up. He did such a thorough job that I am grateful that he did not kill that man. I know he was just upset and stressed out, so I do not hold it against him. I just wanted to know if I should destroy this tape or give it to you? I don't want this evidence against him hurting his bright future. Please call me and let me know what to do when you can. Thanks, dear, and happy Thanksgiving."

I dropped my phone in the wet sink. I was terrified at what I was hearing. I remembered the day in court of Craig's trial and what the victim had said about him.

"Mr. Loomis attacked me from behind. I never saw him coming. I think that he would have killed me if my lady hadn't been there as a witness. Mr. Loomis would probably have killed her too if she wasn't locked inside my truck and calling the police."

I had torn this testimony apart because the female, though a corroborating witness, was squeamish on the stand. She was so nervous that she kept changing her story. I now understand that it was her fear, maybe of Craig, which had made her act that way. At the time, I thought it was because she was lying and could not get her story straight to match that of her man. There had been another witness, but he was a no-show. I wondered if Craig had intimidated him as well.

I felt a combination of shame and anger. I was ashamed that Craig had acted that way. I was also angry that he had acted that way and that he told me a lie. He had made me defend him. He had made me so upset over the injustice of his situation. I had almost given up on being a lawyer because of it, though I never told anyone I felt that way.

I wanted to confront him, but I looked and saw that my phone was covered in running water. I grabbed it out quickly but saw that it was now dead. I almost wished that I had not returned the new phone to Hank. I opened the phone and dried it out as much as I could. I sat the separated components out on the counter with the hopes that they would work again once dried.

I walked down the hallway to find a phone to call Craig. I wanted some answers. However, as I passed the entrance to Craig's three-car garage, I heard a little whimper. It sounded like a kitten, so I went to check to see if a stray had gotten inside by accident. I could really use some kitten cuddling time if it would come to me. Maybe it was not too wild.

I switched on the light to the garage slowly with the hopes that it would not scare the kitten away. Craig had covered all the windows in black garbage bags, which made me wonder how a kitten could have gotten in somehow. I did not hear another sound other than the buzzing of the lights overhead. What I saw made me extremely nervous. I saw that Craig's truck was parked in the first slot. A blue compact car was parked in the second slot. The personalized sticker on the rear window said "Sandy."

I did not realize that Craig could go without his or Sandy's cars. It was possible that they rented a car, which some do to save wear and tear on their own vehicles. I doubted they went on a romantic getaway with someone else, so I was puzzled. I walked cautiously down the wooden steps to see if there was a kitten in the garage. As I walked past Craig's truck, I tripped and fell. I used his hood to steady myself. When I touched his truck's hood, I felt it was hot. Someone had recently driven his truck.

I wondered what was going on here. Just then, I heard another whimper, but it was followed by something else. It was a moan. I rushed over to see where it came from in fear that someone had attacked Craig or Sandy, or both. I cursed myself for not having my cell phone with me in such an important time.

Craig's garage was quite full of boxes, so I had a hard time getting around his truck and Sandy's car to see who had moaned. I practically had to climb over Sandy's hood to get to the third slot in the three-car garage. When I got there, what I saw made me almost pass out.

It was a woman dressed up like some kind of harvest princess. She was wearing a loosely fitting white toga, and on her head was a crown made of corn. The ground was covered in black garbage bags, but she was not lying on the ground. She was tied to what appeared to be a tabletop minus the legs. It was right on the floor. The nubs of where the legs had been sawed off provided the perfect anchor for her hands and feet to be tied with rope. The woman moved, and I saw that she was breathing. She must be unconscious, probably drugged. She began to come out of it somewhat, and when she turned her face to me, I saw that it was Sandy.

I rushed over to her and tried to loosen the ropes. It was difficult at first, but I was able to slide them off the nubs and free her. We made an awful amount of noise, and I feared that we would soon be discovered. I could see that Sandy was coming out of her sleep. I leaped to put my hand over her mouth before she could scream.

I whispered, "Sandy, it's me. Don't scream. I am trying to free you. Did Craig do this?"

Sandy nodded as tears streamed down her face. I removed my hand and whispered again, "I will get you out of here. Do you know where Craig is?"

Sandy shook her head to tell me no. As quietly as possible, I helped her stand up. I whispered, "Can you walk?"

She nodded and I whispered, "Let's go. If Craig shows up, you run and get help. Don't wait for me. I can handle my brother."

Sandy nodded again. Just then, I heard Craig's voice coming from the hallway leading to the garage. In a frantic frenzy, I helped Sandy get the door leading outside unlocked. I made her leave but shut the door behind her. The nearest house was two miles away, and Sandy would need a head start. I would stay and distract him while praying she got to someone for help before he killed me.

I heard the ringing of the bell from the cat collar that I had placed on the window. Craig asked, "Sandy, you didn't get free, did you? What's this, my dear?"

I regretted not fleeing but knew that he would just come after us. We were safer separated, so I decided to face Craig. I stepped out from behind his truck and said, "Craig, Sandy's not here. It's just me."

Craig's smile never faded as he said, "I should have gotten that window fixed. I suppose I am paying for that laziness."

Craig rushed me. Everything went black.

CHAPTER 20

When I woke up, I was tied to a bed in the guest bedroom. My head was really aching, and I was sure that I had a concussion. My vision was a little blurry, and when I was finally able to focus in the dimly lit room, I saw Craig sitting in a chair at the foot of the bed. He had his face propped on his hands. His elbows were resting on his knees. He was staring at me in such a way that I felt that I was being studied.

He said, "What am I supposed to do with you?"

"Let me go, Craig. I am your sister," I said in a forced calm tone.

"Well, is that so? Maybe in this life," Craig said as he reclined back in his seat. Craig was immortal. I did not know what to say. I was surprised. I had no recollection of him.

"So, what now?" I asked as bravely as I could.

"Well, you've blown it for me. I will have to leave and start a new life now. I can't let my purpose be thwarted by a little newspaper title like the Icon Serial Killer. It was bad enough that I had to deal with Marcel to keep things in order, but now that you let Sandy go, I will have to think quickly."

"So, you killed Cliff?" I asked. Tears filled my eyes.

"Yes, I killed the demigod. He will just be born again, like us all. No big deal. I did to him what I did to that little man who saw me defend Johann's honor. Of course, when Cliff found his body along with Morgan's blood, I had to take care of him. It was quite an inconvenience! I needed that blood for today. I had to try to make other arrangements. If only I had fixed that window, you wouldn't have messed this up as well."

That explained why there was so much extra blood in my apartment. Craig must have dumped it so that he could destroy the containers. It also explained why it looked different than I had imagined fresh blood would. Craig seemed to be thinking too hard, so I tried to distract him.

"So, you killed the missing witness?" I asked.

"Well, I had to because I couldn't let them start snooping around here. I needed no extra attention. And of course, that slow fool found where I hid my secrets when he was working on Johann's lawn! I thought he was in jail still, yet here he comes. Who works when they're on trial for murder?"

"And you killed all those girls? How many has it really been, Craig?"

"I lost count. It does not matter. I was not killing them. I was setting them free," Craig said as he leaped to his feet.

When he began to pace the room, I asked, "How did you set them free?"

"They are goddesses—all of them. They were just trapped in their human form. It was a deception, but I have the gift to see past lies. I saw their true nature, and I let them be free. Do you understand me, Alva?"

"No, I don't," I said reflectively.

"I make them become that of their true nature. I saw them for what they really were. When the goddess revealed herself to me—in each time and in each lady—I would set them free. It's not murder. It's freedom. It's strange how I could know a girl for so long and not even know she was a goddess. Like Sandy, I didn't realize who she was until she brought forth such a harvest feast. Then I knew that she was a goddess of harvest. I was going to set her free. She chose me. They all chose me! You have ruined everything. I should kill you, but I need you."

"Need me for what?" I asked as dread soaked my soul.

"I need you to get Aren to make a way for me to get out of the country," Craig said. "If not him, then surely Paul or one of his connections can help me. I need to go soon. Will you call him?"

"I don't have his number. My phone is messed up, and that is where I had it saved," I said.

"I don't mean on the phone, silly. Call him the old-fashioned way."

I was not sure what he meant, so I just called out to Aren. Nothing happened, and Craig busted out laughing. He said, "Quit messing around, Alva." He walked over to me and pulled his hunting knife out of his belt. There was dried blood on it. I could see it and smell it when he put it against my throat and pressed down. It hurt, but he did not cut me much.

When I did not do anything, he said, "Wow, you really don't know how to do it." He removed the knife and said, "Do you know anything at all? Have you not yet remembered?"

"I know a little about Aren and Paul, but not much," I admitted.

Craig returned to the chair at the foot of the bed and used the knife to clean under his nails. He said, "Well, maybe you will remember in a minute how to call him properly. It is an unspoken call. It comes from your spirit. I am surprised you do not know of it since it was what helped you two find one another. I don't know how to teach you but just try to focus. Maybe something will happen soon. If not, we will have to go to Plan B."

I sat for a while and focused, but nothing happened. I tried to think of Aren and the few memories that I had retrieved, but it did not work. I even tried to think of Paul, but no success. Beads of sweat began to form on my forehead. Craig went to get a towel from the bathroom. He wiped off my forehead and looked at me with an eerie kindness.

He said, "You always did have trouble remembering each life. And by the time you remembered, you'd be dead within a year. Seems a waste of a spirit to me. Do you realize that Hank belongs to Helen?"

"Yes," I said flatly.

"And yet you two still got it on? Some things never change. He has been chasing that tail and being a home wrecker for some time now. Did you know that some of us are always born in groups? We are always in one another's lives, whether it be relative, business acquaintance, or friend."

"Why is that?" I asked.

"I don't know. It's a mystery of the universe, but us three are always together. There are no other human immortals in your life."

"That's a relief," I said without sarcasm.

Craig laughed and said, "Tell me about it!"

I said, "Craig, can you loosen the bonds a little? I'm beginning to chaff."

"I can't do that, sis. You know this bed is the key to my remembrance. I know you don't remember, but this is the very bed that mom slept in last."

I began to jerk to get loose. I was lying in the bed that my mom had died in when I was a child. Craig held me down and asked, "Do I have to sit on you or sedate you? Be mindful of sacred history."

"Why is it sacred to you?" I demanded. "She was only our mother in this life," I said in a voice mimicking Craig.

"She was not our mother. She was a goddess—the first goddess that I had ever seen in this life. Our father set her free. He had to tell the cops that she killed herself, so that was how I learned the game. I would set them free and hide the evidence so that the non-believers would not blaspheme and call it murder," Craig said with a proud look on his face.

This was all too much. I asked, "Father killed Mother?"

"No, he set her free. Only a non-believer would say such. You and I are from the very golden age of the god and goddess. We knew what it was for them to walk openly in the world! The Age of Reason caused them to hide, but they will once again reign!" Craig proclaimed.

"How did Father do it?" I asked.

"She challenged him. He began to push her and shove, but she fought back. I was hidden in the closet like I would do to trap spiders. They didn't know I was in there. I liked to watch them do other things too, but this time, it was bad. I was scared, but now I know that she and he were just shaking off the mask. When she revealed herself to him, he made her go asleep. You were crying at the door to get in, so he went out of the room to see you. While he was gone, I crawled out of the closet and saw that she was no longer our mother, but a goddess. She was so peaceful and happy. I knew then that he had done the right thing."

"When I touched her hand, my whole life came back to me. Not just a small section, but it was the complete picture of my eternal life. I knew who I was, and I knew that I must find my goddess. It wasn't until I was in college that I realized that I could not just find my one goddess, but others as well. So, when my landlady revealed her true nature to me, I freed her. So, I began my goddess given duty."

"This is insanity, Craig. If Father killed Mother, it was wrong. You are wrong. You just need help. We can get you help. Paul can heal your mind. Just let me go and we'll go to him. I know where he lives. We can drive there. Or we can go to Aren's house in Huntsville. I know where two of his places are. We can just leave now. No one must know what you did. Please, Craig," I begged.

Craig said, "You know, I never noticed how much you remind me of Mother until just now." He raised his fist, and everything went dark again.

When I came to, I found myself strapped to the same table in the garage. I was wearing a white hooded outfit. I could barely see because the hood blocked my vision. I wiggled my head to clear my view. My head throbbed at the horrible pain. I cried in pain.

Craig returned with something to drink. He said, "If you drink this, the pain will go away."

Instinctively, I opened my mouth for the drink. I was so thirsty, very thirsty, and could think of nothing better than a refreshing drink. If there were drugs in it, maybe the pain would go away. Then I heard a voice speak to me so clearly it was as if another person was in the room with us.

It was Aren's voice, and he asked, "Will you live again so that we may be together forever?"

I looked up and saw that Aren was in fact in the room. There were two of him, or I was having double vision. The two Arens moved around one another in a circle until they formed one Aren. He reached down to me and offered me his hand. I reached for him with my tethered hand, but Craig swatted my hand away and asked what I was doing. I blinked and Aren was now gone.

Craig pushed the cup to my lips. I took a sip, but before I could swallow, my mind cleared somewhat. This was not pain medicine. This was a lethal dose of something that would kill me. It was probably the same concoction that he had used on Morgan and countless others. I spit it out in Craig's face. He slapped me. He tried again, but I used my chin to knock it out of his hands. He was squinting from being spit at, so he was unable to catch the cup. It fell to the floor and spilled empty.

Craig screamed, "I will have to make another batch! I am running low. I will have to feed you drainer if you do that again!"

Craig's anger got the best of him, and he began to beat me. He hit me in the body several times, and when he raised his fist to hit me in the face, I knew that I would again be knocked out. He stopped in midair as a look of wickedness came across his face. He said, "I think this should end now. There is a goddess inside you, even if I must cut it out to set it free."

Craig reached into his pocket and pulled out the knife he had hastily stuck there sometime during my unconsciousness. He said, "Don't worry, I will cover you up when I'm done. No one will find the shell and be able to gawk at it." By shell, he meant my body. I screamed loudly. Craig cringed and took off his shirt and shoved it in my mouth. I choked as I awaited the pain that was to come. I decided to close my eyes with the hope that I would not remember how horribly I had died in this life. In my heart, I told Aren that I would live again with him.

I waited for the death to come, but nothing happened. I tried to brace myself and tell myself that it was only a body, and I would have another one. I was too scared to open my eyes. So, I began to think about Aren. Suddenly, my entire memory came back to me. I remembered everything, and I remembered Craig. He was the boy who had raped me when I lived as a pioneer girl. The settlement had put me to death for being a whore. Craig caused my death.

Then I remembered that during the Civil War, Aren left to go get us food and medicine to stock up for winter. Craig was a local sheriff who had declared martial law. He forced me and the other women to work in the hospital, though there was a great epidemic of fever. I caught that fever and died before Aren could return and bring me medicine. There was none in the hospital because Craig and his men had hoarded all the little medicine that had remained.

Craig was in all my lives, and in all of them, he was involved in my death. Here came my next death, or so I thought. I finally opened my eyes when I heard what sounded like a crash. It was my father, and he was wrestling Craig for the knife. The two fell to the ground, and when Craig rolled over, my father had a knife wound in his chest. He did not move. I was certain that he was dead, and I was next.

Craig approached me and raised his hand to me once again. He was about to plunge the knife in me when the door leading outside, which Sandy had used to escape, burst open. The door shattered, even though it was made of some kind of metal. When the dust settled, I could see that Aren was standing there. In his arms was Sandy. She fell asleep. She had never made it past the yard. If Craig had thought to look, it may have been worse.

Craig said, "Aren, it is about time. I see that Alva finally remembered how to call you."

Aren sat Sandy down in a corner. He looked at my dead father, and then at me. A look of rage filled his face, yet he did not pounce on Craig. He said, "Let her go."

Craig said, "Oh, I can't do that. I must set her free. I must do this for my goddess."

Aren said, "That is not what she wants of you, boy."

"Yes, it is. You don't know what she wants. I know what she wants. She is my mate, not yours!" Craig yelled.

"Why don't you ask me for myself what it is that I desire?" said an airy female voice from outside. Craig began to cry as in stepped Emma Lowe, known to most of the world as the goddess Artemis. Craig rushed to her and held onto her knees. She petted his head like one would do a mangy dog.

"Craig, you have been wrong. This is not what I desire. I no longer seek tribute," Emma said in a soothing voice.

Aren ran over to me and freed me. He held me in his arms, but I was too sore to handle it, so he put me on the wooden steps leading into the house.

Craig was too involved with Emma to care. He looked up to her and asked, "Does this mean you take me back?"

"No, I do not take you back. I regretted taking you in the very first life that you lived. Since then, you have caused destruction. I did not know of your deeds, but Paul seemed to have figured it out. Aren called me, so I came to undo what I have done."

"You cannot kill me!" Craig screamed.

"You are right, I cannot. Our laws prohibit such acts, but why would I bother? Your torment will come soon enough. I will let the human law punish you," Emma replied.

"Then what is it that you will do to me?" Craig demanded.

"I will not let you live another life. I have let all my lovers live on as a favor for their sacrifice, but I will not let you live again." I knew that Emma was a free spirit. She would never keep a lover for more than one lifetime, yet she took one each generation. She must have thousands scattered everywhere throughout time.

Craig declared, "I will live as long as I can since this be my last life to love you." Emma did not respond to him.

Emma said to Aren, "Paul told me that my lovesick one has been causing your mate to die in each life before her due time."

"And why would he do that?" Aren asked.

"How many wars have you started because of your broken heart, my foolish friend?" Emma inquired. Aren looked at the ground in shame. Craig had played us all. Emma was the former goddess of many attributes, but her most known worship was that of the weapon. She had a bow and arrow that she never forsook until she became immortal. Craig was using her love of weapons to get to her. By starting world enveloping wars, he was trying to win her favor and get her attention.

I was the means to his end. But now, it was Craig's end. Craig seemed to know it, as he fell to the ground and touched his face to the cold cement floor of the garage. He begged for mercy, but Emma did not waiver. When he heard the sirens coming, he sat up and waited for the cops to come and arrest him. Emma walked over to me and touched me. The pain left my body for the most part, but there were still cuts and bruises. She said, "Lucky for you that you are female, or else I could not heal you."

Unlike Paul who could heal anyone, Emma could only heal women. When I looked down at my still battered body, Emma said, "Sorry I can't do much more than relieve some pain. I must keep it looking authentic for the paramedics."

The cops rushed in and ascended onto Craig. They cuffed him, and he did not struggle. As they took him into custody, he screamed to Emma, "Don't kill me! My goddess, my love, my icon!" The cops ignored him, as he was a crazy serial killer. In fact, I heard a few laughs from the cops that heard his declaration.

The cops did not keep us for as long as I thought. To them, it was an open and shut case. That belief was solidified when they began to search the house. I found out later that in those clumsy boxes Craig had kept mementos of his many killings. In the end, he had killed twenty girls, my father, Cliff Marcel, and the witness from his trial named Dennis Seabridge. If Dennis had not been a recluse, someone might have noticed that he was missing.

The ambulance made me go to the hospital. They ran several tests and made me stay the night for observation. Their fear was that I had a concussion, but they did not know that Emma had healed me. They made me stay awake the whole night, so when I was finally released, I was exhausted.

Aren stayed with me the whole time I was in the hospital. Paul did not come. I doubted that Aren would tell him where I was. When it was time for me to be released, Aren drove me to a hotel. He paid for everything but honored my request by staying in a separate room. I needed to think. My thinking time became weeks, and after I stayed in the hotel for a whole month, I finally had made my decision about Aren, Paul, and Hank.

CHAPTER 21

The first thing that I needed to do was put a deposit down on my new apartment. Kim had arranged for everything to be put into storage, apart from my father's ashes. I needed to do something with them, as I hated my father. He murdered my mother. Craig turning out the way he had was not his fault, but I still hated him.

Craig sang like a bird for a waiver of the death penalty. He even told that my father had killed my mother during an abusive outburst. It seemed my father was quite abusive to my mother, but I did not ever see it. Craig had hidden in the closet to see that family secret. Father had been too rough on mother one time, so he covered it up and made it look like suicide. When that news broke, I was glad that I was in some anonymous hotel.

Concerning Hank's story, it did not make as big of a splash as I had thought. Ernest did not mention it to me. I still had a job at the law firm, when I was ready to return to it. Larry had offered me the same invitation, but I was through with serving ice cream and cakes. I needed to grow up and have a career instead of a job. I decided to go and tell Larry in person, as he had been so kind to me. He was one of the few people that did not cringe to see me. I was a social leper to some—the sister and daughter of two maniac killers.

I went to Ernest's office first because it was on the way to Creamy's. All the bruises had healed, but I still looked haggard. I felt that some scars would always be inside my heart. I walked inside and found Ernest, who was sitting at his desk reading a file.

When he saw me, he lit up and offered me a seat. He said, "Are you ready to come back? Please don't tell me that you are here to resign."

I had to know one thing before I could come back. I asked, "Did you read Hank Rowling's article on Cliff from a while back?"

"Yes, I did."

"And you're not firing me?"

"No, I'm not."

"Are you mad at me?"

"No, it is not your fault."

"But it was an ethical violation. You should turn me in at least," I said.

"You should know better than that. Do you know what we used to call one another when I first started practicing?" Ernest asked.

"No, what?"

"Brother. We called each other brothers. Us lawyers are all brothers. We need to stick together. What you did was not unethical. It was Mr. Rowling that was unethical. I do hear that he is writing a book. If you can stop that, that would help you from having to visit the Ethics Committee."

"I will try to stop him," I said. I did not want to see Hank again, but it was worth one shot.

"Good, Brother Loomis. Now are you ready to get back to work or do you need more time to heal?"

"No, I am ready to work. Just one caveat, though," I said.

"What is that?" Ernest inquired.

"No criminal cases. Can you please train me in another area of the law?" I asked humbly.

"Of course, dear. We'll work something out, okay? See you Monday then?"

"Yes, see you Monday," I answered. It was Friday afternoon, so I could handle another Monday. I shook Ernest's hand and left the building. I walked a few blocks until I got to Creamy's. I could see Larry was washing dishes as I looked through the window.

When I walked in, he noticed me immediately and came to hug me. After we hugged, he said, "So is this your way of quitting?"

"What gave it away?" I asked.

"Kim returned your suits last week. Plus, I just figured you would ditch us small folk now that you're a big fancy lawyer," Larry jested.

"I've always been a lawyer," I said.

"Yes, but you were a broke one that needed to serve pastries on the side to keep the lights running," Larry said.

"Yes, I know, but I need to grow up. I can't let this opportunity pass me by," I said.

"I agree but promise me that you'll come by often. I'll give you one free milkshake every month if you do," Larry said with a big smile.

After I left Creamy's, I went to my new apartment. It was full of boxes that needed to be unpacked. My couch had not survived the damage by the blood, but there was a small wooden chair from my bedroom that had been set on the floor against the boxes. I pulled it out and sat down and waited. A few minutes later, Paul showed up to see me. I had called him and asked him to come.

Paul was reluctant to see me because he knew what was coming. However, I had asked him to get rid of my father's ashes for me. I wanted him to put them in a place where I never would be able to find them. I would have asked Aren to do it, but I knew that Aren would relent and tell me if I asked. Paul would not. So, it was up to him to do this for me.

He took the ashes from me. The funeral home had put them in a sealed brass container. I thanked him and waited for the inevitable question.

"Have you made your decision?" Paul asked.

"Yes, I have," I said softly.

"It's him and not me?" Paul asked in a stoic manner.

"Yes, I choose Aren. He's my soulmate, but even if he wasn't, I wouldn't want to see you die," I said with wet eyes.

"Why live forever without love?" Paul asked rhetorically.

"If we were together, what would stop you dying the minute we both became mortal? I would be alone, and it would have been in vain," I replied.

"What a reason!" Paul exclaimed.

"Fine, then let me be less selfish. What if I died immediately? There would be no one to heal me anymore if I got sick. You might be stuck without me for a few decades. Could you handle that?" I demanded.

"What of Emma?" Paul asked.

"I know you think she could heal me, but not you. However, I asked her before I made my decision. I called her and asked her what the law was for our choice. I knew it was too good to be true. And she confirmed that for me. If we become mortal, there is no healing allowed ever again for us at an immortal's hand. We cannot receive even one benefit of the gifts of the immortals. It is a true form of forsaking the immortal life."

Paul said, "I accept this because it is what you want. I will continue to wait for you. Maybe you will come back to me when you are at your final life. Then we can be together forever, as mortals will pass to the next world become one. If not as a mortal, then I will wait until I can join you at the end of everything, when immortal and mortal become one."

"Paul, I don't know what to say," I said.

"Then don't say anything. Call me if you change your mind. I will try to find another way for us yet," Paul said with tears in his eyes and a smile on his face. We hugged, and he held me a little too long before he ran away with my father's ashes tucked under his arm. I knew I would see him again, but I felt peace with my decision.

I loved Aren. It all came back to me when I remembered who I was in Craig's garage. I did not just go to him because he was the safer decision. In fact, he was the darker horse of the race. Aren was part of Craig's plan to kill me repeatedly and never even known. Craig used Aren's wars to get Emma's attention, though it had never worked until this life. I still was not certain that I was meant to live a long life. Nothing was ever certain in the love of an immortal.

I was very sad for many reasons. Now that I remembered everything about my former lives, I knew that it was just one continuous life as Craig had called it. I had seen war, famine, disease, and destruction repeatedly. Humans were cruel, but they were also wonderful. There must have been something that had made the Greek gods forsake their throne to take us as lovers.

A few minutes after Paul left, I called Hank. He still had his old phone number. He answered, but I could hear hesitation in his voice. When I told him that I needed to talk, he said he would do it but only in person. I gave him my address, and he showed up twenty minutes later. He looked a little thinner, and he had grown out a little beard and mustache. It seemed that he had not showered very frequently lately, and grooming was not in his priorities.

However, when he saw me, his face lit up. He tried to hide it, but I could see the little light in his soul that permeated through his pores. I caused that light to burn, and it made me sad that I could not relinquish the flame. Hank asked me how I was doing, and the pleasantries were short before we got to the point.

I asked Hank if he was going ahead with his book, and he said yes. When I could not persuade him, I let the issue go. He knew the consequences for me, yet he did not care. Maybe he had pledged me to what he thought was Aren all those years ago. Even though I remembered everything, I did not ever know why he refused to go to the Temple of Ares for the emblem. I just selflessly stepped in for him when he said no. I did not hate him, for now I had eternal companionship with my true love. I was willing to face anything, including torment as a ghost, or even early death for Aren.

I wanted to end some of Hank's suffering. I said, "You don't have to worry about me dying early anymore. Craig was the culprit. Did you know that he was immortal?"

"No, I did not. That explains why he was the killer then. Too bad I can't use that in my book. I'd be laughed off the planet for that one."

"Well, it's over now. So just move on and start a new life. You don't have to be reborn again, no matter what happens to me. I realize that I am going to always choose Aren. I truly love him. You and I barely knew one another. Our marriage was arranged. How can you still burn a candle for me?"

"I just do," Hank said. "Anything else?"

"No," I answered.

"Before I go, let me beg you to come with me. I am going to New York. You can come with me and think things through before you make your final decision," Hank said.

"I have already made it, Hank. I'm sorry," I replied.

"Why won't you come with me?" Hank screamed and grabbed me by both arms. He squeezed me so tightly that I screamed.

"Take your hands off of her," Aren said. He showed up just in time to rescue me once again, though I knew Hank was not dangerous. He was just in pain.

Hank let go and said, "This is fine. The man himself finally makes an appearance. Where were you when she was in danger? Where were you when her very brother was the one who was going to kill her?"

"Hank, you should leave," Aren said coolly.

"How can you be so cruel?" Hank said to Aren. "You keep us alive for a while, but then you torment us. We lose the body you used us for. We become a mist, a vapor, while you choose another lover. I will end this—if not this life, then the next one. In your arrogance and power, you cannot find us. We must find you. So, you won't see me coming. You never do. I always take her away from you. There's never been a thing you can do about it. I will make sure you destroy us all, Ares. It's only a matter of time before you slip up and start another war. Maybe the next will be the one that wipes us all out for good. No more slaves of the fallen gods."

Hank stormed out before Aren could retaliate. Aren rushed over to me and asked me if I was all right. When he saw that I was fine, I asked him what was wrong with Hank. He told me, "Hank and Craig are the forlorn lovers of immortals. The immortals let them live on, but out of mercy or negligence, they never relinquish their immortal life. So, they live on and on. Some were rebellious and were thrown out, while others ran away like Hank. Craig was just another notch for Emma's bedpost, and there are many like him."

"Are they all dangerous? Should I be worried about Hank?" I asked.

"No, he's fine. He loves you too much to hurt you. Don't worry. I will keep you safe. Maybe Craig was truly the reason you died young. If not, we will eventually figure it out."

We left my apartment. I would return to unpack later. Aren had promised to take me for one last vacation to the Smokey Mountains before I had to return to work on Monday. He owned a cabin up there. When we arrived, it was full of red roses. There was champagne waiting for us in the fridge.

Before we could do anything, Aren took me to the bedroom. There was a mirror with a candle underneath it. The candle was unlit, but Aren had a lighter.

He said, "I have a surprise for you."

"What is it?" I asked gleefully.

"This is the Candle of Naught. I know you've never heard of it, but I found it while I was waiting for you to be reborn this last time. Aiden gave it to me."

"Who is Aiden?" I asked.

"He is the former god of death," Aren said.

"You mean Hades?" I asked.

Aren nodded and said, "Yes. This candle has a very special power."

"What does it do?" I asked.

"It will show you what you looked like during your former life. Would you like to see?"

"Which life?" I asked.

"The first one," Aren answered.

"Okay," I said, but I was a little frightened. Aren would not tell me my original name because it was supposed to be the name I had on my last life before I would no longer be able to be properly born again. To speak it again over me might bring my final life. I assumed my original face would do the same harm, but Aren assured me that this was okay.

I closed my eyes as he lit the candle. When I opened them, I saw the face that I had long ago forgotten. Aren was behind me, and he had tears in his eyes. He said, "I have loved all your faces, but now you can see you as I truly see you. When you first touched me in the basement of the library to get your misplaced phone, I saw you as you really are. No more masks. I just wanted you to see your true immortal self."

The candle extinguished by itself. I was now staring at Alva Loomis once again. There was a snaky plume of smoke coming from the smoldering wick. For a second, it seemed to make the shape of an actual snake, and it was around my neck. I felt a choking sensation but found it was just the smell of the smoke that was harming me. I spoke nothing of it and made sure that Aren placed the candle in a safe place away from my sight.

When we laid in bed that night, we spoke of all the things that we had shared in the eternity of our love. Aren held me close that night. It was the first of many. I was so happy to be with my true love. I had lost everything to be with him. Yet, I had gained more in return. As the snow fell and accumulated on the skylight above our bed, I knew that I was finally happy. My icon had finally come home.